NO DEALS MR BOND

Between the Danish island of Bornholm and the
Baltic coast of East Germany a nuclear submarine of
the Royal Navy surfaces under the cloak of
darkness. James Bond and two marines slip quietly
from the forward hatch into their powered inflatable
and set off for a lonely beach where they are to
collect two young women who have to get out in
their socks. Planted to seduce communist agents to
run for cover in the West, they have been rumbled
by the other side. Bond little knows that this routine
exercise is but the prelude to a nerve-racking game
of bluff and double bluff, played with consummate
skill by his own chief M against the East German
HVA and the élite branch of the KGB, formed out of
Bond's old adversary SMERSH.

Bond finds he needs all his wits to negotiate the
labyrinth of double-crossing that is to lead him to a
bewildering showdown in a remote corner of the
Kowloon province of Hong Kong. There, with only
the trusted belt of secret weapons specially devised
by Q branch, he has to fight a terrifying duel in the
dark, with all the cards in the hands of his
opponents. NO DEALS MR. BOND is the sixth and
by far the best of John Gardner's 007 adventures.

About the Author

John Gardner was educated in Berkshire and at St John's College, Cambridge. He has had many fascinating occupations and was variously a Royal Marine Officer, a stage magician, theatre critic, reviewer and journalist.

He is the creator of the *Moriarty Journals*, and the *Boysie Oakes* series and the *Herbie Kruger* trilogy, which has been favourably compared to le Carré's *Smiley* series.

John Gardner was commissioned by Glidrose, the company to which Ian Fleming assigned the copyright in his James Bond stories, to update the series and bring a slightly older Bond into the 1980s. The first of his Bond books, LICENCE RENEWED, was an immediate success, the *Daily Telegraph* passing the verdict that 'Ian Fleming would not be displeased'. It was quickly followed by FOR SPECIAL SERVICES, ICEBREAKER, which the *Standard* claimed was 'just as enjoyable as the originals', ROLE OF HONOUR and NOBODY LIVES FOR EVER.

No Deals Mr. Bond

John Gardner

CORONET BOOKS and JONATHAN CAPE
Hodder and Stoughton

To my dear friend
Tony Adamus

Copyright © Glidrose Publications Ltd. 1987

First published in Great Britain in 1987 by Jonathan Cape Ltd. and Hodder and Stoughton Ltd. in 1987

Coronet edition 1988

Printed and bound in Great Britain for Hodder and Stoughton Paperbacks, a division of Hodder and Stoughton Ltd., Mill Road, Dunton Green, Sevenoaks, Kent TN13 2YA (Editorial Office: 47 Bedford Square, London WC1B 3DP) by Richard Clay Ltd., Bungay, Suffolk

British Library C.I.P.

Gardner, John, *1926–*
No deals Mr. Bond.
I. Title
823'.914[F]   PR6057.A629

ISBN 0-7736-8035-7

CONTENTS

- 1 -
SEAHAWK

THE NAVIGATION OFFICER, like so many of his Royal Navy counterparts, was known affectionately as Vasco. In the red glow of the submarine's control room he now leaned over and touched the captain's arm.

'Coming up to rendezvous, sir.'

Lt Commander Alec Stewart nodded. 'Stop all. Planes midships.'

'All stopped,' came back from the watchkeeper.

'Planes midships,' answered the senior of the two planesmen, who sat in front of the yokes that operated the hydroplanes, controlling the submarine's depth.

'Sonar?' the captain asked quietly.

'Distant activity around Bornholm Island, usual heavy stuff in and out of Rostock, two targets that sound like small patrol boats distant, up the coast at around fifty miles, bearing zero-two-zero. No submarine signatures.'

Lt Commander Alec Stewart raised an eyebrow. He was not a happy man. For one thing, he did not like operating his Trafalgar Class nuclear submarine in forbidden waters. For another, he did not like 'funnies'.

He knew they were called 'funnies' only because he had seen the expression in a novel. He would have called them 'spooks', or maybe simply spies. Whatever they were, he did not like having them aboard, even though the leader held a naval rank. During war games, Stewart had performed facsimile covert ops, but the real thing, in peacetime, stuck in his throat.

When the 'funnies' had come aboard, he had thought the

naval rank was simply a cover, but within a few hours he realised that Seahawk, as the leader was known, was very well informed about the sea — as were his two companions.

Nevertheless, this was all too cloak and dagger for his liking. It was also going to be far from easy for him. The orders, under the heading Operation Seahawk, had been precise but explicit:

> *You will afford Seahawk and his companions every assistance. You will run silent and submerged, making all possible speed, to the following RV.*

Coordinates were given which, after a quick glance at the charts, confirmed Stewart's worst fears. It was a point some fifty miles along the small strip of East German coast, sandwiched between West Germany and Poland, and around five miles offshore.

> *At the RV, you will stand by, remaining submerged, under the direct orders of Seahawk. On no account will you disclose your presence to any other shipping, especially D.D.R. or Russian naval units operating out of nearby ports. On reaching the RV it is probable that Seahawk will wish to leave the boat, together with the two officers accompanying him. They will use the inflatable they have brought with them, and, after departure, you will submerge to periscope depth and await their return. Should they not return after three hours you will make your way back to base, still running silent and submerged. If Seahawk's mission is successful he will probably return with two extra people. You will afford them every possible comfort, returning to base as instructed above. Note: this operation is covered by the Official Secrets Act. You will impress upon all members of your crew that they will not talk about the operation — either among themselves, or to others. An Admiralty team will debrief you, personally, upon your return.*

'Damn Seahawk!' Stewart thought. And damn the operation. The submarine's destination was not the easiest place to reach undetected: under the North Sea, up the Skagerrak, down the Kattegat, skirting the Danish and Swedish coasts, through the narrow straits — always a tricky navigational exercise — and out into the Baltic. The final fifty-odd miles would take them right into East German waters, crawling with Eastern Bloc shipping, not to mention Russian submarines from bases at Rostok and Stratsund.

'Periscope depth.' Stewart muttered the order, observing the hushed atmosphere of the silently operated boat.

The planesmen eased the submarine up slowly from its 250 feet below the surface.

'Periscope depth, sir.'

'Up periscope.'

The solid metal tube slid upwards and Stewart slammed the handles down. He flicked on the night vision switch and made one complete circuit. He could just pick up the coastline, bleak and flat. Nothing else. No lights or ships. Not even a fishing boat.

'Down periscope.'

He knocked the handles up, took two steps across to the radio bank and picked up the internal broadcast microphone. He switched it on with his thumb and spoke in the same low tone.

'Seahawk to control room please.'

Up in the fore-ends, surrounded by red-marked safety equipment and just behind a set of torpedo tubes, in the only space available, Seahawk and his two companions lay on makeshift bunks, four feet above the deck. They were already wearing black rubber diving suits with waterproof holsters attached to their belts. The cumbersome inflatable had been unstowed and lay within reach.

Hearing the captain's order, Seahawk swung his feet on to the metal deck and made his way unhurriedly abaft to the control room.

Only those belonging to the confined inner circle that is

the global intelligence community would have recognised
Seahawk as Commander James Bond. His companions were
members of the élite Naval Special Boat Squadron – officers
known for their discretion and often used by Bond's Service.
Stewart looked up as Bond stooped to enter the control
room.

'We've got you here on time.' His manner showed no
particular deference, merely polite formality.

Bond nodded. 'Good. In fact we're about an hour early,
which gives us a little leeway.' He glanced at the stainless
steel Rolex on his left wrist. 'Can you let us go in about
twenty minutes?'

'Certainly. How long will it take you?'

'I presume you'll surface only partially, so we need just
enough time to get the inflatable blown and paddle out of
your down draught. Ten, fifteen, minutes?'

'And we use the radio signals only as instructed?'

'Three Bravos from you for danger. Two Deltas from us
when we want you to resurface and take us aboard again.
We'll use the exit hatch forward of the sail, as arranged; no
problem there, I trust?'

'It'll be slippery on the casing, particularly on return. I'll
have a couple of ratings out to assist.'

'And a rope. A ladder for preference. As far as I know, our
guests haven't had any experience of boarding submarines
at night.'

'Whenever you're ready.' Stewart felt even more unhappy
about the 'guests' that were to be foisted upon him.

'Right, we'll get shipshape, then.'

Bond made his way back to the Special Boat Squadron
officers, Captain Dave Andrews, Royal Marines, and
Lieutenant Joe Preedy, Royal Marines. They went over the
drill again quickly, each repeating his part in the con-
tingency plan were anything to go wrong. They lugged the
inflatable, its paddles, and the small light-weight engine to
the metal ladder that led to the forward hatch and from there

to the casing and the cold of the Baltic. Two ratings in oilskins were waiting for them at the foot of the ladder, one ready to scramble up as soon as the order came.

In the control room, Lt Commander Stewart took another quick look around through the periscope and as it was lowered he gave the order to surface to casing and 'black light'. As the second command was obeyed the inside of the boat became completely dark but for the glow of instruments in the control room and the occasional flicker of a heavily shaded red torch. One of these was carried by the rating at the foot of the ladder. He moved quickly up the rungs as the soft voice came from the speakers:

'Casing surfaced!'

The rating turned the wheel with a slight clang to unlock the forward hatch. Fresh, cold air poured in from the small circle above. Joe Preedy was first up the ladder, assisted by the dim red glow of the torch held by the rating. Half way up the ladder, Dave Andrews took one end of the inflatable from Bond, hauling it up to Preedy and together the two men heaved the bulky rubber lozenge on to the casing. Bond followed them, the rating passing up to him the paddles and the light-weight engine, the latter among the most heavily classified equipment of the Special Boat Squadron. Easy to handle, with small propeller blades, the I.P.I. can run effectively and almost silently on a fuel supply from a self-sealing tank at the rear of the inflatable.

Finally, Bond ran the air tube up to Preedy and by the time he reached the slippery metal casing the inflatable had taken shape, a long, slim, low cutter fitted with bucket seats and hand grabs.

Bond checked that the two-way radio was firmly attached to his wet suit and balanced himself on the casing while the two S.B.S. men launched the inflatable. The rating held a line from the shallow rounded bow until the paddles and I.P.I. were transferred. Bond then slid from the casing, taking his place in the stern. The rating let go of the line forward, and the inflatable was jerked away from the submarine.

They allowed the little craft to drift clear and Bond took a quick reading from the luminous compass he carried round his neck. He called the reading to the S.B.S. officers, then placed the compass on the plastic well in front of him and using his paddle as a rudder, gave the order to make way. They paddled with long, steady strokes, achieving a respectable speed through the inky blackness. After two minutes, Bond checked their course, and as he did so he heard the hiss of water as the submarine submerged. Around them the night merged with the sea, and it took almost half an hour of hard paddling and constant checking of the compass before they could distinguish the East German coastline. It was going to be a long pull to the shore. If all went well, they would be able to use the engine for a quick sprint back to the submarine.

Over an hour later they were within striking distance of the coast, heading right on course for the safe inlet, its tiny spit of sand showing light against the surrounding darkness. They allowed the craft to drift in, alert and ready, for they were now at their most vulnerable. Andrews, in the stern, raised his unshaded torch and flashed two fast Morse code Vs towards the small stretch of sand. The answer, four long flashes, was returned immediately.

'They're here,' Bond murmured.

'I only hope they're on their bloody own,' muttered Preedy.

As the inflatable drifted on to the beach, Andrews leapt into the water and held the bow rope to steady the craft. Two dark figures came running to the water's edge.

'*Meine Ruh' ist hin.*' Bond felt a little absurd quoting Goethe – a poet of whom he knew little – in the middle of the night on a deserted East German beach: 'My peace is gone'.

'*Mein Herz ist schwer,*' the answer came back from one of the figures on the beach, completing the couplet: 'My heart is heavy'.

The three men helped the pair on board and quickly had them seated amidships. Andrews hauled on the forward rope to bring the inflatable around as Bond set the reciprocal course on the compass. Within seconds they were paddling out again. In thirty minutes they would start the engine and give the first signal to the waiting submarine.

Back in the control room, the sonar operator had been monitoring their progress by means of a short-distance signalling device installed in the inflatable. At the same time he swept the surrounding area, while his partner did the same on a wider scale.

'Looks as though they're coming back, sir,' said the senior sonar operator.

'Let me know when they start their engine.' Stewart sounded tense. He had no idea what the funny business was about, and he did not really want to know. All he hoped for was the safe return of his passengers and whoever they brought with them, followed by an untroubled run home to base.

'Aye-aye, sir. I think … Oh, Christ …' The sonar operator stopped short as the signal came loud into his headphones and the blip appeared on his screen. 'They've got company.' He resumed his commentary. 'Bearing zero-seven-four. He's coming from behind the headland on their starboard side. Fast and light. I think it's a Pchela.'

Stewart swore aloud, something he rarely did in front of his crew. A Pchela was a Russian-built patrol hydrofoil. Though now elderly, carrying two pairs of 13 mm machine guns and the old Pot Drum search radar, these craft were fast and formidable in both shallow water and choppy seas.

'It's a Pchela signature, sir, and he's locked on to them, closing rapidly,' said the sonar operator.

In the inflatable they heard the heavy drumming of the patrol boat's engines almost as they left the shore, pulling away with the paddles.

'Shall we use the engine? Make a run for it?' Dave Andrews shouted back to Bond.

'We'll never make it.'

Bond knew what would have to be done, and he didn't like to contemplate the consequences. He was spared making any decision by Andrews who leaned back and shouted,

'Let him come abreast and be ready for the bang. Don't wait up for me. I'll make my way back overland providing the limpet doesn't get me!' He was quickly over the side, disappearing into the sea.

Bond knew that Andrews carried two small limpet charges that, placed properly, would blow holes directly into the fuel tanks of the hydrofoil. He also knew they would probably blow the S.B.S. man to pieces.

At that moment the searchlight hit them and the patrol craft dropped speed, sinking from the long, ski-like foils which ran under the hull and settling on her bows. A command in German came over the loudhailer, across the closing gap of water.

'Halt! Halt! We are taking you on board so that you can state your business. This is a military order. If you do not stop we will open fire on you. Heave to!'

'Raise your arms above your head,' Bond told Preedy. 'Show you're unarmed, and do as you're told. There will be an explosion. When it happens, drop your heads between your knees...'

'And kiss your arse goodbye,' Preedy muttered.

'...and cover your heads with your arms.'

The patrol boat was low in the water now, engines idle as she drifted in towards the inflatable, the searchlight unwavering. The gap had closed to almost fifty yards before the bows of the patrol boat disappeared in a blinding white flame turning to crimson. A second after the flash they heard the ripping of the explosion, followed by a deeper roar.

Bond raised his head and saw that Andrews had set the mines perfectly. He would, Bond thought. Any good S.B.S.

man would know the exact position for maximum effect on all Eastern Bloc craft, and Andrews had executed the task faultlessly. The boat was on fire her entire length and her bows with their distinctive foils were lifting high out of the water. She went down in less than a minute.

The inflatable had been blown sideways by the blast and was skidding out of control over the water. Bond reached for the light-weight engine. He lifted it over the stern, pushed it well down in position in the water and pressed the ignition button. The little I.P.I. buzzed into life, the propeller blades whirling. Holding its grab handle, Bond could both steer the inflatable and control its speed.

Bond was alarmed at their vulnerability, for the whole area was illuminated by the flames from the doomed patrol boat. Half a dozen queries went through his mind – had the patrol already alerted other vessels along this closely guarded stretch of coast? Was the inflatable now coming up on a land-based or fast ship's radar system? Had Dave Andrews got clear after setting the limpets? Doubtful. Would the submarine have gone deep, preparing to crawl out to avoid detection? That was certainly a possibility, for a nuclear sub was more precious to its captain than Operation Seahawk. He thought on these things as Preedy took up the navigation, using his own compass to guide them.

'Starboard two points. Port a point. No. Port. Keep turning port. Midships. Hold it there ...'

Bond struggled to control the inflatable's progress by heaving on the engine, his hand trailing behind them in the water, desperately holding on – for the engine seemed to be trying to pull itself free from his grip. It took all his strength to keep the little craft moving on course, with constant demands from Preedy to alter to port, then starboard, as they bounced heavily on the water.

He felt spray and wind in his face, and in the dying light of the patrol boat's last seconds he saw their two passengers, hunched in their anoraks and tight woollen caps. It was clear from the set of their shoulders that they were terrified. Then, as suddenly as the hydrofoil had lit the deep black waters, the darkness descended again.

'Half a mile. Cut the engine!' Preedy shouted from the bow.

Now, they would know. Any minute they would discover if their mother ship had deserted them or not.

Stewart had seen the destruction of the hydrofoil on radar, and he wondered if Seahawk and his companions had perished in the explosion. He would give them four minutes. If sonar did not pick them up by then, he would have to go deep and silent, preparing to edge his way out of the forbidden waters. Three minutes and twenty seconds later, the sonar operator said he had them.

'Heading back, sir. Going fast. Using their engine.'

'Prepare to surface low. Receiving party to forward hatch.'

The order was acknowledged. Then the sonar operator said, 'Half a mile, sir.'

Stewart wondered at his own folly. All his instincts told him to get out while they remained undetected. Damn Seahawk, he thought. Seahawk? Bloody silly. Wasn't it an old Errol Flynn movie?

The radio operator heard the two Morse code Ds clear in his headphones just as Bond transmitted them from the almost stationary inflatable. 'Two Deltas, sir.'

'Two Deltas,' replied Stewart with little enthusiasm. 'Surface to casing. Black light. Recovery party clear forward hatch.'

The Seahawk party were pulled on board and slithered down the ladder. Preedy came last, having ripped the sides of the inflatable and set the charge that would destroy the craft underwater, leaving no trace. Stewart gave the order to submerge immediately, going deep and changing course. Only then did he move towards the fore-ends to speak to the Seahawk party. He raised his eyebrows at Bond when he saw they were one short.

Bond did not have to be asked the question. 'He won't be coming back.'

Then Lt Commander Stewart caught sight of the two new members of the Seahawk team. Women, he thought. Women! Bad luck having women aboard. Submarine drivers are a superstitious breed.

2

SEAHAWK PLUS FIVE

IT WAS SPRING, the best time of the year, and London was at its most seductive with golden carpets of crocuses in the parks, girls shedding their heavy winter clothes and the promise of summer just around the corner. James Bond felt at peace with the world as, relaxing in his towelling robe, he finished his breakfast with a second large cup of coffee, savouring the unique flavour of the freshly ground beans from De Bry. The sunshine lit the small dining room of his flat, and he could just hear May humming to herself over the inevitable kitchen clatter.

He was on the late shift at Service Headquarters and so had the day to himself. Nevertheless, when on an office assignment, his first duty was to go through all the national daily papers, and the major provincial ones. He had already marked three small stories that appeared that morning in the *Mail*, *Express*, and *The Times*: one concerning the arrest of a British businessman in Madrid; three lines in *The Times* reported an incident in the Mediterranean; and a full-scale article in the *Express* claimed the Secret Intelligence Service was in the midst of a huge row with its sister organisation, M.I.5, over disputed territory.

'Have you no finished yet, then, Mr James?' asked May accusingly as she bustled into the room.

Bond smiled. It was as though she took pleasure in chivvying him from room to room when he had a free morning.

'You can clear, May. I've got half a cup of coffee to finish. The rest can go.'

'Och, you and your newspapers.' She swept a hand in the direction of the papers spread across the table. 'There's ne'er a happy bit of news in them these days.'

'Oh, I don't know ...' Bond began.

'It's terrible, though, isn't it?' May pounced on one of the tabloids.

'What in particular?'

'Why, this other poor girl. It's spread all over the front page, and they had yon head policeman on the breakfast television. Another Jack the Ripper, it sounds like.'

'Oh, that! Yes.' He had barely read the front pages, which were full of a particularly nasty murder that, according to the newspapers, the police were linking to a killing earlier in the week. He glanced down at the headlines.

TONGUELESS BODY IN WOODSHED.

SECOND MUTILATED GIRL DISCOVERED.

CATCH THIS MANIAC BEFORE HE STRIKES AGAIN.

He picked up the *Telegraph*, which had the story as a second lead.

The body of twenty-seven-year-old computer programmer Miss Bridget Hammond was found late yesterday afternoon. It was discovered in a disused woodshed by a gardener, near her home in Norwich. Miss Hammond had been missing for twenty-four hours. A colleague from Rightline Computers had called at her flat in Thorpe Road after she had failed to turn up for work that morning.

The police stated the case was clearly one of murder. Her throat had been cut and there were 'certain similarities' with the murder of twenty-five-year-old Millicent Zampek in Cambridge last week. Miss Zampek's body was discovered mutilated on the Backs behind King's

College It was revealed at the inquest that her tongue had been cut out.

A police spokesman declared, 'This is almost certainly the work of one person. It is possible we have a maniac on the loose.'

An understatement, thought Bond, tossing the paper to one side. These days, perverted murder was a fact of life, brought closer by the speed of modern communications.

The telephone began to ring and he felt a strange sensation — a prickling at the nape of his neck, and an extraordinary sinking in the pit of his stomach, as though he had a premonition of something very unpleasant about to be, as they said in the Service, laid on him.

It was the ever-faithful Miss Moneypenny, using the simple code they had both mastered so well over the years.

'Can you lunch?' was all she asked after he recited his number.

'Business?'

'Very much so. At his club. 12.45. Important.'

'I'll be there.'

Bond cradled the receiver. Lunch at Blades was a rare invitation from M, which did not bode well.

At precisely 12.40, knowing his Chief's obsession for punctuality, Bond paid off his taxi on Park Lane, taking the usual precaution of walking to Park Street, where that most sought after of gentlemen's clubs can be found, its elegant Adam façade set back from the street.

Blades is unique, an offshoot of the exclusive Scavoir Vivre, which closed not long after its founding in 1774. Its successor, Blades, came into being on the old premises in 1776 and it has remained one of the few gentlemen's clubs to flourish and maintain its standards up to the present day. Its revenue comes almost entirely from the high stakes at the gaming tables and the food is still exceptional. Its membership includes some of the most powerful men in the land who have been shrewd enough to persuade wealthy visiting business associates – Arab, Japanese and American – to use the facilities as guests. Thousands of pounds change hands each evening on the turn of a card or at a game of backgammon.

Bond pushed through the swing doors and walked up to the porter's lodge. Brevett knew Bond as a very occasional guest at the club and greeted him accordingly. Bond could not help thinking of the man's father, who had been porter at the time of the great card game when 007 had at M's instigation unmasked the evil Sir Hugo Drax as a cheat. The Brevett family had been porters at Blades for well over a hundred years.

'The Admiral's already waiting in the dining room, sir.'

Brevett motioned discreetly to a young page boy who led Bond up the wide staircase and across the stairwell to the magnificent white and gold Regency dining room. M was seated alone in the far left corner, away from windows and doors and with his back to the wall, so that he had a view of anyone entering or leaving the room. He gave a curt nod as Bond reached the table and glanced at his watch. 'Bang on time, James. Good man. You know the rules. What d'ye fancy? – bearing in mind we haven't got all day.'

Bond ordered grilled sole with a large salad, asking for the dressing ingredients to be brought, so that he could prepare it himself. M nodded approval. He knew his agent's likes and dislikes as well as his own, and appreciated that it was difficult to get a dressing made to your own liking.

The food arrived and M waited in silence as James Bond carefully ground half a teaspoonful of pepper into the small bowl provided with the ingredients. This was followed by a similar amount of salt and sugar, to which he added two and a half teaspoonfuls of powdered mustard, crushing the mixture well with a fork before stirring in three full tablespoons of oil, followed by one of white wine vinegar, which he dribbled in carefully. He added a few drops of water before giving a final stir and pouring the mixture over his salad.

'Make someone a damned good husband, 007.' The clear grey eyes showed no apology for mentioning marriage, a topic people who knew Bond well steered clear of, and had done since the untimely death of his bride at the hands of SPECTRE.

Bond ignored his Chief's lack of taste and began to attack his fish with the skill of a surgeon.

'Well, sir?' He kept his voice down.

'Time enough, yet not enough time,' M said coolly. 'Words of our late Poet Laureate, not that you'd recognise Betjeman from Larkin, eh?'

'I know a few good ribald rhymes though, sir – The Jolly Tinker; The Old Monk of Great Renown? I can even recite you the odd limerick.'

M chewed on his fish – he too had ordered the sole, but with new potatoes. He swallowed and looked at Bond, his clear grey eyes cold.

'Then recite me one about Seahawk, James. You remember Seahawk?'

Bond nodded, remembering vividly though it was now five years ago. Dave Andrews had been killed on the Seahawk mission and Bond would never forget the days and nights spent in the cramped quarters of the submarine, trying to calm and comfort the two girls.

'What if I tell you the truth about Seahawk?' said M.

'If there's need to know, sir.'

The Service always operated on a need-to-know basis so that all Bond had been told about Seahawk was that he had to take off two agents. He remembered Bill Tanner, M's Chief-of-Staff, saying the two he was to rescue were getting out in their socks, meaning they were leaving fast to save their skins.

Almost to himself, he said, 'They were so damned young.'

'Eh?' snapped M.

'I said, they were very young. The girls we got out.'

'They weren't the only ones.' M looked away. 'We pulled the whole shooting match out over a matter of seven days. Four girls, a young man and their parents. We did it; you brought a couple of girls home. Now, James, two of the girls are dead. You probably read about it this morning. They had new names, new backgrounds. They were untraceable. But someone's got to at least two of them. Brutally killed, their tongues removed. You read about the maniac on the loose?'

Bond nodded. 'You mean...?' he began.

'I mean that both those young women were rehabilitated after doing sterling service for us, and there are still three agents out there waiting for an executioner who cuts out tongues.'

'A K.G.B. hit squad leaving us a message?'

'With each death, yes. They're slicing up Cream Cake, James, and I want it stopped – fast.'

'Cream Cake?'

'Finish your lunch, then we'll take a stroll in the park. What I have to tell you is too sensitive for even these walls. Cream Cake was one of our most effective operations in years. I suppose that's why there's a penalty. Revenge, they say, is a dish best eaten cold. Five years is cold enough, I reckon.'

M did not look at Bond, as they strolled – two businessmen reluctantly returning to their offices – through Regent's Park.

'Cream Cake was a ploy to get our own back. You know what an Emily is?'

'Of course. The jargon's outdated, but I know what it means.'

Bond had not heard the term Emily for years. It was the name their American sister service used to denote special targets of the K.G.B. Emilies had been found mainly in West

Germany. They were usually colourless girls leading dull lives, destined to remain single for the rest of their days. The lack of romance in their lives was often the result of their having to look after an elderly parent so that they had little time to spare – working all day and looking after an ailing mother or father at home. But Emilies had something else in common. They usually worked for a government department, mostly in Bonn, and often as secretaries inside the BfV. The *Bundesamt für Verfassungsschutz* was the West German equivalent of M.I.5, but attached as a department to the Ministry of the Interior, or the B.N.D. (the *Bundesnachrichtendienst*). This intelligence-gathering organisation works very closely with the British S.I.S., the American C.I.A. and the Israeli Mossad.

The K.G.B. had exploited numerous women in the Emily category over the years. A man would suddenly come into an Emily's life and quite quickly the drabness would disappear. She would receive gifts, be taken to expensive restaurants, theatres, the opera. Above all she would feel attractive and wanted. Then the unbelievable would happen – she would sleep with the man. Being in love, nothing else would matter, not even her lover asking her to do little favours such as smuggling a few documents out of the office, or copying some unimportant details from a dossier. Before she knew it, an Emily was in so deep that if things went wrong she had to flee eastwards with her lover. When she was set up in a new life in the D.D.R., or even Russia itself, the lover would disappear.

Bond thought for a second. Emilies had certainly not gone out of style, for there had been several recent defections in that category. Neither were Emilies confined to the female sex.

'We decided to use the Emily ploy in reverse,' M said, cutting through Bond's thoughts. 'But our targets were very big guns indeed, senior officers of the H.V.A. It was they who began the Emily business themselves, and even trained the seducer agents.'

Bond nodded. M spoke of the *Hauptverwaltung Aufklärung*, or Chief Administration, Intelligence – the most efficient organisation next to the K.G.B. in the Eastern Bloc.

'The targets were senior H.V.A. and attached K.G.B. officers, including one woman. We had several sleepers but they'd been left so long that they were really past it. They were married couples we had thought would be of great use. In the end, we used their children. Five families were chosen because of their kids. They were all attractive, in their late teens, over the age of consent, if you follow me?' M sounded embarrassed, as he always did when discussing 'honeypot ops', as the trade knew them. 'We sounded them out. Satisfied ourselves. Slipped in a bit of on-the-ground training. We even brought two of them into the West for a while.' He paused as they passed a group of nannies wheeling perambulators and chatting about their employers.

'It took a year to set up Cream Cake. We had great success, with a little help from others. We put the bite on the woman, who was pure old-school K.G.B., and snaffled a couple of high-grade H.V.A. men. But there was one very big fish who could still be dangerous. Then it was blown with practically no warning. You know the rest. We brought them home and gave them a golden pat on the back, homes, training, careers. We got a lot out of it, 007. Until last week, when one of the girls was murdered.'

'Not one I...'

'No. But it alerted us. We couldn't be sure, of course. Couldn't tip off the police. We still can't. Now they've got a second one, the Hammond girl in Norwich.' He took a deep breath. 'They've signalled loud and clear by this bizarre removal of tongues. It could be K.G.B., it might be H.V.A. – even G.R.U. But there are still two young girls out there and one personable young man. They've got to be pulled in, 007. Brought to a safe place, and put under protection until we've rolled up the hit team.'

'And I'm the one who's going to pull them?'

'In a manner of speaking, yes.'

Bond knew that gruff tone of voice only too well.

M looked away as he continued, 'You see, it's not going to be an easy operation.'

'There's no such thing.' Bond realised he was trying to raise his own sinking spirits.

'This is going to be tough, 007. We know where two of them are – the girls you brought out, as it happens. But the young man's a different kettle of fish. He was last known to be in the Canary Islands.' M gave a frustrated sigh. 'One of the girls is in Dublin, by the way.'

'I can get the girls quickly, then?'

'It's up to you, James.' It was rare for M to address Bond by his Christian name. Today he had done so three times. 'I cannot sanction any saving operation. I cannot give you orders.'

'Ah!'

'In the event of anything going wrong we shall have to deny you – even to our own police forces. After Cream Cake was blown the Foreign Office watchdogs gave strict instructions. The participants were to be hoovered clean, given a face lift and then left alone. We were to make no further contact. If I went to the powers-that-be asking for protection for these people and then used one of them as a tethered goat to deal with the hit team, the answer would come back as callous as …'

'Let them eat cream cake.' Bond spoke sombrely.

'Precisely. Let them die and have done with it. No compromises. No communication.'

'So what do you want, sir?'

'What I've told you. You can have names and addresses. I can point you in the right direction, let you delve into the files, even the murder reports, which naturally we have – er – acquired. That should take you the rest of the afternoon. I can give you leave of absence for a couple of weeks. Alternatively you carry on with your normal duties.

You understand?'

'Point me.' Bond's voice was gritty. 'Point me and give me leave. I'll pull them in ...'

'Nothing official. I can't even let you use a safe house ...'

'I'll see to that, sir. Point me and I'll get them, and the hit team. I'll see to it that nobody but the hit team's masters knows what's gone on.'

The silence seemed to go on for ever. Then M took a deep breath.

'I'll give you names and the file numbers for Registry as we walk back to the shop. After that, you're relieved of duty for two weeks. Good luck, 007.'

Bond knew he needed a great deal more than good luck.

3

DARE TO BE CHIC

The Headquarters Registry was on the second floor, guarded by girls usually dressed in casual jeans and shirts. Until a few years ago the uniform was twin sets, pearls and well cut skirts from Harrods or Harvey Nichols. M rarely went near the Registry since the rules had been relaxed, but he had been as good as his word in giving Bond the information he needed.

In the park, he rattled off names and file prefixes, made Bond repeat them and then told him to take one more turn round the Inner Circle before returning to the high, anonymous building housing the Service Headquarters.

A tall, inscrutable goddess jotted down the file numbers as Bond gave them to her and took the slip of paper to the Watch Officer. There were no questions, not even a raised eyebrow from the Watch Officer, whose name was Rowena MacShine-Jones – known to all as Registry Shiner. Ms Mac-Shine-Jones gave the nod and the computers were set in motion. Within five minutes, the goddess returned with a thick plastic file which was flagged in red, meaning it was Classified A+. The date and the words *These documents must not be taken from the building. Return by 16.30hrs* appeared on the front. Bond knew that if he ignored the instruction to return them, one of the Registry guardians would seek him out and bring the documents back for shredding and burning. Equally, if he tried to get them out of the file, let alone the building, a 'smart card' contained in the spine would trigger a series of alarms.

On his office desk he found a similar file flagged with the

same classification, except this one had to be returned to the Eighth Floor, which meant to M personally.

Within an hour, Bond had been through both sets of files, imprinting the information on his memory. He spent another hour rechecking his memory against the documents After that he returned the Registry file and took the second one up to M's office.

'I think he'll see me,' Bond said, smiling at Miss Moneypenny as he entered the outer office.

'More leave, James? He mentioned you might want to take some.'

'Only for unexpected family business.' Bond looked her straight in the eyes, like any trained dissembler.

Moneypenny sighed. 'Oh, that I could be part of that family. I know what business you fabricate for this kind of leave.'

'Penny, if that were true there's nothing I'd like better.'

The intercom buzzed and M's voice came clearly through the speaker. 'If that's 007, Moneypenny, send him in here and stop your gossiping. The pair of you act like old washerwomen when you get together.'

Moneypenny gave Bond a soulful look, raising her eyes heavenwards. Bond merely smiled at his Chief's crustiness and, seeing the green light come on over M's door, gave a small, courteous bow to Moneypenny and went into the inner sanctum.

'Come to return the grisly papers, sir.'

He placed M's file on the desk. It contained the police reports on the two murders, including the highly disturbing photographs. Violent death is easier to gaze upon in reality than when captured for ever by the camera. The two girls' skulls had been crushed from behind. Their tongues had been removed with almost surgical precision after death; the police officer in charge had commented upon the apparent medical knowledge of the murderer. There was little doubt according to the reports, that the same person, or persons had carried out the executions.

M drew the file towards him without comment. 'Moneypenny said you'd put in an application for two weeks' compassionate leave, 007. True or false?'

'True, sir.'

'Good. Then you can leave right away. I trust things work out for you.'

'Thank you, sir. I think I'll visit Q Branch before I go, but I really do have to get to Mayfair before six.'

M nodded, satisfaction flickering for a second in those icy grey eyes. A look of tacit understanding passed between the two men. Of the three remaining prospective victims, the nearest – Heather Dare – owned a beauty salon just around the corner from the Mayfair Hotel. This was a pleasant coincidence, for Bond occasionlly dined in that hotel's particularly good Le Chateau Restaurant, not merely for the justly excellent food, but for the security offered by its half dozen special alcoved and very private tables, which are well away from the eyes and ears of other clients.

M dismissed Bond with an almost cursory flick of his right hand, and he made his way into the bowels of the building where the Armourer, Major Boothroyd, controlled Q Branch. It happened that the Major was away and Bond found the Branch operating under the expertise of his assistant, the long-legged, bespectacled but unashamedly delicious Ann Reilly, known to everyone in the Service as Q'ute. In her early days with Q Branch, Bond and Q'ute had seen a lot of each other, but with the passage of years and Bond's unreliable timetable, the relationship had become merely friendly.

'James, how nice,' she said in greeting. 'To what do we owe the pleasure? Nothing new brewing, is there?'

'I'm on leave for a couple of weeks. Thought I'd collect some bits and pieces.'

He deliberately played it down. If he had been on normal leave he would have to sign out a CC500 scrambler

telephone. In fact he wanted to pick her brains and maybe
borrow some small new technological device.

'We've got a few pieces on test. Maybe you'd like to take
away a sample.' Q'ute grinned, wickedly alluring. 'Come
into my parlour,' she said and Bond wondered if M had
given her guarded instructions.

They walked briskly down the long room where
shirtsleeved young men were seated in front of V.D.U.s and
others worked through huge lighted magnifiers on electronic
boards.

'Nowadays,' said Q'ute, 'everyone wants it smaller, with a
longer range, and more memory.'

'Speak for yourself.'

It was Bond's turn to smile, though it did not even light up
his eyes. His mind was full of the gruesome photographs of
two young girls battered to death, even though he knew
Q'ute talked of sound-stealing, movement-theft, conceal-
ment and deadly devices.

He left half an hour later with some small items in addition
to the obligatory CC500. This, according to current instructions, would be no use to him, for both M and the Foreign
Office would deny him entirely until the assignment was
completed. At the door of her office, Q'ute put a hand gently
on Bond's arm.

'If you need anything from here, just call and I'll bring it
to you myself.'

He looked into her face and saw that he had been
right – instructions of some kind had been given to Q'ute by
M.

*The participants were to be hoovered clean, given a face lift and then
left alone*, M had said. Bond knew what that meant. It was
like being cut out of some rich relation's will and if he fouled
up, he would suffer the same fate as the Cream Cake agents.

In the Bentley Mulsanne Turbo, tucked away in the underground car park, Bond checked the ASP 9 mm automatic, its
spare clips and the hard steel telescopic Concealable Oper-

ations Baton. With his getaway case, containing a week's
spare clothes, in the boot, he was prepared for what the
instructors called street work. He started the engine and the
car glided smoothly out of its parking slot and up the ramp
into the spring sunshine of London's streets, where he was
conscious of death only a stone's throw from the pavements.

Some twenty minutes later he was on those very pavements, passing Langan's Brasserie in Stratton Street, its
garish red neon blazing even in the afternoon.

At the Mayfair Hotel Bond handed the car over to the
blue-liveried doorman with a discreet Parachute Regiment
badge in his lapel, knowing it would be quickly put on a
parking meter and watched during his absence. From there
to the beauty salon Dare To Be Chic at the end of Stratton
Street took him only three minutes.

The choice of Dare he could understand, for the girl's
German family name had been Wagen, so this was a literal
translation. Where the Heather had come from heaven, and
the Service resettlement officers, alone knew.

The windows of the salon were black, the bold lettering
daring you to be chic in gold accompanied by an art deco
motif of a bobbed-haired woman sporting a cigarette holder.
Inside was a minute foyer, thickly carpeted and with a single
Kurosaki wood block print, which to Bond resembled a
magician's box opened in front of a row of pyramids. The
elevator door was gold and its button was neatly labelled
with the Dare motif.

Bond pressed, stepped into the mirrored cage and was
whisked silently upwards. Like the foyer, the elevator was
carpeted in deep crimson. The lift came gently to a halt and
he found himself in another foyer. Double doors led to the
rooms where clients subjected themselves to heat, facials and
the expertise of hairdressers and masseurs. There was the
same red carpet, another Kurosaki print and to the right a
door marked 'Private'. In front of him a golden blonde
dressed in a severe black suit and blazing white silk shirt sat

at a kidney-shaped desk She looked as though her face had
been cleansed of every particle of dust and grease and each
strand of her hair cemented in position. Her lips parted in an
encouraging smile while her eyes asked what the hell a man
was doing in this woman's preserve. Bond felt about as
welcome as when he visited his sister Service, M.I.5.

'Can I be of help, sir?' She spoke in the accents of a shop
assistant emulating an aristocratic drawl.

'Quite possibly. I wish to see Ms Dare,' said Bond, giving
her his patently insincere smile.

The receptionist's expression became fixed as she said she
was most terribly sorry but Ms Dare was not in this afternoon. The reply lacked conviction and the eyes flickered an
instant towards the door marked Private. He sighed, took
out a blank card, wrote one sentence on it and pushed it
towards the girl.

'Be a darling and take this to her. I'll mind the store. It is
very important, and I'm sure you wouldn't want me to walk
in on her without being invited.'

When the girl hesitated, he added that Ms Dare could look
at him on the monitor — inclining his head towards the
security camera high up in the corner by the door — and if she
did not like what she saw he would move on. The blonde still
could not make up her mind, so he added that it was official
and flashed his ID — the impressive, fully laminated one with
coloured lettering rather than the real thing, which was plain
plastic in a little leather folder.

'If you'll wait one moment I'll see if she's come back. Ms
Dare was certainly out earlier this afternoon.'

She disappeared through the private door and Bond
turned to face the camera. On the card he had written, 'I
come in peace with gifts. Remember the gallant sub-
mariners.' It took five minutes but it worked like a charm.
The golden girl showed him through the door, along a
narrow corridor and up some steps to another very solid-
looking door.

'She says to go straight in.'

Bond went straight in to find himself staring down the
wrong end of a piece of gunmetal blue which, by its size and
shape, he recognised as a Colt Woodsman — the Match
Target model. In the United States they would call it a
plinking pistol, but a plinking pistol can still kill and Bond
was always respectful in the presence of any such weapon,
particularly when it was held as steadily as this, and pointed
directly at him.

'Irma,' he said in a slightly admonishing tone. 'Irma,
please put away the gun. I'm here to help.'

As he spoke, Bond noted that there was no other exit and
that Heather Dare, née Irma Wagen of Operation Cream
Cake, had placed herself in the correct position, with legs
slightly apart, back against the left hand side of the rear wall,
eyes watching and steady.

'It *is* you,' she said without lowering the pistol.

'In the flesh,' he replied with his most genuine smile,
'though to be honest I wouldn't have recognised you. The
last occasion we spent time together you were a bundle of
sweaters, jeans and fear.'

'And now it's only the fear,' she said without a trace of a
smile.

Heather Dare's accent held no vestige of German. She had
adopted her cover entirely. She had become a very poised,
attractive lady with dark hair, a tall slim frame and long,
shapely legs. Her elegance went with the business she had
managed to build up over the last five years, but underneath, Bond sensed a toughness, maybe even ingrained
stubbornness.

'Yes, I understand about the fear,' he said. 'That's why
I'm here.'

'I didn't think they'd send anybody.'

'They didn't. I was simply tipped off. I'm on my own, but
I do have the training and skills. Now, put the gun down so
that I can get you away to somewhere that's safe. I'm going

to haul in the three of you that are still alive.'

Slowly she shook her head. 'Oh no, Mr...'

'Bond. James Bond.'

'Oh no, Mr Bond. The bastards have got Franzi and Elli. I'm going to make certain they don't get my other friends.'

The Hammond girl's real name was Franziska Trauben; while Millicent Zampek had been known as Eleonore Zuckermann.

'That's what I said.' Bond took a pace forward. 'You'll go to a safe place where nobody's going to find you. Then I'll take care of the bastards myself.'

'Then where you go, I go; until it's over, one way or another.'

Bond had experienced enough of women to realise that this stubbornness could neither be fought nor reasoned with. He looked at her for a moment, pleased with her slender build and the femininity which lay under the well-cut grey suit set off by a pink blouse and thin gold chain and pendant. The suit looked very French. Paris, he thought, probably Givenchy.

'Do you have any ideas how we should handle it then, Heather? I do call you Heather don't I, not Irma?'

'Heather,' she murmured very low. After a pause she said, 'I'm sorry, I called the others by their original names. Yes, I've thought of myself as Heather ever since your people sent me out into the real world with a new name. But I have difficulty thinking of the old gang in new guises.'

'On Cream Cake you were interconscious? I mean, you knew one another? Knew what each target was?'

She gave a brief nod. 'By real names and by street names. Yes, we were interconscious of each other, of the targets, of our control. No cut-outs. That's why Emilie and I were together when you picked us off that little beach.' She hesitated, then frowned, shaking her head. 'Sorry, I mean Ebbie. Emilie Nikolas is Ebbie now.'

'Yes, Ebbie Heritage, isn't it?'

'That's correct. We happen to be old friends. I spoke to her this morning.'

'In Dublin?'

Heather smiled. 'You are well informed. Yes, in Dublin.

'On an open line? You spoke on an open line?'

'Don't worry, Mr Bond ...'

'James.'

'Yes. Don't worry, James, I said only three words. You see, I spent some time with Ebbie before this salon got started. We made a simple code for speaking on an open line. It went, "Elizabeth is sick", and the reply, "I'll be with you this afternoon".'

'Meaning?'

'The same as "How's your mother", which was the Cream Cake warning, slipped into a conversation. "Mother" was the trigger: "You're blown. Take the necessary action.'

'The same as it was five years ago.'

'Yes, and we're about to take that necessary action again now. You see, James, I've been in Paris. I flew back this morning. On the aeroplane I saw the report of the murders. It was the first I knew of it. Once would have put us on guard, but twice, and with the ... the tongue ...' For the first time she sounded shaken. She swallowed, visibly pulling herself together. 'The tongues made it certain. It's a charming warning, isn't it?'

'Not subtle.'

'Warnings and revenge killings are seldom subtle. You know what the Mafia does to adulterers within a family?'

He nodded sharply. 'It's not pretty, but it makes its point.' For an instant he recalled the last time he had heard of such a murder, with the man's genitalia hacked off.

'The tongue makes a point too.'

'Right. Then what does "Elizabeth is sick" mean?'

'That we've been blown. Meet me where arranged.'

'Which is?'

'Which is where I'm going, on the Aer Lingus flight from

Heathrow at 8.30 tonight.'

'Dublin?'

Again she nodded. 'Yes, Dublin. I'll hire a car there and head for the rendezvous. Ebbie will have been waiting there since this afternoon.'

'And you did the same for Frank Baisley, or Franz Belzinger? The one known as Jungle?'

She was still tense, but she gave a little smile. 'He was always a joker. A bit of a risk-taker. His street name had been Wald, German for forest. Now he calls himself Jungle. No, I couldn't get a message to him because I don't know where he is.'

'I do.'

'Where?'

'Quite a long way off. Now, tell me where you are meeting Ebbie.'

She hesitated for a second.

'Come on,' urged Bond, 'I'm here to help. I'm coming with you to Dublin anyway. I have to. Where do you plan to meet?'

'Oh, we decided a long time ago that the best way to hide is in the open. We agreed upon Ashford Castle in County Mayo. It's the hotel where President Reagan stayed.'

Bond smiled. It was sound professional thinking. The Ashford Castle Hotel is luxurious and expensive, and the last place on earth a hit team would think of looking.

Then he asked, 'Can we look as though we're having a business meeting? Do you mind if I use your telephone?'

She sat down behind her long desk and locked the Woodsman in a drawer. Then she spread papers around and pushed the telephone towards him. Bond dialled the Aer Lingus reservation desk at Heathrow and booked himself on flight EI 177, Club Class, in the name of Boldman.

'My car's just around the corner,' he said as he put down the receiver. 'We'll leave here about seven o'clock. It'll be dusk and I presume all your staff will have left.'

She glanced at her neat Cartier watch and her eyebrows rose. 'They'll be finished very soon now...'

As though on cue, her telephone rang. Bond guessed it was the blonde because Heather said that yes, they should all leave. She was working late with the gentleman who had called and she would make sure that the building was locked. She would see them all in the morning.

As the glowing spring day faded and the grumble of traffic from Piccadilly dwindled, they sat and talked, Bond gently probing her about Cream Cake. He learned quite a lot more than he had gathered from the files that afternoon. Heather Dare held herself responsible for the panic call to all five participants, 'I'm sorry, Gustav has cancelled dinner.' She had been working their prime target, Colonel Maxim Smolin, who during that period was the second in command at the H.V.A. She told him unwittingly a great deal about herself and about the inner workings of Cream Cake, alerting him to a few deceptions left out or excised from the files.

At five to seven he asked if she had a coat, and she nodded, going to the small, built-in wardrobe and slipping into a white trenchcoat that was far too easily identifiable, and very definitely French, for only the French can make raincoats that have flair. He ordered her to lock up the Woodsman. Then, together, they left her office, switching out lights as they went, and into the elevator cage, hissing down to street level. The lights went out of their own accord just as they reached the small ground floor foyer and, as the doors opened onto gloom, Heather screamed and the attacker came at her like a human typhoon.

- 4 -

DUCKING AND
DIVING

THE MAN WHO hurled himself into the elevator cage must
have thought that Heather was alone. Later Bond realised
that all he would have seen from the gloomy foyer would
have been the white trenchcoat, for Heather had taken a step
forward as the doors swung open. Bond was thrown against
the glass side of the cage and, taken by surprise, he was
uncertain whether to reach for the pistol or baton. But he
could not afford to hesitate. The assailant already had one
hand firmly on Heather's shoulder and was spinning her
round, his other arm raised high, holding an object that
looked like a large hammer. Desperately fighting to regain
his balance as he slithered against the glass, Bond struck out
with his right leg, aiming a hard, straight blow with his heel
forced forward, in the direction of the intruder's lower legs.
He felt his shoe make contact and heard a muffled grunt as
the man missed striking Heather with the hammer by
inches, instead smashing the rear mirror glass of the cage.

As the attacker tried to recover his balance, Bond was
tugging the collapsible baton from its holster on his right hip.
He flicked it down sharply so that the telescoped steel clicked
into place, making a formidable weapon, and he struck out
at the man's neck. He went down without even a cry. There
was just the dull thud of the steel baton, followed by a
scraping noise as the killer's head hit the splintered glass.

Suddenly there was silence, punctuated only by the sound
of Heather's little choking sobs. Bond reached out to see if

there was an emergency light switch inside the elevator cage. His hand touched the control panel and the doors began to close. They opened again as the safety mechanism came into play when they hit the assailant's legs sprawled out into the foyer. The same thing happened three times before Bond found an override button and the cage was flooded with light.

Heather was hunched in the far corner, away from the inert body clad in black jeans, black rollneck and gloves. The man's hair too was dark, but the crimson streaks of blood lent a macabre, punk-like effect. The shattered mirror reflected the gory patches and the great star-shaped cracks produced a kaleidoscopic picture of black and red.

With his right foot, Bond heaved the body over. The man was not dead. His mouth had fallen open and his face was patterned with cuts from hairline to mouth where his face had hit the glass. Some of the slashes looked quite deep, but the quick breathing was audible, and the blood seemed to be flowing normally. When consciousness returned, he would probably feel more pain from Bond's blow than the cuts.

'A couple of aspirins and he'll be as right as rain,' Bond muttered.

'Mischa,' Heather said vehemently.

'You know him?'

'He's one of the heavies they kept in Berlin; Moscow-trained.' As she spoke, Heather seemed to be pushing herself away, attempting to put as much space as possible between herself and the man she recognised as Mischa. All the time, the doors kept closing and opening against Mischa's legs, sounding a regular tympanic beat in the background.

'Persistent things, elevator doors,' said Bond as he bent over the unhappy Mischa. He probed around and finally pulled from under the body the weapon meant for the back of Heather's skull. It was a brand new carpenter's mallet. He weighed it in his hand, a heavy wooden hammer with a king-size head. Then he wiped the handle with his handkerchief and put it back on the floor. Bending again, he began to go over the body, searching for any other weapon that might be concealed.

'He doesn't even have loose change or a pack of cigarettes,' Bond announced, straightening up. 'Do we, by any chance, Heather, have another way out of this wretched building? A fire escape or something?'

'Yes. There's a metal zig-zag thing at the back of the salon. I had it put in when we refurbished the place. Why do you ask?'

'Because, sweet lucky Heather — and you've been damned lucky — friend Mischa did not come alone. Not if comrade Colonel Maxim Smolin did for the two other girls and meant you to go by the same unpleasant route.'

'But Maxim wouldn't...' she began, then after a pause asked, 'Why?'

'Mischa carries nothing else on him, only the instrument to bludgeon you to death. There's no knife; no little medical instrument for the swift removal of tongues — and that's the trademark isn't it?'

She gave a small, frightened nod. Bond kicked the mallet to the back of the cage, grabbed the unconscious Mischa by the scruff of his rollneck and, lifting him without effort, pushed him out into the foyer. Once Mischa was free of the doors, Bond slammed the heel of his hand on to the up button. They made the silent ascent to the entrance of the beauty salon. Heather switched off the security alarms in a neat metal cupboard set into the wall. Then she pushed open the double doors.

'No lights,' Bond ordered. 'Lead me.'

He felt her hand, remarkably cool for one who had just escaped death, clasp his as she negotiated her way past the basins and dryers of the hairdressing salon, then into a corridor punctuated with clinical white doors. A final door, with the sign Emergency Exit visible in red overhead, opened with a push bar, and the cool of the evening hit them as they emerged on to a metal platform. From there you could almost reach out and touch the neighbouring buildings. To the right, narrow swaying steps zig-zagged down.

'How do we get out? At the bottom, I mean,' Bond asked, looking down. He could see nothing but a tiny square courtyard surrounded by tall buildings.

'Only key-holders can use the exit. We have four sets, one for each of my managers – hairdressing, beauty consultant, massage – and one for me. There's a door into a passageway that runs alongside the car showroom and a door at the other end. The same key works for both doors. The far door takes you into Berkeley Street.'

'Go, then! Go!'

She turned towards the fire escape, one hand on the guard rail, and at that moment Bond heard the thudding of feet running towards them from the other side of the door.

'Quick!' He did not raise his voice. 'Get down there and leave the doors open for me. There's a dark green Bentley parked opposite the Mayfair. Go into the foyer and wait for me. If I arrive in a hurry with both hands showing, run straight to the car. If my right hand's in my pocket and I'm taking my time, lose yourself for half an hour, then come back and wait. Same signals at half-hour intervals. Now, move!'

She seemed to hesitate for a second, and then went down the metal stairs which seemed to shake precariously as her speed increased, while Bond swivelled towards the exit. He drew his ASP 9 mm, holding it low against his hip. The thudding grew louder and when he thought the distance right, Bond pulled back sharply, opening the door. He did it the text book way, leaving just enough time to check that his targets were not policemen – who were likely to be unfriendly if they thought he was a criminal intruder.

By no stretch of the imagination were these men police, unless London's forces had taken to using Colt ·45 automatics without warning. The men who had been pounding down the passage slithered to a halt as soon as Bond showed himself. Oddly, they had put the lights on in the corridor so that they could be seen quite clearly; though Bond was aware that he was an equally good target, even standing sideways, as he'd been taught so often on the small arms course. There were two of them, well-muscled hit men, one moving fast behind the other.

The one ahead, to Bond's right, fired, his big ·45 sounding like a bomb in the confines of the corridor. A huge piece of the door jamb disintegrated, leaving a large hole and sending splinters flying. The second shot passed between Bond and the jamb. He felt the crack of the bullet as it cut the air near his head, but by this time he too had fired, low to damage only feet or legs with the wicked little Glaser slugs always loaded in the ASP. The men would have been easy to take out with that ammunition. The No.12 shot suspended in liquid Teflon within the soft bullet would explode inside the body. But Bond had no desire to kill anybody. M's message had been clear enough: 'In the event of anything going wrong we shall have to deny you even to our own police forces.' He had no intention of being denied by his Service and sent up for murder to the Old Bailey. He squeezed the trigger twice, one shot to each wall, and heard a yelp of pain and a shout. Then he turned about and hurtled down the fire escape. Glancing below, he saw no sign of Heather.

He thought he heard another shout from above as he reached the first door, which Heather had left open. Bond raced through, slammed it after him and put up the Yale catch. He tore down the passage to the street door. Seconds later he was in the street itself. He turned left and left again, keeping both hands in sight. Instantly the hotel doorman appeared with the car keys and unlocked the Bentley. Bond tipped him lavishly and smiled casually at Heather as she came across the road from the hotel entrance.

The car was parked facing Berkeley Street. He slid left into the street, then around Berkeley Square. At the top he bore

left again, then right, past the exclusive Connaught Hotel,
and left into Grosvenor Square, Upper Grosvenor Street and
the heavy traffic of Park Lane.

'Keep an eye open,' he told Heather, who sat silently at his
side. 'I presume you can spot a tail. I'm going through the
park, down Exhibition Road and then right towards the M4.
I take it I don't really have to tell you the rules, but in case
you've forgotten...'

'I don't forget,' she snapped back at him. 'We are ducking
and diving, aren't we?'

'Yes, according to the rule book. Never fly straight for
more than half a minute. Never walk ahead without watching your back. Always mislead.'

'Even when they know you're there,' she added tartly.

'That's right.' Bond smiled, but the streak of cruelty still
played around his mouth. 'What, incidentally, were you
going to do about luggage, Heather?'

'I had a case packed at home. There's nothing I can do
about it now.'

'We'll have to buy a toothbrush at the airport. Anything
else can wait until we get to Ireland. Are you booked under
your own name?'

'Yes.'

'Well, you're going to cancel it. Let's hope the waiting list
isn't too long. We'll call from a service station. Those two
must have been Smolin's men as well, expecting to find your
battered corpse and remove your tongue. From what I saw of
them, they seemed to be quite capable of it.'

'Did you...?'

'Kill them? No, but at least one of them's hurt; maybe
both. I didn't stop to find out. Now, think of a good alias.'

'Smith'

'No. The house rules are not Smith, Jones, Green or
Brown. You'll have to produce something more convincing.'

'Arlington,' she said. 'Like Arlington Street. That sounds
distinguished.'

'It's also the American cemetery. Perhaps it's a bad omen, but it'll do. Are we still free of company?'

'There was a Jaguar XL behind that I didn't like the look of, but it turned off into Marlowes Road. I think we're clear.'

'Good. Now listen, Heather. You cancel your Aer Lingus booking, and try to get a seat in the name of Arlington as soon as we arrive. I'll take care of anything else. All right?'

'Whatever you say.' She was reasonably calm. He could detect only the merest tension in the cool, collected voice. It was impossible for him to deduce how professional she really was.

They stopped at the first service station on the M4, about three miles from the Heathrow exit. Bond directed her towards the telephone booth that was free while he loitered by the next one, waiting as a woman appeared to dial every number she had in a little black book. In the end Bond was able to take Heather's place. She nodded to him, confirming that she had cancelled her flight. Bond delved into his telephone number memory and dialled the British Airways desk at Heathrow. He asked if there were seats available on the 20.15 shuttle to Newcastle. Assured that there were, he asked them to hold two in the names of Miss Dare and Mr Bond.

Back in the parking area, using the opened car boot for cover, Bond slid the baton and his ASP pistol into the lined compartment of his getaway case. There the weapons were entirely safe from detection by airport scanners, and almost as secure from discovery by search. In the last resort he would have to use his Service permit but then every Special Branch officer of the Irish Garda would know he was in the Republic.

Within fifteen minutes they had reached the airport and Bond drove the Bentley to the long term car park. During the bus ride from the car park to the terminal building he explained his plan for getting on the Dublin flight to Heather. It was something he had pulled off before.

'They don't often have accurate passenger listings for the internal shuttles. And we shall be going through the same gate to get to our shuttle as the passengers for the Irish flight.'

He went on to tell her exactly what she should do if she was unable to get a seat on the Aer Lingus Flight 177.

In the first stages they were to go their separate ways, meeting up only when, as Mr Boldman, Bond checked in at the Dublin desk. He also suggested that she try to buy a small carry-on flight bag and the bare essentials.

'Not that you'll ever be able to buy anything really essential at Heathrow,' he added, his mind darting back to those halcyon days when airports and railway stations could provide practically everything around the clock.

They got off the bus at Terminal One. It was just twenty minutes to eight, and they both moved quickly. Heather went to the Aer Lingus desk and Bond to the shuttle area, where he picked up the tickets booked in their real names, paying for them with his own credit card. Carrying his small case, he walked briskly back to the Aer Lingus check-in, collected his ticket in the name of Boldman and waited until Heather reappeared with a small, very new-looking overnight bag she had bought at the airport shop.

'I was able to get toothpaste, a brush, spare underwear and some scent,' she said.

'Good. Now let's head for the Newcastle shuttle,' said Bond.

As they passed down the ramp and through the gates to the walkway, showing their tickets to the security guards, Bond checked on the departures monitor that Flight EI 177 was already boarding at Gate 14. There was the usual crush around the shuttle check-in, and he took the boarding cards for them both. They had no difficulty slipping quietly to the back of the queue and then back through the door into the walkway again. Bond allowed Heather to go well ahead of him towards Gate 14. If anyone was looking for them, it would be confirmed that they had checked in for the New-castle shuttle.

If M had broken the rules further and had people watching at a discreet distance, they would not discover the Dublin booking until too late. But Bond was thinking more of Smolin's people, who could well be searching the airport and making enquiries already. That instinctive sense acquired over long years of experience with SMERSH and SPECTRE was well tuned, but Bond picked up nothing. He neither felt nor saw anyone watching on behalf of Smolin.

They boarded Flight EI 177 separately and sat three rows apart, not joining up again until they had gone through the green customs channel at Dublin airport an hour later. Outside it was raining and dark, but Bond felt quite ready for the lengthy drive to County Mayo. While Heather went off to see if the main airport shop was open, where she could buy clothes, Bond hired a car at the rental desk. They had a Saab available – his preference as a Bentley Turbo was out of the question – and he filled in the necessary forms, using his Boldman licence and credit card. A red-uniformed girl smiled like a true Irish colleen and had just told him she would take him down to the car when he turned to see Heather a few yards away, leaning against a pillar. She looked stunned, her face chalk white. As Bond came up to her, he saw a copy of the Dublin *Evening Press* in her hand.

'What is it, Heather old love?' He spoke gently.

'Ebbie,' she whispered. 'Look.' She raised the newspaper for him to see the headlines. 'It must be Ebbie. The bastards.'

Bond felt the hairs rise on the back of his neck. In bold print, two inches high, the headlines shouted, GIRL BAT-TERED TO DEATH AND MUTILATED IN HOTEL GROUNDS. He scanned the report. Yes, it was the Ashford Castle Hotel in County Mayo, and the girl, who was unidentified, had been battered to death. Part of her body had been mutilated. Yes, Bond thought, it had to be number three – Ebbie Heritage, or Emilie Nikolas. Smolin, if indeed it was Colonel Maxim Smolin behind the murders, must have two teams operating. As he glanced at the trembling Heather, Bond knew they were not safe anywhere.

'We'll have to move fast,' he told her softly. 'Now, follow that nice girl in the red uniform.'

- 5 -
JACKO B

IT WAS NOT merely what in Ireland is called 'soft weather'. The rain lashed against the windscreen so that the tail lights of other vehicles were barely visible. Bond drove with excessive care while Heather sat hunched next to him, crying.

'It's my fault...three of them gone...Ebbie now. Oh, Christ, James...'

'It's not your fault. Get that out of your head,' he said, but he understood how she felt, having heard the whole story from her in her office only a few hours ago.

With the news of another violent death spread over the front page of the *Evening Press*, Bond knew it would be folly to head straight for Ashford Castle. He turned on to the airport exit road, was narrowly missed by a battered yellow Cortina with a wire coathanger for an aerial, and then turned off before reaching the main road which runs into Dublin from the north. There was a sign to the International Airport Hotel, and he knew the place well. He parked the car near the hotel entrance and looked at Heather.

'Stop crying.' It was a quiet command, not ruthless or uncaring, but a command nevertheless. 'Stop crying and I'll tell you what we're going to do.'

At that moment, if asked he would not have been able to tell anyone what he expected to do, but he needed Heather's confidence and co-operation. She sniffed and looked at him with red eyes.

'What can we do, James?'

'First we're going to book into this hotel, just for the night.

I'm not taking advantage of the situation, Heather, but we'll have to book one room. One room, and I lie on a sofa pulled across the door. We are Mr and Mrs Boldman. I'm taking a double room only for your protection. All right?'

'Whatever you say.'

'Then do something with your face and we'll go in looking like an ordinary English couple – or maybe an Irish couple, depending on what sort of voice I'm in.'

Inside, Bond managed a soft Dublin accent. He booked the room, commenting on the weather to the somewhat straitlaced girl at the reception desk.

The room was comfortable, but without frills; a one-night stopover place. Heather flopped on to the bed. She was no longer crying but looked tired and frightened.

Meanwhile, Bond had made some quick decisions. M had pushed him towards this job and underlined that he had no official status, but he had his own contacts, even here in the Republic of Ireland. As long as he did not cross lines with the Embassy, he saw no reason for not taking advantage of them.

'We'll get food shortly,' he said. 'In the meantime, why don't you freshen up in the bathroom while I make a couple of calls.'

Even if Smolin was after them, with the entire H.V.A., G.R.U. and K.G.B. backing him up, it was unlikely the telephones of the International Airport Hotel had an intercept on them. Dredging his memory, Bond dialled a local number and was answered after three rings by a woman who did not give the number.

'Is Inspector Murray in?' Bond asked, still using the Dublin accent.

'Who wants him?'

'One of his lads, tell him. He'll be knowing when he speaks.'

She made no comment, and a few seconds later he heard the deep voice of Inspector Norman Murray of the Garda's Special Branch.

'Norman, Jacko B here.'

'Oh? Jacko is it? And where are you, Jacko?'

'Not over the water, Norman.'

'Lord love you, what the hell are you doing here, then? Not mischief, I hope – and why didn't I know you were in the country?'

'Because I didn't advertise. No, not mischief, Norman. How's the charming Mrs Murray?'

'Bonny. Rushing around all day and playing squash half the night. She'd be sending her love to you if she knew we'd talked.'

'Don't think she should know.'

'Then you are on mischief. Official mischief?'

'Not so you'd notice, if you follow me.'

'I follow you.'

'You owe me, Norman.'

'That I know, Jacko. Only too well. What can I do for you?' There was a slight pause. 'Unofficially, of course.'

'For starters, the Ashford Castle business.'

'Oh Jasus, that's not in our court, is it?'

'Could be. Even then, it would be unofficial. Have they identified the girl yet?'

'I can find out. Ring you back, shall I?'

'I'll call you, Norman. You're there for the next hour or so?'

'You'll get me here. I'll be home after midnight. I drew the late shift this week, but the wife's out with her squash pals.'

'You hope.'

'Away with you, Jacko. Call me back in ten or fifteen minutes. Okay?'

'Thanks.' Bond quickly rang off, praying that Murray would not run a check with the Embassy. You could never be sure how Branch people would react, either side of the water. He dialled another number. This time a jaunty yet oddly guarded voice answered.

'Mick?' Bond asked.

'Which Mick would you be wanting?'

'Big Mick. Tell him it's Jacko B.'

'Jacko, you rogue,' the voice roared at the other end of the line, 'where are you then? I'll bet you'll be after sitting in some smart hotel with the prettiest girl any red-blooded man would fancy right there on your knee.'

'Not on my knee, Mick. But there is a pretty girl.' He glanced up as Heather came out of the bathroom, her face scrubbed. 'A very pretty girl,' he added for Heather's benefit. She did not smile, but grabbed her handbag and retreated into the bathroom again.

'There, what did I tell you?' Big Mick's voice gave a great guffaw. 'And if there's a woman in the picture, Jacko B, then there's trouble, or I don't know you at all.'

'Could be, Mick. Just could be.'

'What can I do for you, Jacko?'

'Are you in work, Mick?'

He gave another hearty laugh. 'Sort o' in and out. This and that, if you know what I mean.'

Bond knew what he meant. He had known Big Mick Shean for the best part of fifteen years, and while the Irishman walked a slender tightrope as far as the law was concerned, Bond had a dozen reasons to trust him, and any one of his companions, with his life. Bond had trained him in certain crafts such as back-watching, on-the-ground surveillance and losing a tail.

'Would you have any clean wheels, Mick?' He knew that if Big Mick did not have a car he could soon get one.

'I might have.'

'You'll need maybe three, with a couple of fellas to each.'

There was only a short pause, half-a-beat too long

'Six fellas and three sets of wheels. What's in it?'

'A couple of days' work. Usual rates.'

'Cash?'

'Cash.'

'And danger money?'

'If there's danger.'

'With fellas like you there's always danger, Jacko. What's the deal?'

'Straight and true as a dog's hind leg. I might be needing you to look after me and the girl – at a distance.'

'When?'

'Probably in the morning. As I say, two days, maybe three.'

'Give us a ring about midnight, Jacko. If it's you, the cars have to be respectable...'

'And reliable.'

'I was just going to say that, so.'

'We want a nice little country drive, that's all.'

Big Mick appeared to hesitate again. His voice had dropped and was serious when he next spoke. 'It's not to go into the North at all, Jacko, is it?'

'The opposite direction entirely, Mick. No worries on that score.'

'Lord love you, Jacko. We don't do politicals, if you follow me.'

'I'll call back around midnight.'

'You do that.'

Bond cradled the telephone just as Heather came out of the bathroom again. She had repaired her face and her hair was now perfect. He smiled at her warmly.

'What a pity, you look so good, Heather.'

'What do you mean?'

'Because I'd like to take you out to dinner. Dublin boasts some excellent restaurants. Unfortunately...'

'We daren't show our faces.'

'No. I fear it'll have to be sandwiches and coffee here in the room. What would you like?'

'Could we have a bottle of wine instead of coffee?'

'Whatever you say.'

He called room service and discovered they had smoked salmon sandwiches, which he ordered with the best bottle of

Chablis on the list. He also retrieved the baton and his gun from the getaway case. He didn't intend being caught by the oldest trick in the book, a substitute for the waiter bringing their order – one of the few details they got right in bad movies. Before the waiter arrived, he picked up the telephone again and dialled Inspector Murray as he had promised. The call was short. He knew exactly how long it would take Murray to get a trace on his number and so pinpoint him at the International Airport Hotel. In the field you never trust anybody.

'Norman? Jacko. You have anything?'

'It'll be in the morning papers, Jacko. But there's something else I want to talk to you about.'

'Just give me what's going in the papers.'

'Local girl, Jacko. No form. Part-time chambermaid, name of Betty-Anne Mulligan.'

'Ah. They got any ideas down there?'

'None at all. Good girl. Twenty-two years. No current boyfriends. Family's cut up no end.'

'And the mutilation?'

'I think you know, Jacko. You've had a couple on your side of the water. Betty-Anne Mulligan's head was bashed in and she had not a tongue in her mouth. Removed after death. It was very professional they tell me.'

'Nothing else?'

'Only the clothes she was wearing. The raincoat and headscarf.'

'Well?'

'Not hers, Jacko me boy, not hers. They belonged to a guest at the hotel. It was a lovely bright day when Betty-Anne went in to work. The rains came mid-afternoon and she had a long walk home. Two miles and no coat or covering for her head. A guest took pity on her ...'

'What name?'

'Miss Elizabeth Larke – with an e, Jacko. Would you be knowing anything about that?'

'No,' Bond answered honestly, 'but I might by tomorrow. If I do I'll give you a call.'

'Good man, now...'

Bond had been looking constantly at his watch. He had about thirty seconds before he might be traced.

'No, Norman. There's no time. Your questions will have to wait. Will the guest's name be in the papers?'

'It will not. Neither will the news about the tongue.'

'Good. Oh, and Norman, this is completely unofficial. I'll be in touch.'

He heard Murray exclaim, 'Jacko...' as he rang off. For a full minute he sat looking at the telephone, then the waiter knocked at the door, interrupting his thoughts.

'Heather, did you often have meetings with Ebbie? I think I asked you before, but I need more details.'

They ate the sandwiches, and drank a '78 Chablis. It was a good year but vastly overpriced. Heather held out her glass for more.

'We met two or three times a year.'

'And observed the field rules?'

'Yes. We were very careful. We booked hotels under names we concocted...'

'Such as?'

'She was always Elizabeth. I was Hetty. Our surnames were birds and fish. She was a bird, I was a fish.'

'Ah. Did you keep a list?'

'No. Each time we met we arranged the name for the next meeting.' She laughed, a jolly, almost schoolgirl laugh. 'Ebbie and I were very close. She was the best friend I ever had. In my time I've been Miss Sole, Miss Salmon, Miss Crabbe. We changed the spelling slightly, as in Miss Pyke, spelled with a y.'

'And what are you this time?'

'You've made me Miss Arlington, but I would have gone as Hetty Sharke, with an e.'

'What about the bird?'

Her eyes brimmed, and he thought she was about to break down again so he told her gently to take her time. She nodded, gulped and tried to talk. Then she had another go and managed to speak in a small voice.

'Oh, we laughed a lot. She's been Elizabeth Sparrow, Wren, Jay, Hawke, with an e.'

'And this time?'

'Larke.'

'With an e, naturally.'

'Yes.' So Miss Larke, safely staying at the Ashford Castle Hotel, was Ebbie Heritage. Had she just been kind, lending the poor little chambermaid her raincoat and scarf, or had she spotted someone, and if so would she now get out fast?

'Did you have a fallback if anything went wrong?'

Heather nodded. 'Every time. But this was an emergency. We made plans for something like this the first time we met after our rehabilitation. If anything went wrong, or I didn't show, she was to have gone to Rosslare, to the big hotel that looks over the harbour, the Great Southern. That was in case we had to make a dash for it on the ferry. But, now...' She trailed off, the tears close again.

Bond looked at his watch. It was gone eleven. For a second he wanted to put Heather out of her misery, to tell her that Ebbie was alive and well. But experience told him to keep the information very close to his chest.

'Look, Heather, tomorrow's going to be a tough day. I'm going downstairs for a few minutes. You are not to open the door to anyone except me. I'll give you a Morse V knock — tap-tap-tap-bang — twice. If anyone else comes, keep silent. And don't answer the telephone. Get yourself ready for bed. I'll avert my eyes when you open up...'

'Oh, Lord, James, I'm a big girl. I've been in the field, remember.'

She giggled, which signalled a tiny doubt in Bond's mind. Here was a trained field agent, who had been entrusted with possibly the most important target in the Cream Cake operation, yet she appeared to be slightly drunk on less than half a bottle of Chablis. That just didn't ring true. She seemed to be an enthusiastic amateur trying hard for professional recognition. He slipped into his jacket.

'Right, Miss Heather Dare. No door opening, except at my knock; and no answering of the telephone. I won't be long.'

Downstairs, Bond went into the bar and bought a vodka and tonic, offering an English ten pound note. The change came entirely in Irish money, as though there were no difference in the rate of exchange, so he persuaded the barman to give him three pounds' worth of ten pence pieces to feed one of the telephone boxes in the foyer.

He took his time checking the bar, coffee shop and foyer, even walking into that odd well, furnished with black imitation leather seats, that occupied most of the foyer like some kind of bunker. There was nobody there who raised his suspicions. Not a smell, nothing untoward, as his old friend Inspector Murray would have said. When he was absolutely certain, he went over to the telephones near the door, looked up the Ashford Castle Hotel in the directory and dialled the number.

'I'd like to speak to one of your guests, Miss Larke,' he told the distant switchboard operator. 'Miss Elizabeth Larke.'

'Just one moment.' There was a click on the line, then she said, 'I'm sorry, sir, Miss Larke checked out.'

'When? I'm really calling for a friend who was to meet her at your hotel, a Miss Sharke, S-h-a-r-k-e. There wouldn't be a message left for her?'

'I'll have to put you through to Reception.'

There was a short pause then another voice announced, 'Reception.'

Bond repeated his question. Yes, Miss Larke had left a message to say she had gone on ahead.

'You don't know where?' Bond asked.

'It's a Dublin address.' The girl paused as though

uncertain whether she should give it. She relented and
rattled off Ebbie's Dublin address near Fitzwilliam Square.

Bond thanked her, rang off and then dialled the Garda
Special Branch number in Dublin Castle.

'Jacko again, Norman,' he said when Murray came on the
line.

'You just caught me. I was getting out early. Hang on a
minute.' The minute stretched a little. Murray was putting a
trace on the call.

'Right, man. I wanted a word with you anyway.'

'That you'll get, probably tomorrow, Norman. One question: do you think the boys in Mayo will have finished with
Miss Larke — the guest who was so kind with her raincoat?'

Another pause: one, two, three. Murray was holding on to
give the engineers time.

'Well?' prompted Bond.

'I suppose so, if they had her forwarding address. I spoke
to the Super in charge of the case. She was no suspect; as
gentle as a lamb, he said. Lamb and Larke, eh?' he said with
an explosion of laughter.

'Thanks, Norman.'

Bond quickly put down the telephone. Murray knew him
as Jacko B on an official basis. The name had been Bond's
telephone crypto for the Republic of Ireland — his 'blower
name' as old hands called it — for a long time. In fact, he
thought, it must be wearing thin now, but nobody had
thought of changing it. They had worked together a couple of
times, and Murray had no illusions about the Service he was
dealing with when Jacko B contacted him. They had an
edgy, suspicious, though firmly defined relationship. In all
probability Murray would, after three conversations and
having no idea of his whereabouts, be on to the Resident at
the Embassy in Merrion Road.

It was not yet midnight, but Big Mick was never very far
away from a telephone. Piling the loose change on top of the
public telephone, Bond dialled the number. Mick answered

straight away.

Once the bona fides were established, he said, 'I have the cars and the men. Just give me the details, Jacko.'

Bond gave him the number of the hire car, then said, 'Around ten, maybe ten-thirty, tomorrow, you should pick us up near the Green. We'll have parked and be walking up from Grafton Street. What have you got, Mick?'

'A maroon Volvo, a dark blue Audi and an old Cortina, dun-coloured, with plenty of go under the bonnet. Where are we going and how do you want us?'

'We'll be taking the direct route to Rosslare. I want one of you well ahead, let's say the Cortina, with the Volvo and Audi close to me. Box me in if you can, Mick. Don't make it too tight, nothing out of the ordinary. Flash me if we have any persistent company. Flash twice if you see a dark complexioned man with close-cropped hair and a square face who struts rather than walks...'

'He won't be doin' much strutting in a motor.' Big Mick sounded caustic.

'He's military; Germanic. That's the only description I can give you,' Bond said wearily, realising that a word picture of Maxim Smolin was not the easiest thing to produce over the telephone. He had seen the man only once, in Paris about three years ago; seen him once and been through his file a dozen times. There were seven covert photographs in the file but they did not help. Dragging his thoughts back to Big Mick Shean, Bond said, 'See you tomorrow, and thanks, Mick. Will money from the usual place be okay?'

'You're a gentleman, Jacko. Tomorrow, then.'

He cradled the telephone and was about to go up to the room again when he thought of one more chore. Perhaps he was being over-cautious, but he could not help feeling most uneasy. On the way to the elevator he paused by the internal guest telephone and dialled their room number. He frowned as he heard the engaged tone. Heather had disobeyed him

and the knowledge added to his present anxiety. When he
reached the bedroom, Bond gave the Morse Code V knock
twice, quickly. The door opened, and a pink and white figure
scampered back to the bed. He closed the door, put on the
chain and turned to look at her, lying there with a half smile
on her face. On the bedside table the telephone was off the
hook. He nodded towards it.

'Oh.' She smiled more widely, moving from under the
bedclothes so that they dropped back, revealing a bare arm,
shoulder and part of one breast. 'I'm terrible with
telephones, James. I can't stand not answering them, so I
took it off the hook.' She replaced the instrument and looked
at him from the bed, the sheet and blankets falling to reveal
both breasts. 'If you want to sleep here, James, I wouldn't
complain.'

She looked so vulnerable that it took a great deal of will
power for Bond to refuse the offer.

'You're a sweet girl, Heather, and I'm flattered.
Exhausted, but flattered, and tomorrow's another day. It'll
be a tough old day as well.'

'I just feel so...so alone and bloody miserable.' And, with
that, Heather turned over, pushed her head into the pillow
and pulled the sheets up.

Bond quietly removed one of the spare pillows from the
bed, and took off his jacket and trousers. He wrapped himself
in the short silk robe from his getaway case and then in a
blanket he found in the wardrobe. Then he literally stretched
himself across the doorway, one hand resting lightly on the
butt of his automatic pistol.

Eventually he drifted into sleep.

Suddenly he woke with a start. It was five o'clock and
someone was gently trying the handle of the door.

- 6 -
BASILISK

SILENTLY, JAMES BOND rolled out of his blanket, drawing the pistol as he did so. The door handle turned slowly, then stopped, but by that time Bond was at Heather's side of the bed, shaking her naked shoulder with his gun hand. The other he pressed gently over her mouth. She made small grunting noises as he bent low and whispered that they had company, that she should keep silent and get on to the floor, out of sight. She nodded and he took his hand away. He returned to the door, keeping to one side. More than once he had seen what bullets could do to people through doors. Gingerly he slipped the chain, then, standing well back, sharply pulled the door open.

'Jacko? Hallo there.'

Even in the light from the corridor, he recognised Inspector Murray's tall frame and the smiling shrewd face peering into the room.

'What the hell!'

Bond stepped behind him. In one fast movement he shut the door and snapped the lights on, pushing the Garda Special Branch man just hard enough to put him off balance. Murray stumbled forward, grabbing for the bed, but Bond had him in a neck choke, the ASP's muzzle just behind the policeman's right ear.

'What are you playing at, Norman? You'll get yourself killed creeping about like that. Or have you got an armed posse surrounding the hotel?'

'Hold it, Jacko! Hold it! I come in peace – alone and unofficial.'

Heather slowly appeared from the other side of the bed, her frightened eyes looking straight into the Inspector's merry face.

'Ah,' he said, his mouth splitting into a friendly smile as Bond slightly relaxed his grip, 'ah, and this would be Miss Arlington, would it, Mr Boldman? Or shall I call you Jacko B?'

Keeping the pistol close to Murray's head, Bond released him from the choke. With his free hand he found the Garda issue Walther P.P.K. in a hip holster. He removed the gun, sliding it well out of reach across the floor.

'For a man of peace, you come well prepared, Norman.'

'Oh, come on Jacko, I have to carry the cannon. You're knowing that as well as I – and what's a wee gun between friends?'

'It could be death.' Bond sounded cynical. 'You knew I was here all the time then? And Miss Arlington?'

'Ach, man, of course. But I kept it to myself. We just happen to have a red alert on at the moment and your face came up at the airport. Lucky I was on duty at the Castle when it came in on the Fax. I telephoned the Brits' chief spook, old Grimshawe, at Merrion Road and asked if he had any extra bodies over here, or if he expected any. Grimshawe tells me the truth. We work better that way. It saves a lot of time. He said no spooks and no extra-curricular activities, so I believed him. Then you rang me, and I got interested.' His eyes twinkled as he turned back towards Heather. 'You wouldn't be Miss Larke's friend, Miss Sharke, would you, dear?'

'What?' Heather's mouth hung open.

'Because if you are, then it's bloody bad security, and not up to the standards we've come to know and love. Names like Larke and Sharke attract attention. They're stupid, which we are not.'

Bond stepped back. 'Mark him well, dear, stupid he is not,' he said, mimicking Murray's accent, which was more

lowland Scots than Dublin. As he always said, 'I was born in
the North, educated in the South, take my holidays in
Scotland or Spain and work in the Republic. I don't feel at
home anywhere.'

'It was rather stupid, Norman, to come trying my door
handle at this time of night.'

'And when else should I try it? Not in broad daylight,
when I have to account for every movement I make.'

'You could have knocked.'

'I was going to knock, Jacko. Another thirty seconds and
I'd have knocked. Tap, tap, bloody tap.'

The men looked at each other, neither believing the other.

'I'm not here for the fun of it.' Inspector Murray produced
his cheerful smile. 'I'm here because I owe you in a big way,
Jacko, and I always repay.'

That was true. Four years ago, Bond had saved Murray's
life just on the Republic's side of the border, not far from
Crossmaglen; but that incident would remain buried in the
secret archives of Bond's Service.

Heather pulled the clothes off the bed, wrapping them
around her and trying to pat her hair into shape at the same
time. It was an interesting and revealing series of movements
which had both men gazing at her in silence. When she was
decent, Murray sat himself on the bed, swivelling his body in
a vain attempt to watch both Bond and Heather at the same
time.

'Look, girl,' he said, 'Jacko will tell you that you can be
trusting me.'

'Don't even think about trust, Miss Arlington.' Bond's
face remained impassive.

Murray sighed. 'All right. I'll just be giving you the facts.
Then I can get home to a cup of cocoa and my sleep.'

They sat as though staring each other out. Finally Murray
spoke again.

'Your Miss Larke, now – the one that lent the poor young
girl her coat and scarf...'

'What...' Heather began, but Bond shook his head imperceptibly, signalling that she should not react.

'Well, your Miss Larke appears to have gone to earth, as they say of foxes.'

'You mean she's not...?' Heather began again.

'Shut up!' snapped Bond.

'My God, Jacko, can't you be the masterful one when you've a mind?' Murray grinned, took a breath, then started to speak again. 'There was a Dublin address.' He looked around, first at Heather and then at Bond, his face a picture of innocence. 'A nice little address in Fitzwilliam Square.' He waited but received no comment so with a shrug continued: 'Well, as they would say in London, somebody's gone and turned over the drum.'

'You mean this Dublin address given by someone called Larke?' Bond asked.

'Whose name is not Larke, I suspect, but Heritage. Ebbie Heritage.'

'This woman, Larke or Heritage...' said Bond.

'Ach come on, Jacko, don't play the goat with me. You know bloody well, if you'll pardon me Miss...er...Sharke?'

'Arlington,' said Heather decidedly. She seemed at last to have got herself under control.

'Yes.' Murray clearly did not believe a syllable of the name. 'I've told you, the address provided by Miss Larke really belongs to a Miss Heritage. Both are missing. The apartment in Fitzwilliam Square's been done over.'

'Was it burglary? Vandalism?' asked Bond curtly.

'Oh, a bit of both. It's one hell of a mess. I'd say a professional job dressed up to look like enthusiastic amateurs. The interesting thing is that there's not a single piece of correspondence in the place. They even ripped up floorboards. Now what d'you think of that?'

'You've come out here at dawn just to tell me this?'

'Well, you showed interest in the Ashford Castle business. I thought you should know. Besides, me knowing what kind of work you're engaged in, I thought there was something else I should put your way.'

Bond nodded for Murray to continue.

'Did you ever hear of a fella called Smolin?' Murray asked with supreme disinterest. 'Maxim Smolin. Our branch in London, and I presume the people you work for as well, have him under the stupid code name of Basilisk.'

'Mmm,' Bond grunted.

'You want this joker's life history, or do you know it already, Jacko?'

Bond smiled. 'Okay, Norm…'

'And don't you be after calling me Norm, either, or I'll have you in the Bridewell on some trumped-up charge that'll ban you from the Republic for life.'

'Okay, Norman. Maxim Anton Smolin; born 1946 in Berlin of a German lady, Christina von Geshmann, by a Soviet General, called Smolin, whose mistress she was at the time. Alexei Alexeiovich Smolin. Young Smolin took his father's name but his mother's nationality. He was educated in Berlin and Moscow. His mother died when he was only a couple of years old. Is that your man, Norman?'

'Go on.'

'He entered the military via one of those nice Russian schools; I forget which one. It could have been the 13th Army. Anyway, he was commissioned young, then sent to the *Spetsnaz* Training Centre — for the élite, if you like that kind of élite killer. Young Maxim found his way by invitation into the most secret arm of the Military Intelligence, the G.R.U. That's the only way you get into the G.R.U., unlike the K.G.B. who'll take you off the streets if you make them an offer. From there by a series of postings, Smolin came back to East Berlin. And he returned as a high-ranking field officer of the H.V.A., the East German Intelligence Service.

'He's everything, our Maxim: a mole within a warren of moles, working with the H.V.A., which has to work with the K.G.B., yet all the time doing little jobs on the side because he's really a member of the G.R.U.'

'You have the man to a T.' Murray beamed at them. 'You know what they say about the G.R.U.? They say it costs a rouble to join, and two roubles to get out. Almost an Irish saying, that. It's very difficult to become a G.R.U. officer. It's even more difficult to jump over the wall once you're in because there really is only one way out — in a long box. They're very fond of training foreigners, and Smolin is only half Russian. They tell me he holds great power in East Germany. Even the K.G.B. men there are in awe of him.'

'Well, Norman? Have you something new to tell us about him?' asked Bond.

'You know, Jacko, the whole world thinks that we have only one problem on this divided island, the North and the South. They'd be wrong and I'm sure you're aware of it, so. Your man Basilisk arrived in the Republic two days ago. Now, Jacko, when I heard of that terrible thing at Ashford Castle, I recalled there'd already been two just like it over the water, and a little quotation came to mind.'

'Oh yes?'

'There's something most pertinent been written about your Soviet General Staff Chief Intelligence Directorate — your G.R.U. The fella was a G.R.U. defector, name of Suverov. He was writing about people who can't keep quiet, who leak secrets. He wrote, "The G.R.U. knows how to rip such tongues out!" Interesting, Jacko?'

Bond nodded, looking solemn. The historians of the intelligence services tended to dismiss the G.R.U. as having been swallowed by the K.G.B. 'The G.R.U. (Soviet Military Intelligence) is completely dominated by the K.G.B.', one writer had maintained. Another had written, 'It is an academic exercise to consider the G.R.U. as a separate entity'. That was wrong on both counts. The G.R.U. fights hard to keep a separate identity.

'Penny for them, Jacko?' Murray was making himself comfortable on the bed.

'I was only thinking that the cream of the G.R.U. are richer and more deadly than their opposite numbers in the K.G.B. Men like Smolin are better trained, and have no scruples at all.'

'And Smolin's here, Jacko and...' He paused and the smile vanished from his face to be replaced by a hard look, 'And we've lost the bastard, if you'll pardon the language again, Miss Dare.'

'Arlington,' Heather mumbled without conviction. Bond saw that she looked both nervous and a little sad.

Norman Murray lifted his hand and tilted it. 'Dare, Wagen, Sharke, so who's counting?' He yawned and stretched. 'It's been a long night. I must away to my bed.'

'Lost him?' Bond asked sharply.

'He did the vanishing trick, Jacko. But Smolin's always been good at vanishing – he's a proper Houdini. Talking of Houdini, Smolin's probably not the only one that's on the loose in the Republic.'

'Don't tell me you've lost the Chairman of the Central Committee as well?'

'It's no time to be joking, Jacko. We've had a small tip off. Nothing elaborate, but a straw in the wind.'

'A straw to clutch at?'

'If it's the truth, you wouldn't be after clutching at this one, Jacko B.'

'Well?' Bond waited.

'The word is that someone much higher up the ladder than Smolin is in the Republic. I've nothing firm but the word's strong enough. There's someone here from the top. Now that's all I can give you. I'll be saying goodnight to you both, then. And sweet dreams.' He rose, walked to the corner of the room and retrieved his Walther.

'Thanks, Norman. Thanks a whole bunch,' said Bond, walking him to the door. 'Can I ask you something?'

'Ask away. There's no charge.'

'You've lost sight of Comrade Colonel Smolin...'

'Yes. And we haven't even had a sniff at the other one – if he's here at all.'

'Are you still looking for them?'

'We are, in a way, of course. Manpower's your problem, Jacko B.'

'What would you do if you cornered either of them?'

'Put him on an aeroplane to Berlin. But those fellas would complain and dodge into that den of iniquity in Orwell Road. You know, the one that's got about six hundred pieces of aerial and electronic dishes on the roof. Bit of an irony, isn't it? The Soviets having their Embassy in Orwell Road, and building a forest of communications hardware on top of it. That's where your man would hide.'

'And he's not there at the moment?'

'How would I know, so? I am not my brother's keeper.'

They came into St Stephen's Green from Grafton Street, with Heather clutching bulging carriers from Switzers and Brown Thomas. Bond walked two paces behind her and slightly to the left. He carried one small parcel and his gun hand hovered across the front of his unbuttoned jacket. Ever since Norman Murray had left the hotel he had been increasingly uncomfortable about the way things were turning out. Heather had been furious that he had not told her Ebbie was alive.

'But why didn't you tell me? You knew how I felt. You knew she was alive…'

'I knew she was probably alive.'

'Then why couldn't you have the decency to tell me?'

'Because I wasn't certain, and because your precious Cream Cake strikes me as having been a lash-up operation from the start. It's still a lash-up.'

He stopped himself from saying more, for his humour was rapidly fraying at the edges. In theory Cream Cake had been a good operation, but if Heather was typical of the five young people chosen to carry it out, the Operations Planners were criminally at fault. There would never have been time to train them properly. Yet the fact that their parents were in place was considered to be enough.

Their names ran repeatedly through Bond's mind like a gramophone record stuck in a groove: Franzi Trauben and Elli Zuckermann, both dead, skulls crushed and tongues neatly removed; Franz Belzinger, who liked to be called Wald; Irma Wagen herself and Emilie Nikolas, who should be in Rosslare. He asked himself why Franz liked being nicknamed Wald. But no, he told himself, he must start thinking of them by their English names, though much good they had done them. He must think of the dead Bridget and Millicent and the living Heather and Ebbie; of the presumably living Jungle Baisley.

While he thought about these five characters, Bond was conscious of the other dark figures, especially Maxim Smolin, whom he had seen so many times in grainy surveillance photographs and jumpy films, distorted through fibre-optics lenses, and — only once — in the flesh, as he came out of Fouquet's on the Champs Elysées. Bond had been sitting almost opposite at a pavement café with another officer and even at the distance provided by that wide street with the distractions of its traffic, the short, tough, military figure of Smolin had a profound effect on him. It may have been the way he carried himself like a professional soldier, but exaggeratedly so; or perhaps it was his look, the eyes never still, and his hands held with one fist clenched, the other flat making a tough cutting edge. Smolin appeared to radiate energy and a malevolent power.

The seventh protagonist, the 'someone higher up the ladder than Smolin', unnamed by Norman Murray, threw a much darker shadow over the entire business.

Bringing his mind back to the present, Bond noticed the rain had gone, yet there was a chill in the air and gunfire-smoke clouds raced each other over the rooftops. They paused for the traffic lights and Bond caught sight of the

black-bearded, tousled-haired Big Mick Shean at the wheel
of a maroon Volvo. The Irishman showed no sign of recognition but Bond knew he would have already identified the
parked car and he and Heather as they waited for the lights
to change. They crossed the road on the green light and
began to walk slowly. He had told Heather not to rush.

'It should be the same routine you use when lighting a fuse
on an explosive charge. Walk away. Never run in case you
trip.'

She had nodded. She obviously knew something about
explosives, so there had been some field training, he supposed. During the journey to Rosslare he would go through it
piece by piece.

They did not cut across the Green but sauntered along the
north side, heading for the east side where the car was
parked. As they drew level with the Shelbourne Hotel, Bond
almost froze. Glancing across at the famous hotel, he saw for
only the second time in the flesh the precise, compact figure
of Colonel Maxim Smolin, accompanied by two short,
heavily built men. The three were descending the steps,
looking left and right as though expecting transport.

'Don't look towards the Shelbourne,' Bond muttered
under his breath. 'No, Heather, don't look,' he repeated,
quickening his pace as she reacted. 'Keep walking. Your ex-
lover just came out of his cave.'

ACCIDENT

THERE WAS NO point in trying to run. Smolin knew Heather clothed and unclothed, and Bond reckoned that Smolin would know him on sight as well. After all, his photograph was in the files of probably every intelligence agency in the world. All he could hope was that in the traffic and with Smolin's obvious concern over his own transport, he would not have spotted them. But he knew the chances were slim. Smolin was trained to single out the most unlikely faces among a crowd of thousands.

Gently taking Heather's arm, Bond guided her around the corner, almost imperceptibly increasing their pace as they walked towards the car.

He felt the familiar, unpleasant tingling around the back of his neck – like a dozen small, deadly spiders unleashed in the nape hair. It was not one hundred per cent accurate, but Bond was realistic enough to know the odds were very high on Colonel Maxim Smolin's eyes watching their retreating backs. He was also probably smiling at the coincidence of catching sight of his former lover in the middle of Dublin. Or, Bond wondered, was it simply coincidence? In this business coincidence was usually a dirty word. M always maintained there was no such thing, just as Freud had once said that, in conditions of stress and confusion, there was no such thing as an accident. Once inside, Bond scanned the mirror as he twisted the key in the ignition and clipped on his seat belt. The traffic was heavy, but he just caught the flash of a dun-coloured Cortina passing behind them with a dark blue Audi close on its bumper. Already he had seen Big Mick at the wheel of the maroon Volvo, so all the cars were circling the Green. The trick would be to get out successfully and on to the road to the outskirts of Dun Laoghaire, then along the coast. The route would take them through Bray and Arklow, Gorey and Wexford, then down to Rosslare. A trick it certainly would be, for they might have to circle the Green more than once to get into position, and that meant passing the Shelbourne again.

Gently Bond started to back out from his parking space, waiting a little impatiently for a gap to appear in the traffic. When he saw the opportunity, he reversed the car very fast, slammed the gear into first and took off at some speed. Seconds later he was tucked neatly in behind the Audi.

They circled the Green once and there was no sign of Smolin and his two large companions outside the Shelbourne. The Cortina left them at that junction and went straight on towards Merrion Row and Baggot Street. By the time they reached the same point a second time, Big Mick was behind them so that the Saab was tightly boxed in, with the Cortina well ahead and out of sight as the forward scout. Glancing in the mirror, Bond saw Big Mick's craggy face split into a grin at the successful link-up. In the back seat Heather's shopping rolled around, slipping and sliding as Bond threw the car from one lane to another. He wanted to get out of Dublin as soon as possible.

'Why did he like to be called Wald?' Bond asked suddenly.

They were now well away, approaching Bray in a steady stream of traffic, with its great church, looking almost French, dominating the small town.

Heather had been silent, allowing Bond to concentrate, while they had negotiated the pleasant, if crowded, roads that took them out of the city, past Jury's Hotel and the anachronistic Royal Dublin Society in Ballsbridge. At his question she started in her seat.

'Wald? You mean Franz? Jungle?'

'I'm not talking about the Black Forest, old love.'

Bond's eyes scanned the road ahead, the mirrors and instruments, making regular checks every thirty seconds. Yet his mind was balanced between driving and the interrogation he wanted to conduct. Heather was silent, as though she was preparing her answer.

'It was odd. You've seen his photograph? Yes, well, he was so good-looking with his blond hair, clear skin, and so fit and slim, that he looked like those old photographs you see of Hitler's ideal German – a true Aryan.'

'So why did he like to be called Wald?' he repeated a little impatiently.

'He was vain.'

'And what's that got to do with it?'

They had stopped for some traffic lights. Bond's car was close to the Audi's rear, with Big Mick's Volvo separated from them by two lorries.

'About the work, he was vain. He said he could always hide from anybody. He had this idea that no one would ever find him if he didn't want to be found. It would be like searching a dense forest. I think it was Elli who said we should call him Wald, and that pleased him. He is a little full of himself – is that the right phrase?'

Bond nodded. 'Hence Jungle Baisley now. Looking for him would be like looking for a particular tree?'

'That's about it. Or like a needle in a haystack.'

Now Bond was even more concerned. 'You say Elli gave him the nickname. You five met together regularly?' That would have been almost suicidally bad security, he thought. But there were many things about Cream Cake that pointed towards bad security.

'Not often, no. But there were meetings.'

'Were they called by your controller?'

'No. Swift saw us one at a time. We had regular meetings in safe houses; rendezvous in shops or parks. But you must understand that we all knew each other since we were children.'

Bond thought they were almost children when this monstrous plan was conceived. Two were dead for sure, the others had prices on their heads and their tongues. Smolin would not rest until they were all safely in their coffins. And what of Swift, their control? There had been a great deal about Swift in the files M had put his way. Swift was a street name, his real identity carefully hidden, even in the official documents. But Bond knew the man behind that name. He was a legend among case officers, one of the most experienced and careful people in the business. He had been given the name Swift because of the speed at which he worked on his clients: swift and sure-footed. He was not the kind of man to make errors. Yet if Heather had told Bond the truth about the way Cream Cake had ended, Swift's judgment had let him down at last.

They passed through lush green countryside. A few cottages sent up drifting smoke from their turf-burning fires. It was a land that was tranquil, if untidy – untidy like Cream Cake. Quickly, Bond went through it again in his mind.

All five had parents who had been sleepers, handing over only the odd piece of useful intelligence. Yet all of them were very well placed. Bridget's father was a lawyer, with some important officials among his clientele. Millicent's parents were both doctors who had a number of intelligence community people on their lists. The other three came from military or para-military families: Ebbie's father was an officer with the Vopos, Jungle's and Heather's were German officers working out of the Karlshorst barracks, which housed both intelligence buildings and the Soviet Headquarters in East Germany. It was easy to see how a few years ago those five young people had shone out when the Planners thought of compromising key targets in East Germany.

Bridget was to set her cap at a member of the East German Politburo and Millicent was to make herself available to one of the seven K.G.B. officers serving under a paper-thin 'advisory' cover at Karlshorst. Ebbie had a Major of the East

German Army in her sights. Jungle and Heather were in charge of the greatest prizes — Fräulein Captain Dietrich, the woman officer in charge of the civilian executive staff of the H.V.A., well known for her taste in younger men, and Colonel Maxim Smolin.

Smolin, who had fallen for Heather hook, line and sinker, or so the record said. Bond recalled every detail of that file: 'Basilisk set the girl up in a small apartment five minutes' drive from the Karlshorst Headquarters, where he spent most of his off-duty hours with her. After any "business" trip abroad he brought back luxuries.' There followed a list ranging from expensive hi-fi equipment to what the French term 'fantasy' gifts from Paris. Attributed to Swift, the list was outstanding for its detail. Dates and items were given in one column, the time Basilisk spent away in another, with a full account of his movements. It was the only list so itemised.

Fräulein Captain Dietrich also gave presents to Jungle but Swift did not appear to have such full intelligence about those. There was even less information about the relationships between the other three operatives and their targets. From the beginning Bond had wondered whether this was a complete operation, or whether only two people, Dietrich and Smolin, were really wanted, the rest being merely makeweights or even distractions. Bearing in mind the way Swift had misjudged the operation, he would have to sift the details again and again. As they were passing through a village of around five hundred inhabitants, which seemed to have a cathedral, twelve garages and twenty bars, he said, 'Tell me about it one more time, Heather.'

'I've told you all of it.' She spoke in a small, weary voice, as though she did not want to discuss Cream Cake ever again.

'Just once more. How did you feel when they told you?'

'I was only nineteen. I was precocious, I suppose. I saw it all as a joke. It wasn't until later that I realised how deadly the whole business really was.'

'But you felt excited?'

'It was an adventure, for heaven's sake. If you were just nineteen and they told you to seduce a not unattractive woman older than yourself, wouldn't you have been excited?'

'It depends which way my feelings ran politically.'

'What is that supposed to mean?' Her shredded nerves were showing now.

'Were you a politically aware young woman when they approached you for this exciting adventure?'

She gave a long sigh. 'If you really want to know, I was disenchanted with the whole scene. To me everyone talked rubbish: East, West, North, South, whatever – the Communist Party, the Americans, the British. Maxim used to say, "When it comes to politics and religion, it's a fairground."'

'Really?' Bond was surprised at this sudden revelation about Smolin's views on political matters. 'And what did he mean by that, I wonder?'

'He meant you paid your money and took your choice. But he used to say that once you'd taken that choice it bound you hand and foot. He said that Communism was the nearest thing in politics to the Roman Catholic Church. Both of them had rules from which you could not deviate.'

'But you were trying to make him deviate. You were doing your best to make him a convert.'

'In a way, yes.'

Bond grunted. 'You had met him before?'

She sighed again. 'I've told you. He was a regular visitor to our house.'

'And he'd already shown an interest in you?'

'Not particularly.'

She hesitated, then launched into a long speech. Colonel Smolin may not have been the greatest looking man around, but he was attractive. There was no real physical attraction at first sight but he had something. Then Smolin was made even more attractive to her when the matter was fully explained. First her father had said he was fighting against the powers that had split her country in two. Then the man she had come to know as Swift, her controller, had been more blunt.

'He's a bastard,' Swift had said at her first briefing, 'a grade A bastard who wouldn't think twice about hanging his own mother with piano wire. He's a professional spycatcher and spykiller who doesn't mind if he's wrong from time to time. We're asking you to get yourself into his bed, make him rely on you, share his thoughts with you, share his fears, and, in the end, his secrets.'

'Maxim wasn't really as bad as Swift painted him.'

Bond had already sensed that she still clung to some hidden nostalgia about the affair with Smolin. 'I expect the executioners' mistresses at Auschwitz and Belsen said the same thing while they ate their *Kirschtorte*.' He had no time for sentiment as far as men like Smolin were concerned.

'No!' Heather almost shouted. 'Read my report. It's all there. Maxim was an odd mixture of a man, but a lot of stories about him are just not true.'

'So that's why he's got a team out now hunting down you and your friends? That's why he's tearing tongues out?'

She remained silent, staring ahead. Bond gave her a quick glance. He could have sworn that there were tears in her eyes.

'And you just went out and caught him, netted him, bedded him and reported the pillow talk back to Swift?'

'I've told you!' She almost shouted at him. 'How many more times, James? Yes, yes, yes. I hooked him. I even became fond of him. He was good to be with: kind, thoughtful, gentle and very loving. Too loving.'

'Because you misjudged the moment of truth?'

'Yes! Must I go through it again and again? I told Swift that I thought he was ready. God ...' She was indeed near to tears now. 'Swift told me to bring him home, to lay the news on him.'

Bond concentrated on the road. 'And what happened when you laid the news on Maxim Smolin?'

Heather took a deep breath and opened her mouth. At that moment they started to go into a bend leading on to a long stretch of open road flanked by scrubby hedges. Big Mick, a couple of hundred yards behind, flashed his lights and in the driving mirror Bond saw two cars squeezing in on the Volvo fast so that the road was filled with the three vehicles. Though he had not driven this route for years, Bond had an odd sense of *déjà vu*. In his mind there was a picture of an accident, flashing blue lights and police flagging them down. Even before seeing what lay ahead, he felt the fear tighten in his stomach. Behind, the two flanking cars appeared bent on squashing the Volvo.

Then they were round the bend and on to the straight road that was, just as he expected, littered with débris, warning signs and flashing lights. He shouted to Heather to brace herself. Ahead, there was a Garda car, an ambulance, the remains of a dun-coloured saloon that could have been a Cortina, and an Audi on its side crushing the hedge. There was also a heavy lorry, across the road. Bond was in no mood for lorries. He braked with his left foot and tried to spin the car, even though he knew that by now the road behind him would be blocked by a crushed Volvo — unless Big Mick had supernatural powers.

Heather screamed, the car slewed sideways and kept going, gathering speed in spite of Bond's attempt to control it. Too late, he realised that the road surface had been covered with a thick slick of oil.

The scene of the crash was coming up with amazing speed. Bond fought the wheel, feeling the rear coming round much too fast and knowing there was no way to avoid collision. When it came, there was a sense almost of anti-climax. A grinding crunch brought them to a halt.

Bond automatically reached for his gun but was already too late. The doors were wrenched open and two men in

Garda uniform pulled Heather and Bond out of the car,
using an expert and very painful arm-lock. Dazed, Bond
wondered where his gun had gone. He tried unsuccessfully
to resist and became aware that they were being hustled into
the ambulance, where four other men were waiting to take
over.

For members of an ambulance team, they appeared far
from concerned about injuries. By this time Heather was
screaming loud enough to wake the dead. She was silenced
by one man chopping her sharply on the side of the neck with
the edge of his hand. She went down just as the doors closed
and the ambulance began to move. The man who had hit her
caught her falling body and hoisted it on to one of the
stretcher beds.

From the front a fifth man appeared, yet they seemed in no
way crowded. Later Bond realised that they were in a very
large ambulance, probably a refurbished military vehicle. It
picked up speed, its klaxon sounding. Above the wail the
fifth man spoke.

'Mr Bond, I believe? I'm afraid there's been a minor
accident and we have to get you away from the site as fast as
possible. I'm sorry to inconvenience you, but this is essential
for everyone's safety. I'm sure you understand. If you would
just sit down and remain quiet we'll get along nicely, I'm
sure.'

There was no doubt about it. Colonel Maxim Smolin had
a great deal of charm, even when it was laced with threats.

- 8 -
COCKEREL OR WEASEL

THE AMBULANCE SWAYED and bounced, slowed, swayed again, then accelerated. Bond reckoned they had very quickly left the main road and were probably doubling back. They could be edging up into the hills, even climbing through the wild and craggy Wicklow Gap. He glanced at Heather, who lay unmoving on the stretcher bed, and hoped that the force of the blow had not done her any serious damage.

'She'll be fine, Mr Bond. My men had orders not to kill, merely to render unconscious.'

Close to, Smolin was an even more impressive figure, and his quick response to Bond's anxious look showed an intelligent and observant awareness.

'And your people are well trained in how to kill and not quite kill, I'm sure.' He almost added Smolin's name, but held back.

'Trained to perfection, my dear sir.'

Smolin spoke nearly faultless English, though a discerning ear would pick up the fact that it was just a shade too perfect. His charm of manner took Bond by surprise, yet behind it there was an undeniable sense of absolute power and confidence. Smolin was a man who expected to be obeyed, who knew that he would always be in control. He was somewhat taller than Bond had supposed from his previous two sightings, and his body was fit and well-muscled under the expensive anorak, cavalry twill trousers and rollneck.

Smolin looked hard at Bond and there was the trace of humour in his dark, slightly oval eyes. The smile around his mouth appeared amused rather than mocking.

'May I ask what all this is about?'

Bond had to speak loudly above the engine noise and rattling of the swaying ambulance. Either the driver was unused to handling such a vehicle or they were indeed on a difficult mountain road. The smile turned into a short, almost pleasant chuckle.

'Oh, come on now, James Bond, you know well enough what it's about.'

'I know that I was giving a lift to a lady friend of mine, and suddenly I find we're kidnapped.' He paused, then added with mock puzzlement, 'And you know my name! How the hell do you know my name anyway?'

This time Smolin gave a full-blooded laugh. 'Bond, my dear good fellow, don't make me into a fool.' He nodded his head towards Heather. 'Do you know who your lady friend is and what she has done? I suspect you know exactly what she has done and exactly who I am. After all, my file is with many foreign agencies. Surely the British Secret Intelligence Service has a dossier on me, just as my own Service has one on you? You know everything about the operation called Cream Cake, and I would be most surprised if you did not have all the details of the punishment at present being dealt out to its protagonists.'

'Cream Cake?' Even Bond was pleased with the convincing mixture of query, bewilderment and surprise.

'Operation Cream Cake.'

'I know nothing about cream cakes — or chocolate éclairs!' Bond was pacing himself now, allowing time to build up a good, healthy anger. 'I do know that Heather asked me to give her a lift...'

Smolin gave a rueful smile. 'Would this be after the little problem in her beauty salon last night?'

'What problem?'

'You're trying to tell me that you were not the man who was with her when some ill-advised idiots tried to kill her in London? That you're not the man who drove her to the airport...' A hint of uncertainty crept into the smile.

'I bumped into her in the departure lounge at Heathrow.' Bond stared at him unwaveringly. 'I've met her only once before. Look, what's this all about? And why did you set up that road block? Are you a terrorist involved in the North or something?'

He was sizing up the opposition while playing for time. Heather still lay unconscious, Smolin sat quite close to him and the four other men were distributed around the ambulance. Two were in front, the other two by the doors. All were clinging on hard for the roller coaster ride. He could not drag the charade on for much longer and, as they had disarmed him, neither could he contemplate escape.

'If I didn't know who you are and had not watched you making your own security precautions, I might just wonder if I'd got the wrong man.' Smolin was smiling again. 'But the set-up, together with the weapons you were carrying. Well...' He allowed the conclusion to hang in the air.

'And what of your set-up?' Bond asked innocently.

'I suspect the arrangements were exactly as you would have made in similar circumstances. We had a back-up in radio contact watching you while we went on ahead. We simply closed off the far end of the road a mile farther on. Then we shut off the road behind you when we had you in our zone. It's the old funnel principle.'

Bond could dissemble no longer. 'They teach you those kind of skills in that centre of yours on the old Khodinka airfield, do they Colonel Smolin? The place where most of you end up, one way or another, either neat in a box in the crematorium, or alive and screaming because you've betrayed your Service – the organisation you jokingly call "The Aquarium"? Or do you learn them in your offices on Knamensky Street?'

'So, Bond, you do know about my Service. You know about G.R.U. And you know about me too. I'm flattered – and happy that I was right about you.'

'Of course I know, along with anyone who takes the trouble to read the right books. We have a saying in my Service that the tricks of our trade are far from secret. You have only to find the right bookshops in the Charing Cross Road and you can learn it all: tradecraft, addresses, organisation. It just requires a little reading.'

'Rather more than that, I suspect.'

'Perhaps, because the G.R.U. likes to let the K.G.B. have the glory, pretending to be backseat boys who bow to the grey men of Dzerzhinsky Square. Yes, we do know you're more fanatical, more secretive and therefore more dangerous.'

Smolin's smile was overtly happy. 'Much more dangerous. Good, I'm glad we know where we stand. It has been a long-held ambition of mine to meet you face to face, Mr Bond. Was it you, perhaps, who concocted the ill-conceived Cream Cake plan?'

'There you have me, Colonel Smolin. I know nothing of such an operation.'

One of the drivers shouted something from the front of the ambulance and Smolin said, almost apologetically, that they would soon have to take measures to ensure Bond and Heather were silent. The ambulance slowed down, lurched, leaned heavily to the left so that it was necessary to hang on tight as they bumped over rough ground. Gradually they rumbled to a halt. From the front came the sound of the cab door being slammed shut. Then the rear doors were opened and a short, red-faced man dressed in the dark uniform of an ambulance driver peered in.

'They are not here yet, Herr Colonel,' he said to Smolin in German.

The Colonel merely nodded in an off-hand way, and told them to watch and wait. Bond craned his neck in an attempt to see out of the rear. A view of trees backed by rocky slopes bore out his original feeling that they had taken a route into the bleak Wicklow hills.

'Get the girl ready.'

Smolin half turned his head, giving the order to one of the men in the front. The man fumbled with a briefcase and Bond saw a hypodermic syringe being prepared. He made a move towards the syringe bearer, whose partner immediately produced an automatic pistol, the muzzle pointing steadily at Bond. Smolin raised an arm, as though both protecting and restraining Bond.

'It's all right. The girl will not be harmed, but I think she should be put under a mild sedation for a while. We have a long drive ahead, and I don't want her to be conscious. You, friend Bond, will lie on the floor in the back of the car that will arrive at any minute. You will have your face covered and as long as you behave, no harm will come to you.' He paused, smiled, then added, 'Yet!'

Heather moved slightly and groaned, as though regaining consciousness. The man with the syringe quietly prepared her for the injection, which he gave skilfully, sliding the needle through the skin of her bared forearm at a neatly calculated angle.

'So, James Bond, you say that you know nothing of any operation coded Cream Cake?'

Bond shook his head.

'And I suppose,' Smolin continued, 'you've never heard of Irma Wagen?'

'It's a name not known to me.'

'But you do know Heather Dare?'

'I met her once before we saw each other in the airport departure lounge, yes.'

'And where did you meet her, "once before the airport departure lounge"?'

'At a party. Through friends.'

'Friends as in professional friends? I believe, in the

terminology of your Service, "friends" are other members of
that Service. Or, at least, your Foreign Office refers to them
as "the Friends".'

'Ordinary friends. A couple called Hazlett – Tom and
Maria Hazlett.'

He gave an address in Hampstead, knowing it could be
checked with impunity, for Tom and Maria were an active
alibi couple. If asked, even in a roundabout way, whether
they knew Bond or Heather they would answer, 'Yes, and
isn't Heather wonderful?' or 'Of course, James is an old
friend.' They would also have a surveillance team on to the
questioners in double quick time. That was what the Service
had trained them to do.

'So you would claim you did not know that Irma Wagen
and Heather Dare of the Dare To Be Chic beauty salon are
the same person?'

'I've never heard of any Irma Wagen.'

'No. No, of course you haven't, James. You must call me
Maxim by the way. I do not respond to the diminutive, Max.
No, you haven't heard of Irma, neither of the doomed Cream
Cake operation.' His smile did not change, but the disbelief
rang through his words. Then he came out and said it aloud.
'I just do not believe you, James Bond. I cannot believe you.'

'Please yourself.' Bond gave the impression of complete
lack of concern.

'Where were you driving Fräulein Wagen, whom you
know as Heather Dare?'

'To Enniscorthy.'

'Why should she want to go to Enniscorthy?' Smolin
shook his head, as though to underline his disbelief. 'And
where were you going that enabled you to be able to help her
that way?'

'We simply recognised each other at the airport and sat
next to one another on the aeroplane. I told her I was going
to Waterford and she asked if she could cadge a lift.'

'What were you going to do in Waterford?'

'Buy glass, what else? I'm very fond of Waterford crystal.'

'Of course you are. And it's so difficult to buy in London, isn't it?' The heavy sarcasm betrayed Smolin's Russian side.

'I am on leave, Herr Colonel Smolin. I repeat, I know of no Irma Wagen and have never heard of an operation called Cream Cake.'

'We shall see,' Smolin replied smoothly. 'But just to clear the air, I will tell you what we know of this ludicrously named operation. It was what used to be called a honeytrap. Your people baited it with four very young and attractive girls.' He held up four fingers, grasping one for each name, as though ticking them off. 'There was Franzi Trauben, Elli Zuckermann, Irma Wagen and Emilie Nikolas.' He laughed pleasantly again. 'Emilie is a good name when you consider that we always spoke of our honeytrap targets as Emilies. But you know all that.' He ran a hand through his dark hair. 'Each of these girls had a well placed target, and they might have got away with it but for the fact that I was included.' Suddenly his whole demeanour altered. 'They used *me* as a target for their games. Me, Maxim Smolin, as though I could be caught and netted by a slip of a girl with about as much idea of how to set up an entrapment as a raw recruit.' His voice rose. 'That's what I can never forgive your people for doing. Sicking an amateur on me; so amateur that she gave the game away within minutes of her first pass at me, and eventually brought down the whole nasty little network. Your Service, Bond, took me for some kind of fool! A professional would have been different but an amateur like her,' he jabbed a finger towards Heather's prone body, 'an amateur I can never forgive.'

So, this was the real Smolin – proud, arrogant, and unforgiving.

'Surely the *Glavnoye Razvedyvatelnoye Upravleniye* also uses casual labour from time to time, Maxim?' Bond asked the question with the ghost of a smile.

'Casual labour?' A fine spray of spittle clouded the air in

front of Smolin's lips as he spat the words out. 'Of course we would train casual labour but never would we use it against a target of my importance.'

There he had it. My importance. Colonel Maxim Smolin regarded himself as inviolable, essential to the smooth running of one of the topmost secret organisations within the Soviet Union. The other was Bond's older enemy, the one-time SMERSH, now totally reorganised as Department 8 of Directorate S, following their loss of credibility as Department V as in Victor. Smolin was breathing heavily, and Bond felt that old and ice-cold hand trace an invisible finger down his spine, an indication of fear. He recognised the stone-hard face of a killer, the muscular body, that brightness in the dark eyes.

From far away came the sound of a car's horn. It gave three short blasts followed by a longer one.

'They're here,' said Smolin, speaking again in German.

The ambulance doors were opened, revealing the full view of green slopes strewn with outcrops of grey rock and a half circle of trees. They were parked well off the road. Two cars, a BMW and a Mercedes, were making slow progress towards them. Bond looked at Smolin and cocked his head towards Heather.

'I honestly have no knowledge of this Cream Cake business.' He spoke quietly, hoping that in his blind rage Smolin might believe him. 'It sounds more like a B.N.D. job than our people...'

Smolin turned. 'It was your Service, James Bond. I have proof, believe me; just as you must believe we'll sweat you until your very bones turn to water. There are still a couple of mysteries that need solving, and I'm here to solve them.'

'Mysteries?'

The cars were near now and two of the men had descended from the ambulance, preparing for the transfer of their prisoners.

'We have dealt with two of that nest of spiders – Trauben

and Zuckermann. You might recognise them better as Bridget Hammond and Millicent Zampek. They were small fry, but they had to be squashed. This girl – my girl – may hold some of the answers in her tiny brain; and there's another yet to come. Nikolas – Ebbie Heritage. Those two, and you, should fill in the gaps before we send you to hell and damnation.'

If he wanted Heather and Ebbie alive, why had he sent the thug with the mallet and the two who chased them down the fire escape? Smolin had spoken of the incident earlier as 'some ill-advised idiots trying to kill her'. The most devious of ideas filtered into Bond's mind as he watched Heather being carried to the Mercedes. He was surprised to see the driver loading the packages they had bought in Dublin into the boot. They had moved with great speed, Bond thought, to get everything out of his rented car in so short a time. But then the G.R.U. were organised on military principles and the kidnap would be run with military precision. This was the first time he had been up against the G.R.U., and he was impressed by their strict standards.

In Moscow, they worked out of that decorative mansion at 19 Knamensky Street – once the property of a Tsarist millionaire – and were constantly at loggerheads with the K.G.B., who always claimed to have the upper hand, even though the G.R.U., by virtue of its military roots, was effectively set apart from the larger and better known intelligence and security service.

He felt Smolin's arm on his shoulders.

'Your turn, Mr Bond.'

They frogmarched him to the BMW, where they drew a thick sack over his head, handcuffed his wrists securely behind his back and forced him on to the floor. The sack smelled of grain, making his throat dry in a matter of minutes. He heard the sound of the ambulance starting up, and felt Smolin's feet pressing down on his back as he took his seat. A moment later, the car started and they began to move away.

Smolin had said, 'The honeytrap...was baited with four very young and attractive girls.' Only the four girls had been mentioned. He had not spoken of Jungle Baisley and Fräulein Captain Dietrich, whom Heather had described as one of the two prime targets. Why? As he concentrated on trying to deduce their speed and direction, a more sinister scheme began to take shape. Was Jungle not yet blown as a member of the network? Had M performed a neat piece of misdirection when briefing him, or was there something more dangerous at work? Was there a connection with Norman Murray's rumour of an officer more senior to Smolin in the field? Was Smolin under pressure?

He remembered Murray's smiling face as he said, 'Maxim Smolin...a stupid code name – Basilisk.' Bond delved into what little he knew of mythology. The basilisk was a particularly revolting monster hatched from a cockerel's egg by a serpent. Even the purest and most innocent humans perished by looking at the basilisk's eyes. The creature would lay the whole world to waste but for its two enemies, the cockerel and the weasel. The weasel was immune and the basilisk died at the sound of a cock's crow.

Bond wondered whether he was a cock, a weasel, or neither.

- 9 -
SCHLOSS GRUESOME

By Bond's reckoning, they drove for roughly three hours. After half that time he lost all sense of direction, although his instincts told him they were crossing their own path again and again. In the dark, stuffy sack, cramped and uncomfortable on the floor of the car, he tried to work out exactly where they might be heading. When he was forced to abandon this, he began to examine the various theories that had first come to mind in the ambulance.

He did not doubt that Smolin's threat to get a full rundown on Cream Cake from them would be carried out. The man's reputation was enough to convince him of that. If Norman Murray's vague information bore any truth, Smolin might not be entirely his own man. If the huge arrogance he had shown in the ambulance had been dented, it could be that the G.R.U. officer would act irrationally and that could be Bond's lever. He knew that it was now up to him somehow to influence events.

They stopped once. Smolin did not leave the car but said to Bond, 'Your lady friend appears to have woken up, so they're taking her for a short walk. She is quite safe. She will anyway remain docile for a while yet.'

Bond moved, trying to shift his position, but Smolin's heel came down hard on one shoulder, almost causing him to shout with pain. He realised that his interrogation, when it came, would not be conducted along sophisticated lines but rather in an atmosphere of brutality.

Eventually they seemed to leave the well made road and follow an upward course on a rougher track. They were moving at around thirty miles an hour and bouncing a good deal. Then they met a good surface, turned slightly and came to a halt. He heard the engines dying and doors opening. He felt fresh air on his body. Smolin moved and hands pulled away the sack and freed his wrists.

'You can get out of the car now, Mr Bond.'

Bond blinked, adjusting to the bright light as he tried to massage life back into his arms. Stiffly, he pulled himself on to the seat and then through the door. His legs felt as though they did not belong to him, while his back and arms ached so that he could hardly move. He had to clutch at the car to steady himself.

It took several minutes for him even to stand properly, and he made good use of the time to examine the surroundings. They seemed to be on a circular driveway in front of a solid grey building with a square tower at either end. The top of the building was castellated with rows of tooth-like battlements and the main door was of heavy oak, set in a Norman arch. The windows bore similar decoration. The whole, Bond thought, added up to a typical early Victorian neo-Gothic castle. This one, he saw, had a number of twentieth-century refinements, such as a large number of antennae sprouting from one tower and a big satellite dish aerial on the other. The building was set in a green bowl at least three miles wide. There was no sign of trees or other cover.

'Welcome.'

Smolin was in a peaceful mood now, apparently at his most charming. As he spoke, Bond saw Heather being helped from the Mercedes parked in front of them. He could hear dogs barking from behind the main door, together with the sound of bolts being drawn back. Seconds later the doors swung open, and three German Shepherds raced on to the gravelled drive.

'Hey, Wotan, Siegi, Fafie. Hey-hey!' called Smolin.

The big, sleek-coated dogs bounded towards Smolin with obvious pleasure. Then, as they sensed Bond, one turned and bared its fangs, growling.

'Good, Fafie, good! Stay! Watch!' All this Smolin said in German, and then to Bond, 'I should not make any sudden moves if I were you. Fafie can be particularly vicious once I've told him to watch someone. They're well trained, these animals, and they all have a good killer instinct – so take care.' He stopped petting the other two Shepherds and quietly motioning towards Bond, said, 'Siegi, Wotan. Watch! Yes, him. Watch!'

Two men had come through the door, followed by a young girl with fluffy blonde hair. She was dressed in a claret coloured tight silk shirt and a pleated skirt, which lifted and flared around her legs as she started to run towards Heather, calling out in German, her eyes shining and her face a picture of happiness. She turned and moved with an almost innocent sexuality, as though she was unaware of her body and its beautiful proportions. Bond's heart sank as he heard the words.

'Heather – Irma – they have you safe as well. I thought we were going to be left out in the cold. But they haven't let us down.' She was close to Heather now, embracing her.

'A small deception, I'm afraid.' Smolin looked at Bond, as Heather gasped, 'Ebbie? What...'

'Inside!' Smolin's voice cut loudly across the several conversations that had started up among his men and the bewildered girls. 'Everybody inside! Now!'

The men closed in, the dogs circling as though on guard. They seemed to be particularly concerned with Bond and the two girls, herding them through the door into a vast flagstoned hallway. It was dominated by a stripped pine gallery running round three sides and a wide staircase.

Heather appeared to be calm, still under the effect of the drugs, Bond supposed, but Ebbie trembled visibly. There was horror in her wide blue eyes as she looked towards Bond.

Recognition slowly dawned as she recalled that night, five years before, when Bond and the Special Boat Squadron men had plucked Heather and herself from the German coast.

'Is he?' Ebbie spoke loudly, turning towards Heather and half raising a hand to point accusingly at Bond.

Heather shook her head and said something quietly, glancing quickly first at Smolin and then at Bond, who glanced around the hallway, taking in everything: the dark blue velvet of the curtains, the three doors and one passage that led off to other parts of the castle, and the large eighteenth-century portraits, so much at odds with the group now gathered there.

Smolin snapped orders at the two men who had appeared with Ebbie. The four from the ambulance and the two who had driven the cars stood near the door. From their manner and the distinct bulges beneath their clothes it was obvious that all of them were armed. Armed to the teeth, Bond thought. As though the very thought produced the fact, he saw a folded machine pistol appear from behind one of the drivers' backs. There would be more of those and probably other men as well – watchers on the rim of the grassy bowl. Men, guns and dogs; locks, bars and bolts; and a long haul across open ground if they were even to get that far.

'Irma, my dear, bring Emilie over here, although I think she knows Mr Bond.'

Bond was pleased to see that Ebbie had regained enough wit to cloud her face with a puzzled expression.

'I don't think...' she began.

Smolin spoke coldly. 'How remiss of me. Mr Bond, you do not know Fräulein Nikolas – or Miss Ebbie Heritage as she now prefers to be called?'

'No, I haven't had the pleasure.' Bond walked over with his hand outstretched and gave Ebbie's a reassuring squeeze. 'This really is a pleasure.'

He meant this last remark, for, now he was close to Ebbie

Heritage, Bond sensed a desire he rarely felt on first meeting a girl. Through his expression he tried to convey that all would be well, a difficult task as the German Shepherds moved with him, not aggressively but still letting him know of their presence.

'How strange,' Smolin commented, 'I could have sworn that she recognised you out there, Bond.'

'He…' Ebbie began. Then, as her confidence returned, she said, 'He reminded me of someone I used to know. Just for a second. Now I see he's English, and I've not met him before. But, yes, for me also it is a pleasure.'

Good girl, Bond thought to himself, looking towards Heather and trying to pass on a reassuring look to her also. Heather's eyes did not appear to be properly focused, but she managed a firm, confident smile. For a moment, Bond could have sworn that she was trying to convey him a message of deeper significance. It was as if they had already reached a mutual understanding.

'So.' Smolin was standing beside them. 'I suggest we eat a hearty meal. A full stomach before work, eh?'

'What work, Colonel Smolin?'

'Oh, Maxim. Please call me Maxim.'

'What kind of work?' Bond repeated firmly.

'There is much talking to be done. But first you must see your quarters. The guest accommodation is good here in…' He paused, as though stopping himself from giving away their location. Then he said, with a contented smile, 'Here, in Schloss Varvick. You recall Schloss Varvick, James?'

'It's familiar,' he said with a nod.

'As a boy you probably read of it in Dornford Yates. I forget which book.'

'So, for the want of a better name, Maxim?'

Smolin nodded. 'For want of a better name.'

'Then this is your base in the Republic of Ireland? Schloss G.R.U. Or perhaps Schloss Gruesome?' said Bond without a smile.

Smolin exploded with laughter. 'Good. Very good. Now, where is our housekeeper? Ingrid! Ingrid! Where is the girl? Somebody get her.'

One of the men disappeared through a service door and a few seconds later returned with a dark, sharp-faced, angular woman. Smolin ordered her to show his 'guests' to their quarters, adding that Miss Heritage was already nicely settled in.

'You won't be cramped,' he said as he stood hands on hips and head thrown back. 'There is a communal sitting room, but you each have a separate bedroom.'

Two of the men closed in on them and Smolin ordered Fafie to follow. The thin figure of Ingrid moved up the stairs silently as though she walked on a cushion of air. Yet her movement appeared sinister rather than graceful.

'It is very comfortable.' Ebbie's voice was strong and pleasant. 'I quite enjoyed it last night, but then I thought it to be sanctuary.'

Her English was not quite so flawless as Heather's but she seemed at least initially to have a more outgoing personality. Heather, he felt, had disappeared into the shell of her long legs, slim body and beautiful mask of a face. Ebbie was full of fun and had an unselfconscious sense of her own attractiveness. She held herself well as though to show off her fine body.

The little group, followed by Fafie, climbed to the gallery, and turned right along the polished pine floor. At the end of a short corridor was a solid door, also in pine. This led into a large sitting room decorated in heavy mid-European style with flock wallpaper, a buttoned sofa, matching chairs and solid oak side tables. A card table with ball and claw feet, a Gothic break-front bookcase reaching almost to the ceiling containing only magazines piled into the shelves and a heavy bureau filled the remaining space. Three dark German prints of mountain scenes, with clouds gathering between valleys, in ugly wooden frames hung on the walls. The floor

was of the same polished pine with a number of thick rugs
placed haphazardly around a central oblong carpet. Bond
was deeply suspicious of rugs. It also worried him that the
room had no windows. There were three doors besides the
entrance, one in each wall, which Bond took to belong to the
bedrooms.

'I have the room over here,' said Ebbie as she went to a
door set almost opposite the entrance. 'I hope nobody
minds?'

She looked Bond straight in the eyes, then invitingly
through slightly lowered lashes. She stood with one leg
forward, bent at the knee, showing the curve of her thigh
under the thin material of her skirt.

'First come, first served, as my old Nanny used to say,' he
said, nodding at her. Then, turning to Heather, he told her to
take her pick. She shrugged and went to the door on the left.
Sinister, Bond thought, recalling the old theatrical tradition
of the pantomime devil making his entrance stage left: *e
sinister*, the side of evil omen.

The whole tangle of questions and theories came into the
open again. Where did Jungle Baisley fit in? Had M misled
him? Had Swift really made a terrible error of judgment in
telling Heather to activate Smolin? How was Smolin so well
briefed about his movements, and why had he felt it necessary to distance himself from the London incident, when
Heather had almost died? Had the delicious Ebbie lent her
raincoat and scarf to the Ashford Castle chambermaid on
purpose?

He entered his bedroom and found the furniture equally
oppressive. There was a huge bed with the head intricately
carved in solid oak, a heavy free-standing wardrobe and an
old-fashioned marble topped washstand doubling as a dressing table. The bathroom was modern, in unlikely avocado
green, with pine surrounds to the tiny cupboard, a bath built
for a midget and even a bidet squeezed between the bath and
lavatory. Bond went back into the bedroom to find one of the

men standing in the doorway holding his getaway case.

'The lock is, I fear, broken,' he said in English. 'The Herr Colonel ordered the contents inspected.'

The Herr Colonel can take a running jump, thought Bond. Aloud, he thanked the man. It was highly unlikely that they had found anything to interest them. His two overt weapons, the ASP and the baton, had been removed, but they had left his cigarette lighter, wallet and pen – all three from Q Branch with Q'ute's blessing. It struck Bond as odd that so far Smolin had not subjected him to a body search, which could easily have revealed items secreted in his clothing. Such an oversight was out of tune with his reputation.

As Bond was about to open the getaway case, he heard the two girls talking loudly in the sitting room. Quickly he went out, motioning them to stop – pointing at the telephone and fighting to remind them that the rooms were almost certainly bugged.

He needed to find some way of talking unheard to the girls, to discover the three key questions Heather had been instructed to ask Smolin, and more details about Swift. Once they could have crowded into one of the bathrooms, turned on all the taps and talked. But that old dodge had long gone out of the window with modern filtering systems that cut out extraneous sound. Even talking in whispers with a radio on at full volume was no longer safe.

He strode to the bureau and tried the flap. It was not locked and sure enough, writing paper and envelopes had been left in the pigeon holes. Taking some of the paper, he gestured at the girls to sit down near one of the heavy side tables and carry on talking while he went to the door and looked out. They must have been very sure of themselves, for the door was unlocked and there appeared to be no guards in the corridor.

Back at the table, seated between the girls, he bent over the paper and took out his pen. Writing quickly, trying to

make some logic of his own confused suspicions, he se
questions in order of importance. The girls were flagging
their conversation becoming stilted, so he asked Ebbie how
she had been picked up.

'It was done by telephone. After the girl's murder.'

Ebbie moved a fraction closer to him, her hand brushing
his arm. Bond started to write his questions, two to each
sheet of paper, and double sets, one for Ebbie, another fo
Heather.

'They telephoned you?'

'*Ja*. They said I was to leave as soon as the police had no
use for me. I was to drive to Galway, to the Corrib Grea
Southern Hotel and they would contact me there.'

She allowed her shoulder to press hard against his arm
leaving in its wake a tingling sensation that he found
decidedly pleasant.

Bond passed two sheets of questions to Heather, and a
couple to Ebbie, miming for them to write replies. Heathe
had a pen, but Ebbie looked lost, so Bond gave her his
Meanwhile he continued the conversation, as though
desperate to know the answers.

'And they said they were from Britain?'

There was a slight hesitation, for Ebbie was trying to
write. Then she said, 'Yes, they said they came from the
people we used to work for.'

She smiled at him, revealing small, perfect teeth and the
tantalising pink tip of her tongue.

'You had no doubts?'

'None. They seemed to be perfect English gentlemen
They promised me one night at a safe place, then an
aeroplane would come and I would go to some other place.

She frowned and continued to write, still allowing her arm
to press against Bond's shoulder.

'Did they say anything about Heather?'

There was an agonising silence while she wrote some
more.

'Safe. They say she is safe and will be coming soon. I never...'

He turned to Heather, who had apparently been writing without trouble. 'You were unconscious in the ambulance,' he said, giving her a broad wink so that she would not be disturbed by what he was going to say. 'Smolin talked to me about something called Cream Cake. Do you know about that?'

Her jaw dropped, her mouth starting to form the word 'but', then she remembered their audience and said she was not to speak of it. The whole business had been a despicable trick; neither she nor Ebbie were responsible for it.

'It was a mistake,' she repeated, 'A most horrible mistake.'

Bond leaned over and began to read what they had already written, his eyes moving quickly first down one page, and then the other. As he read, the suspicion that had started earlier returned. At that moment the door burst open to reveal Smolin flanked by two of his men. There was no point in trying to hide the papers, but Bond pulled them off the table, hoping to misdirect Smolin's gaze by rising to his feet.

'James, I'm surprised at you.' Smolin's voice was soft, almost soothing and therefore more threatening. 'You think we only listen to what we call our guest suite? We have *son et lumière*, my friend – sound and pictures.' He gave one of his regular laughs. 'You would never guess how many times we've compromised people in these rooms. Now, be a good fellow and hand over the papers.'

One of the men stepped towards them, but Heather snatched the sheets from Bond and headed for her bedroom door, light and very fast on her feet. The man sprang at her in a rugger tackle, missed and fell against the wall as her door slammed and the key turned in the lock.

Smolin and the other man had automatics in their hands, while the other man who had fallen was back on his feet, pounding on the door and shouting in German for Heather to come out. But there was no sound until eventually the door opened and Heather stalked haughtily into the room. From behind her, smoke curled out of a metal waste bin.

'They're gone,' she said in a matter-of-fact tone, 'burned. Not that they would have meant much to you, Maxim.'

Smolin took one pace forward and hit her hard in the face, first with the back of his hand, then the palm smashing into her cheeks. She staggered with the blows and then straightened up, her face scarlet.

'That's it. Enough!' Smolin drew in a breath through his clenched teeth. 'We won't wait for food. I think the time has come to talk – and talk you will. All of you.'

He turned back to the door and shouted for more of his men, who came noisily up the stairs, weapons drawn.

'You first, I think, James.' Smolin's finger was aimed like a dagger.

There was little point in struggling as two of the men seized Bond's arms and hustled him out along the corridor and down the main staircase.

Ingrid stood overseeing the whole incident like a thin black insect, surrounded by the growling dogs. The men pushed Bond through one of the other doors, down another pine staircase and along a passage. They sat him down in a small room, bare but for a metal chair bolted to the floor. Handcuffs were snapped on his wrists and ankles, shackling him to the arms and legs of the chair. He was conscious of the two men standing behind him, while Smolin, his face set in cold anger, was directly in front of him.

Bond braced himself for physical pain or, even worse, the ordeal the Soviets always spoke of as a chemical interrogation. He did everything they had taught him, emptied his mind, putting in layers of rubbish and forcing the truth deep into his subconscious. When it came, Bond was shocked into mind-bending fear. Smolin, the main target of Cream Cake, spoke very quietly.

'James,' he began, 'when M took you to lunch and then for

that walk in the park and explained Cream Cake to you, saying they would deny you if anything went wrong – what was your first thought?'

Smolin had started with the very truth that Bond had buried most deeply and would have given his interrogator only under the heaviest pressure.

- 10 -
INTERROGATION

FOR WHAT SEEMED an eternity Bond felt as though his mind had been struck by a whirlwind: listening devices planted in Blades? Directional microphones? Sound stealing in the park? A penetration of M's office? Of M himself? Impossible. Yet Smolin knew. M's first private briefing had been in the park, and it was the last piece of information Bond would have revealed. But Smolin had it, and if he was party to that knowledge, what else did he know, and how?

Bluff could not last long, but he must try to spin it out.

'What briefing? What park?'

'Come, James, you know better than to try that. I'm a case-hardened G.R.U. officer. We're both aware of the way our organisations can be penetrated. Let us say that Cream Cake was detected long before we allowed the four girls to discover they were blown.'

'As I know nothing of this Cream Cake, I can't be any help to you.' Still only four girls, he thought, and no mention of the one man.

Smolin shrugged. 'Do you want me to do it the hard way, James? We all make mistakes from time to time. Your people made a mistake with Cream Cake. We made a blunder in letting the network get away in their socks, as your people say.' He gave his most unpleasant laugh. 'In the case of Cream Cake, I suppose we should say they got away in their stockings, eh?' He looked hard at Bond, and it seemed, incredibly, as though he was trying to pass some secret message. 'All of them being young women, eh?'

'I don't know what you're talking about,' Bond said

quietly. 'I haven't the faintest idea what this Cream Cake business is. I gave a lift to a girl I met at a party, and ended up with the G.R.U. around my neck. I haven't denied what you obviously do know, that I'm a member of one of Britain's secret departments. But we're not all privy to every hare-brained scheme. We work on a need-to-know basis...'

'And your Head of Service, M, decided that you did need to know, James. Yesterday in Regent's Park, after you lunched together at his club, he told you the story, with many of its twists and turns; not quite all of them, though. Then he said he'd be obliged if you'd tidy things up, bring in the members of the Cream Cake team. He offered you the information but said he could not sanction your actions. If you got into a mess neither he nor the Foreign Office could bail you out. They would have to deny you. It was up to you and, like the headstrong field man you are, you took him up. Now, my question was, what did you feel when he laid that little lot on you?'

'I felt nothing because it didn't happen.'

There was a long pause as Smolin sucked in air through his teeth.

'Have it your own way. I'm not going to play any games. No strong-arm stuff. I haven't got time to waste. We'll do it with a small injection. My report has to be ready later tonight when we expect an important visitor.'

He turned, speaking to the guards in a mixture of German and Russian. From what Bond could understand, he was telling them to bring in the medical instruments, then leave him alone. The taller of the two men asked if he needed assistance.

'I can do my own recording. The prisoner is secure. Now get on with it.'

Smolin's manner made them jump to obey, and one man was back in a few seconds, wheeling a small medical trolley.

Smolin dismissed him and moved towards one of the walls. For the first time, Bond saw a row of small switches, which Smolin carefully threw down. Then he turned back to the trolley and started to prepare a hypodermic syringe. Meanwhile he spoke very softly, not even looking in Bond's direction.

'I've turned the sound off, so we cannot be overheard. One of those guys is K.G.B. – very bad news. And there are others planted in my team. Only two of them can be trusted as G.R.U. men, and even they might find themselves in a situation where they cannot obey my orders. You should know that this injection will be nothing more harmful than distilled water. It was the only way I could engineer matters so that we could be alone.'

'What the hell are you talking about?' Bond found his own voice dropping to a whisper. He had to be careful. He could not trust a man of Smolin's reputation.

'I'm speaking to you about truth, James Bond.' Smolin lifted the syringe and picked up a small vial. He slid the needle through the skin of the vial, filled the syringe and squirted a small spray to eliminate any bubbles of air. 'I'm talking about how I escape with Irma. I'm sorry, I mean Heather. I've been able to hide the fact that Wald Belzinger – your Jungle Baisley – was ever part of Cream Cake. I did that to shield myself and Susanne.'

'Susanne?' asked Bond as Smolin took his arm to give the injection.

'My colleague, Susanne Dietrich. I hid her little affair, and the conspiracy. I also warned the four girls so they could get out before the K.G.B. caught up with them. That was none of Heather's doing, though of course she thinks it was her fault, that she made her play for me too soon.' He slid the needle in and Bond did not even feel it. 'If anyone should come in, act as though you're doped to the eyeballs. In fact it would be a good idea if you just let your head go back and closed your eyes anyway.'

'As I understand it,' said Bond, still hardly above a whisper, 'it was you, the resident G.R.U. mole inside the

H.V.A., who blew the whistle on the girls.' Christ, into the trap, he thought. I've admitted it.

Smolin bent down close to Bond's ear, pretending to make him comfortable. 'Yes, I had to blow the whistle, as you put it. Believe me, James, I blew it only a matter of seconds before K.G.B. sounded their own alarm. And now? Well, I can't keep the heat off much longer. First, it is a K.G.B. team – two teams to be exact – who are killing off the Cream Cake agents. Second, my guess is that tonight's honoured guest will bring with him news that Wald Belzinger has had it away on his toes, as the London criminal fraternity would say, with my good colleague and friend, Susanne Dietrich.'

'Really?' Bond wanted to listen, not comment. Already he had gone too far.

'She went on leave two weeks ago and hasn't returned. The K.G.B. officer in charge of cleaning up the case will have put two and two together by now and there will be an A.P.B. out on Belzinger, or Baisley. It puts me right in focus, which means I too must jump, as I have promised, if the going gets rough.'

'Promised whom?'

'My dearest Heather for one; her case officer, Swift, for another. And your own Chief, M, for good measure.'

'Are you trying to tell me, Maxim, that you have been a defector in place for the last five years?'

'Quite'

'And you expect me to believe you? You, the half-Russian, half-German, scourge of the D.D.R.'s intelligence service? Hated by more people than either of us would care to count? The dedicated officer with allegiance only to Moscow? I can't buy it. It just doesn't add up.'

'That is exactly why you should buy it, James. It is the only thing you can do, because if you don't you're dead. So am I, come to that. You, Heather, Ebbie, me and eventually Susanne and Baisley. We're all headed for oblivion if you don't buy it and act on it.'

'Prove it to me, then, Maxim.'

'Haven't I done that? Haven't I done it by asking you about your reaction to M's briefing? There was no way I could get that except from the horse's mouth.'

Bond waited, still wary. He examined his own mental and physical state and knew he was not drugged. This was all very real and Smolin's story became more probable the more he heard.

'James, the job we're in — it's like living within a set of Chinese boxes and never knowing exactly who or what is in which box. I know about the telephone call you received yesterday morning, about your lunch at Blades and your walk in the park. I know you spent the afternoon going through the files and what happened at Heather's beauty salon.' He paused, looking very serious now. 'I tried hard to head off that bloody K.G.B. team but it was too late. I know about the escape, your double-switch at Heathrow and your telephone conversations here — including those with Inspector Murray.' He leaned forward in the chair, putting his face close to Bond. 'You see, I have committed the cardinal sin within any intelligence organisation. I knew what Heather was when she made her first pass at me and I checked out the others. At any moment I could have hauled them all in, but I did not.'

'Why?'

'Because when I was approached I wanted to be approached. I wanted to get out. I knew it; had to live with it. Heather offered me a way of escape and like a fool I took it. And what happened? They asked me to stay in place; to become even more of a monster than before. What better cover, James?'

'Who asked you?'

'Heather, whom I love dearly, then Swift and finally M.'

'Where?'

'In a safe house in West Berlin. On a day trip. M agreed to keep Heather under wraps. I agreed to work for him. We set

up codes, contacts, cutouts, and so it went on until the
K.G.B. began to sniff around what had really been happening five years before. It's only a matter of time before they
link me with Cream Cake. Then unless I can jump it's
Moscow and a quick bullet if I'm lucky; one of the cancer
wards or the Gulag if I'm not. The same goes for you, James.
For all of us.'

Bond had yet to be convinced that this was the complete
story.

'If this is true, why wasn't I told?'

For a stomach-churning second he again realised that
even in discussing events with Smolin he was answering
questions, providing a skilled interrogator with all he
required.

'Need-to-know. Your cunning old M is too wily a bird.
You were the man for the job, but you didn't have to know
about me. It was a chance in a million that we would meet.
M's instructions to me were to watch from a distance and let
you get the girls out, then pick up Jungle.' His eyes narrowed
and the creases of anxiety showed in his forehead. 'I don't
think he realised that I was so surrounded by K.G.B. and
that I couldn't call off their hit team. Also, up until late
yesterday he had no idea of the latest developments. We
spoke during the early hours of this morning, first through
Murray, who had contacted him, and later on a secure line.
M thought I might still have a chance of staying in place. But
he was wrong. I've almost certainly been blown, James, and
I must get out. I need your help because we have been
thoroughly penetrated by K.G.B. I've told you, at least one
is in my team, and probably more than one. The real threat
here is that bitch of a housekeeper, Ingrid. She's certainly
K.G.B. Black Ingrid, as they call her in certain circles, is
deputy and probably mistress of the man after your Cream
Cake team. Beware of her, my friend. It might look as though
those damned dogs regard me as their master, but I assure
you the dogs are doubles too. Ingrid's their real controller.

She can countermand my orders to them any time and they will obey.' He gave a humourless smile. 'And before you ask, yes they were trained in that windowless complex behind the walls and wire on the old Khodinka airfield.'

What had Smolin to lose by telling him all this – or for that matter, to gain?

'If I go along with you, Maxim, what do you need from me? You have a plan, have you? Like getting me to take you and the girls to Jungle Baisley's hideout so you can put the lot of us in the bag?'

'Don't be stupid, James. You think the K.G.B. won't know where he's hiding out by now? You think they won't have double-checked Susanne's movements? By this time, those two are probably as near to being in the bag as we are.'

'And who's this honoured guest you've been talking about? The one due in tonight?'

'At last you ask.' His expression was clear and calm; the calm before the hurricane strikes.

'Well?'

'You know me as Basilisk, yes? Cryptonym, Basilisk, yes?'

'Yes.'

'Do you, then, James, happen to know the cryptonym Blackfriar?

Bond felt his heart thump, and stomach turn over wildly. 'Christ!'

'Quite. Our guest is Blackfriar.'

It took a few seconds for Bond to assimilate the information.

'Konstantin Nikolaevich Chernov. General Chernov.'

'Christ,' Bond repeated, 'Kolya Chernov?'

'As you say, James, Kolya Chernov – to his few friends. The Chief Investigating officer of Department 8, Directorate S, which was once Department V, and before that...'

'SMERSH.'

'With whom you have had dealings on several occasions.' Smolin spoke slowly, as though each word had a hidden meaning. 'And Konstantin Nikolaevich has a reputation that makes my own appear blameless.'

Bond frowned. Not only was he aware of General Chernov's reputation but knew his file intimately. Kolya Chernov was responsible for dozens of black operations that had caused mayhem within both the British and American intelligence communities. He was also a man of crude and cruel cunning. Bond guessed he would be hated by many in the Russian services as well. Blackfriar was a living nightmare to Bond's Service.

He conjured up a picture from the photographs on the file: a slim, tall man with his body well toned by exercise. Blackfriar was known to be a health fanatic who neither smoked nor drank alcohol. His IQ went off the scale, and he was well established as a dirty tricks planner of immense ingenuity. He was also a tenaciously shrewd investigator. His file showed that he had sent at least thirty members of the K.G.B. and G.R.U. to their deaths or the Gulag for infringements of discipline. One defector was on record as saying, 'Being what he is, Blackfriar has the knack of scenting even the tiniest deviation at ten paces, and he follows it up like a hell-hound.' Bond closed his eyes and let his head droop. Suddenly he felt both exhausted and worried, not for himself, but for the two girls.

'It must be important if he's coming into the field,' he murmured.

'It is the first time in my own memory.' Either Smolin was a very good actor or he was filled with dread even discussing the General. 'Let me tell you, James, when I first blew Cream Cake, it was a matter for the Germans, for H.V.A. and of course G.R.U. It has taken time for K.G.B. to sniff out the existence of Jungle, the turning of Susanne Dietrich and of Maxim Smolin.' He banged his own chest with a balled fist.

'It has taken them five years.' Bond's voice was flat, as though his mind was elsewhere.

'Four, to be exact. It was last year that K.G.B. reopened the files and decided to investigate the case, going over our heads. They do not like G.R.U. to feel that they are an élite body. They dislike our methods, our secrecy, our way of recruitment from within the Army. I have heard Chernov himself say that we smack of the hated S.S. from the Great Patriotic War.

'At first the reinvestigation was fairly low grade. They did some cross-checking here and there. Then Chernov arrived in Berlin. I flashed warnings to your people, but I dared not make a move. After only a week there were a number of field changes and it didn't take a lot of brain to work out that the K.G.B. were boxing me in. I have been watched and monitored for the past six months. It is Chernov's own team who are on the loose and his orders are that the girls are to be rooted out, killed and left with their tongues cut from their mouths – as the French say, *pour encourager les autres.*'

'So you do all in your power to assist Blackfriar, eh, Basilisk? You pick up Ebbie and go to great lengths to trap Heather and me on the road.'

'Only on Chernov's orders. I've told you, K.G.B. are all around us. I thought of botching the job, but how could that help? James, I want your help. I need to get out now and take you and the girls with me. In front of the others, naturally, I have to keep up a pretence of obeying Chernov's orders. But not for long.'

'If you want to prove your intentions to me, Maxim, tell me where we are. What is the location of this castle?'

'It's not far from where we picked you up. The track to the road is about two miles. At the entrance we turn left and it's straight on downhill until we reach the Dublin–Wicklow road. In an hour, two hours at the most, we can be at the airport and away.'

Bond still lay back with his eyes closed. 'If I accept your version, I too need help.'

'You have it. Don't move suddenly but I'm unlocking the cuffs now. I have your gun with me – a nice piece of work, the ASP 9 mm. There…'

Bond felt the heavy metal drop into his lap. 'So we just shoot our way out?'

'I fear we would be outnumbered. We could probably deceive my own men, but certainly not Black Ingrid, and those Chernov has planted.'

'Again assuming I accept your word, how long have we got?' Bond's hands were free now. He could feel the cuffs drop away.

'An hour. An hour and a half with luck. He has to land here while there is still enough light.'

'And the girls, where are they being housed?'

'They've been locked in the guest suite, I expect. Those were my orders. The problem is getting to them. After an interrogation such as I am supposed to be making, you would be semi-conscious. The men will be waiting with a gurney trolley to take you along the passage. Then they'll carry you up the stairs. There.'

Bond felt the shackles on his legs being freed. 'Do you have any suggestions?'

He lifted the ASP, weighing it carefully to be certain there was a magazine in place. It was something he had practised many times, even in the dark, with empty magazines, blanks and the real thing. Now it was fully loaded.

'There is one way…' Smolin began, then wheeled round as the door smashed open to reveal Ingrid with the three dogs straining at their leashes.

'Ingrid!' Smolin used his most commanding tone.

'It's all been very interesting.' Ingrid's voice was thin and sharp. 'I have made certain changes to the interrogation room since you were last here, Colonel – on General Chernov's orders, naturally. For one thing, the switches for recording have been reversed. The General will be fascinated by the tapes. But we have listened long enough. He will be here soon, and I want you all locked away before he arrives.'

As though reading each other's thoughts, Smolin leaped to the left, while Bond rolled out of the chair, moving right.

Ingrid shrieked in German at the dogs, 'Wotan, *Rechts*! *Anfassen*! Fafie, *Links*! *Anfassen*!'

The dogs sprang, snarling, and as Fafie's teeth fastened on his gun arm, Bond had a fleeting view of men standing behind Ingrid, and the third dog, Siegi, straining to go in for the kill.

DOG EAT DOG

BOND FELT A searing pain as Fafie's jaws fastened on the lower part of his arm, making the fingers of his right hand open involuntarily so that the gun dropped heavily on to the floor. He was aware of Ingrid's harsh shouting above the snarling of the dogs, Smolin cursing in a mixture of Russian and German and the stale stinking smell of Fafie's breath on his face. The dog held on, still growling, his head moving from side to side as though he were trying to wrench Bond's arm from its socket.

Bond smashed his free hand with full force into the dog's genitals, as he had been taught. The growl changed into a yelp of pain and for a second the jaws relaxed. Bond used that brief moment to roll and bring his right hand up to the animal's throat. His thumb and fingers found the windpipe and he pressed as though to tear out the dog's larynx. His left arm whipped around, catching the beast by the scruff of the neck, but by this time the shock of pain and the dog's instinct for danger had given Fafie renewed strength. The yelp changed back into a series of chilling snarls and it took all of Bond's depleted reserves just to hang on. He could feel the deepening pain where Fafie had lacerated his arm, and the growing weakness. But, like the dog, he knew he was fighting for his life. He increased the pressure on the dog's windpipe.

He could hear the little leathery instructor from the training school as clearly as during the first of many kill-or-be-killed courses. 'You never throttle anyone, or anything, like they do in the movies, with both hands. Always use the one-handed choke for good results.'

Screw in with the hand on the windpipe and use all your strength at the back of the neck with the other arm. He put action to the thought as Fafie threshed around in an attempt to pull clear. For one brief moment, Bond allowed his natural love for animals to creep into his consciousness. But for no more than a second. This was life and death. Fafie wanted his blood.

'Fafie! *Anfassen! Anfassen!*' Ingrid shrieked: 'Fafie! Hold him! Hold him!'

But Bond had summoned a last surge of strength. His fingers cut through Fafie's thick fur, pressed harder with his left arm. He could feel the animal begin to lose consciousness. Then suddenly Fafie's jaws relaxed and the body became a dead weight.

Bond continued to act as though he were wrestling with the dog, glancing sideways to check where the ASP had fallen. He rolled, grunted and moved, trying to give the impression that Fafie was still fighting him. He felt strangely cool and calculating now, conscious of pain, but determined to get his hands on the automatic, which lay to his right, just within his grasp.

He looked towards Smolin and saw with horror that he was lying back with Wotan covering him, fangs bared ready to be buried into his victim's throat if Smolin moved. That one look told Bond that the Colonel could not risk even the twitch of an eyebrow, for Siegi was in reserve, held on a chokechain, and after Siegi the men he had seen crowding in behind Ingrid.

Bond broke through the barrier of pain screaming from his damaged arm. Using Fafie as his shield, he rolled to the right, reached for the ASP, rolled again and fired two shots at Siegi. He let off another single round as Wotan turned from his captive, and the dog caught the full force of a Glazer slug, knocking him back against the wall. A fourth shot, directed low and towards the door, struck the jamb and carved a great hole through wood and plaster. The men scattered but shock rooted Ingrid to the floor.

'No more!' Smolin shrieked. He was on his feet now, lunging towards Ingrid. He caught one wrist and jerked her arm down hard, then towards him and away, so the luckless housekeeper hurtled across the room. She fell against the far wall with an unpleasant cracking sound, all the time screaming in rage, frustration and agony. Then she slid silently down the wall and sprawled, a black heap, on the floor.

Smolin had an automatic in his hand and was shouting towards the shattered doorway, 'Alex! Yuri! I am your senior officer. K.G.B. have mounted a despicable plot against us. You are with K.G.B. men now. Turn. Turn on them. They are traitors and can only bring discredit and death upon your heads. Turn now!'

For a couple of seconds, silence hung in the passageway, then there was a cry, followed by a shot and the sound of blows. Smolin nodded at Bond, signalling him to take up a position on the right of the door, while he pressed himself against the wall on the opposite side. There was another shot, a shout and the noise of a struggle.

Then a voice called in Russian, 'Comrade Colonel, we have them. Quickly, we have them!'

Smolin nodded towards Bond, and together they threw themselves into the passage. As they jumped Smolin yelled in English,

'Get them all, James! All!'

Bond needed no second bidding. To his right two men attempted to overpower a third, while another lay unconscious. It required three quick shots from the ASP to dispatch the group. The deadly Glazer slugs did their work, the first exploding in the right side of one of the struggling men and spreading half its load into the stomach of the one grappling with him. The second took out the man on the floor. The final shot did not allow the fourth man time even to know what hit him.

The noise of the shots was deafening in the narrow

passageway; and doubly so as Smolin loosed off two rounds
from his automatic. Bond turned to see that he too had
scored. The two corpses, one spreadeagled, the other an
untidy pile, bore witness to Smolin's accuracy.

'A pity,' Smolin muttered, 'they were good men, Alex and
Yuri.'

'There are times when you have no option. You've proved
yourself now, Maxim. How many are upstairs?'

'Two. I should think they're with the girls.'

'They'll be down any minute then.'

'I doubt it. Up there you don't hear much that goes on in
this basement.' He was breathing hard. 'We've used it many
times. Strong men have screamed down here while people in
the rooms upstairs have made love and heard nothing.'

Bond heard Smolin's words but the world around him
began to swim and go out of focus. He was aware of the hot
stickiness of his arm and a blinding pain which started at the
source of the heat and spread throughout his body. He
retched twice, hearing Smolin calling his name from a long
way off. Then he lost consciousness.

He dreamed of snakes and spiders. They slithered and
crawled around him as he tried to get out of a dark and
twisting maze, ankle deep in the revolting creatures. He had
to make it. There would be dim light at the end of the tunnel.
Then it would disappear and he was back where he had
started, deep in the earth, surrounded by a red glow. There.
There it was again, the light at the end, but a large snake was
dragging at his legs. He had no sense of fear, just the
knowledge that he had to get out. But another snake had
joined the first and smaller reptiles wrapped themselves
around his legs, pulling him down. Now one of the reptiles
had him by the arm, squeezing, sinking fangs into it, causing
a pain that broke through the blackness. He looked and a
nest of spiders crawled into the wound made by the snake.
Other spiders, large, fat and furry were on his face, stuffing

themselves into his nostrils and forcing their way into his mouth so that he had to cough, splutter and spit them out. He was gagging on the spiders, but somehow he must have managed to get nearer to the tunnel's end, for light was hurting his eyes and a voice called his name:

'James! James Bond! James!'

The snakes and spiders were gone, leaving only a wrenching pain in his arm. A face swam into his vision, the face of a girl. The lips moved.

'James. Come on. It's okay.' The face blurred and he heard the voice say, 'Heather, he's coming round.'

'Thank heaven for that.'

Bond's eyes fluttered, opened and closed, then opened fully and he saw Ebbie Heritage.

'What ...?' he said.

'You're okay, James. It's okay now.'

He moved and was aware of the throbbing in his right arm and that something was constricting it.

'There's not much time.' Maxim Smolin was easing Ebbie to one side. 'You'll be fine, James, but ...' He looked at his wristwatch.

Everything came flooding back in sharp detail. Smolin straightened up. He stood, looking down at Bond, with one arm around Heather Dare's shoulders.

Bond took a deep breath. 'Sorry. Did I pass out on you?'

'Not surprisingly,' said Smolin. 'That damned dog's teeth went deep. How does it feel?'

He moved his arm. 'Numb. It's uncomfortable but I can use it.'

'Ebbie acted nurse,' said Heather. 'We have a lot to thank you for, James. Maxim told us what happened down there.'

'I only cleaned the wound,' said Ebbie. 'The dogs were in good condition. I don't think there's any danger of poison. We used the strongest antiseptic known to man.'

'And the most expensive.' Smolin gave a wry smile. 'The last of the Hine 1914 Vintage. Smooth. Very smooth.'

Bond groaned. 'Smooth, magnificent and totally wasted. I'm sorry.'

'It went in a good cause,' said Smolin. 'Can you sit up? Stand?'

Unsteadily, Bond eased himself up. They had lain him on the sofa in the guest suite. He tried to stand, but his legs began to go from under him. He had to cling to one of the sofa arms to steady himself. Ebbie rushed to hold him, her hands strong and experienced.

'Thank you, Ebbie. Thank you for everything.' He moved carefully, trying out his muscles. Slowly the power returned. 'Thank you, Ebbie,' he repeated.

'We're in your debt. This was nothing.'

'What happened to the others?' Bond asked Smolin. 'Your men up here?'

'They're taken care of.'

The G.R.U. man's face went blank, reminding Bond of his own reaction when an unpleasant piece of work had been finished. It was always best to erase that kind of thing from memory. People who recalled too much either started to enjoy it or cracked under the guilt.

'And Ingrid?' he asked.

'She's alive; resting. She's conscious but she won't be going far. Several bones are broken.' His tone became urgent. 'James, we have to get out. You remember Blackfriar? He could arrive any time. We must be away before he lands.'

'Who's Blackfriar?' asked Ebbie, startled.

Smolin's mouth was set grimly as he said, 'General Chernov from K.G.B.'

Bond nodded. 'Blackfriar is evil, clever and very good at his work – which he appears to enjoy. I'll be okay, Maxim.'

He took several deep breaths and glanced smiling at the girls. Heather appeared to have abandoned her haughty airs and now gazed at Smolin with wide, adoring eyes.

'Yes, I'm sure you'll be okay, James,' said Smolin acidly.

'You're the one who's been injured but you'll survive. I'm thinking of the rest of us.'

'The cars are…?'

'Here, yes.' The Colonel shook his head impatiently. 'We have cars, James. What you don't seem to realise is that we're sitting in a natural bowl overlooked on all sides. To my knowledge there are at least ten men out there with a full armoury. They're K.G.B. too. There are four at the main entrance alone. If we start to drive away, they'll want to know why but I don't think they'll stop to question us. The guys up on the hills and at the gates don't ask questions either. They're snipers.'

'Dog eat dog, eh?'

'Shoot first. Worry about the questions later.'

'Would they shoot at a prime target?'

'Yes. You, me or the girls. No doubt about that. Blackfriar has been constantly in touch with this place – its real name is Three Sisters Castle incidentally, and it has been used by K.G.B. and G.R.U. for the past ten years. But he's been on the radio. I've had a look at the scratch pads in the Communications Room. Your name and mine have been passed along the line. Blackfriar's last order is that nobody leaves until he gets in. Anyone who tries has to be stopped.'

'I said prime target,' Bond repeated. He was gradually starting to feel better, his mental processes becoming sharper. 'Such as General Konstantin Nikolaevich Chernov. Would they fire at him?'

'You mean we should take him with us? Grab him?'

'Why not?'

'Because he will not be alone.'

'Well, why not simply use him as cover? How's he coming in?'

'By helicopter. He's got plenty of unofficial transport over here – all legal, of course. The Republic's not the place to play games with illegal transport. But he won't risk coming in when it gets dark. There are no facilities here for light aircraft once the sun's gone.'

'He'll land near the castle?'

'We usually come in directly in line with the main entrance and fly up it. We land out in front, close to where the cars are parked.'

'Who'll be with him?'

'At least two bodyguards, his adjutant and a skilled interrogator. They'll be armed. And they're all highly efficient.'

Bond's arm gave a sudden stab of pain, making him wince.

'James, are you all right?'

Ebbie was at his side, one hand resting on the injured arm, her face troubled. She had the kind of deep blue eyes which he found irresistible and lips that asked to be kissed.

Bond nodded. 'It's just a twinge, nothing serious.' He reluctantly dragged his eyes from Ebbie and back to Smolin. 'We've *got* to get out, whatever the risks. It strikes me that they are lessened if we go just as the General arrives. Which is the best car, Maxim?'

'The BMW. It's a good model to start with, and this one's been souped up.'

Bond began to pat his clothes. He asked Smolin for his gun, surreptitiously checking that he still had his other secret equipment. Smolin produced the ASP from the table, together with the spare magazines and the baton. Bond dismantled and reassembled the weapon. Then he asked, 'We're agreed, then? We make a run for it as soon as the chopper appears?'

The others nodded, but Smolin did not look altogether happy.

'Maxim?'

'Yes. The only other way would be to go now and risk their full firepower. I'd be happier if we'd had the time to take them out.'

'Are you going to arm the girls?'

'He already has.' Heather had certainly become more confident and professional. Bond made a mental note to ask her why she had offered herself to him so blatantly at the Airport Hotel – but that was not a question he could put to her in front of Smolin.

He now asked, 'Do you have the BMW's keys?'

Smolin nodded.

'Then what are we waiting for? We should get down to the main doors. Maxim, why don't you walk out to the car? That would be natural enough. Play around with it and give us a yell as soon as the chopper appears.'

As they went down the stairs, the castle seemed cold and cheerless. Outside there was still plenty of light, although the sky was starting to redden in the west, but the flagstoned hall retained an almost ghostly chill.

'It's going to be a lovely sunset,' said Bond smiling cheerfully, mainly to keep the girls in good spirits. He knew from Smolin's face that escape from this place was not going to be easy. At the door he asked Maxim how they should place themselves when they reached the BMW.

'Is it all right if Heather comes in front with me? You, James, go in the back with Ebbie. We should all keep down as low as possible.'

'That's fine by me,' said Ebbie, grinning happily at Bond.

'We should open all the windows,' he said, 'in case we have to return fire.'

'Right,' said Smolin with a curt nod. 'I think that would be most wise.'

'Can I have a private word with you, Maxim,' asked Bond, taking Smolin's arm and pulling him to one side. 'If we do get clear, where should we head for?'

'Out of this country, for a start. But there's no hiding place from Chernov – not in the long run.'

'Have you any idea where Jungle and your colleague Susanne might be?'

'Do you know where they were last sighted?'

'Yes, and you?'

'In the Canary Islands.'

'That's what I heard, but I should think it's old news by now.'

'It was a week old when M gave it to you. I think they'll have moved on, but once we're clear I'll have burned my boats. That means we'll get no help from my people...'

'And very little from mine, if we're sticking to M's rules.'

'Chernov will expect us to head for Dublin, Shannon or one of the ports – Rosslare or Dun Laoghaire.'

'We'll have to do that if we're going to get out.'

Smolin gave him a fast sideways glance. 'Not necessarily. I still have some contacts we can use. So do you, in fact. But I could get us out quietly.'

It was Bond's turn to look anxious. 'I can't go into the North, you do know that? It's off-limits to my department; strictly M.I.5 territory. I would really be *persona non grata* if I turned up there. "Five" are very touchy about it.'

'I'm not thinking about the North,' said Smolin. 'If we do get out, we'll have to pull some kind of deception. We'll make them think we're heading for Dublin, then double back. I want to get us into west Cork. From there I know how we can be moved out with the minimum fuss. Okay?'

Bond nodded. 'You'll be at the wheel, so you take the lead.'

Smolin gave his first cheerful smile for some time. 'At least I know where we can switch cars,' he said with some pleasure, as though he had only just thought of it. 'I also know a nice quiet hotel where they're unlikely to think of looking for us.'

'Well...' Bond began, then changed his mind. 'How many telephones have they got in this place?' he asked, as though suddenly struck with another idea.

'There's one here, in the hall,' said Smolin pointing to a small table set under the stairs. 'There's one in the Communications Room – the door to the left at the top of the stairs – and one in the main bedroom, that's the next door along.'

'They're all extensions of the same number?'

'Yes.' Smolin gave the number, which Bond instantly committed to memory. 'The line in is in the Communications Room, where they keep the radio equipment. The others in the hall and main bedroom are the extensions. Why?'

'I just have a little idea. Keep the girls happy. Get them outside with you. It'll only take ten minutes.'

Smolin raised his eyebrows. 'If we've got ten minutes. This is necessary?'

'I think so, yes.'

Bond gave a cheerful smile and turned away, taking the stairs as quickly as he could. His arm did not hurt so much, but he still felt weak.

The Communications Room was small, with most of the space taken up by banks of radio equipment, tape machines and a computer ranged against the longest wall. They were set on modern office desks, which were littered with pads, blotters and calculators. The telephone stood on the central desk, in front of the main radio. Almost before he was in the room, Bond had unclasped his belt and begun to remove the ingeniously hidden miniature tool kit put together by Q'ute some time ago. It contained an assortment of compact tools, detonators, picklocks, wire and fuses, folded into an almost flat leather container.

Bond removed the top from a small plastic cylinder and selected a screwdriver head that would easily fit the screws on the underside of a standard telephone. He slid the head into the other end of the tiny cylinder, which became a handle. Then he removed the four screws at the base of the instrument. With the telephone open, he took out his wallet and extracted a small packet that Q'ute had given him just before he had left the Headquarters building. It contained six tiny black grains, each with two wires trailing from it. He changed the screwdriver head, this time taking one used by jewellers.

The grains were the latest advance in what at one time was known as a 'harmonica bug'. It took Bond less than four minutes to attach one of the bugs to the appropriate terminals and then close the telephone up. He breathed a silent thank you for these skills, which he had learned many years ago from Q Branch's special telephone instructor. He was a perky cockney called Philip, known to all at the Regent's Park Headquarters as Phil the Phone.

Bond next went to the main bedroom and quickly inserted another of the tiny devices in the telephone there. Downstairs, he went through the same routine with the third instrument.

Smolin and the girls were outside, and the sun was quickly sinking. Bond had hardly completed his work on the last telephone when Smolin opened the door and called out, 'I'm going to the car, James. He should be here by now. All right?'

He squared his shoulders, pushed open the heavy front door and walked slowly towards the BMW. He played around with the boot for a while before going to sit behind the wheel to operate the central control to open the windows. They heard the first sound of the helicopter's engine in the distance. Smolin started the engine, leaned over and opened the passenger door, shouting for them to come on.

Hardly had they reached the car, with the helicopter clearly visible against the red glow of the sky, when the first shots came down from the overlooking hills. They were warnings, smacking against the driveway, well away from the car. Inside Maxim Smolin was crouched over the wheel and the others as near to the floor as they could get. Ebbie, close to Bond, tensed as a second round of bullets hit the ground near by.

Smolin took off like a racing driver. He weaved as he went,

building up speed to take the bumps along the rough track that led to the main entrance two miles on.

The helicopter had turned away from its first run in, as though alerted by the gunfire. It circled low and came, as Bond had hoped, between them and some of the marksmen. He could see that it was a version of the big twin-finned, double-rotored KA-25 – the Hormone as NATO dubbed it.

'If we do get out,' Heather shouted, 'where are we heading for?'

'If we make it!' Smolin yelled and at that moment they heard the roar of the helicopter just over the roof, and the sudden rattle of automatic fire kicking up the dust and stones to their right. Bond raised his head and watched as the cumbersome machine turned on its own axis and started to run in again, towards them, its two huge rotors whirling fore and aft. He felt the downdraught of the Hormone battering the car like a gale. It was low and chopping in alongside them, one man half out of the rear sliding door manning a machine pistol.

Bond had the ASP clasped in his right hand. He fired twice and felt the kick as the marksman was cut straight out of the door, taking part of the fuselage with him. Bond steadied his hands, lifted the weapon slightly and fired another two rounds at the lower rotor blades. The Hormone faltered and began to fall away. The forward rotors whined as a section of one blade was torn off.

Smolin let out a roar of laughter. 'You got the bastards!' he shouted, 'The stinking, rotten bastards! There they go...'

Bond glanced back through the rear window and saw the helicopter put down with a jolt that almost crushed one of the wheels of its undercarriage, sending it into the fuselage.

'They won't get that fixed at the local garage in a hurry,' he muttered.

Then the bullets hailed down on them again and he had to

fold himself flat on the floor, so close to Ebbie that he could smell the fresh scent of her body.

'Let's get the hell out of here,' Smolin called. 'Hang on tight! I'm going to take a short cut.'

- 12 -
STRANGE MEETING

IN THE RAPIDLY DARKENING landscape the forward lights of
the grounded helicopter blazed down the main track, bar-
ring any exit there but a suicide dash. Smolin heaved the
BMW away, swinging it over the uneven rutted meadow
towards the rising ground. It lurched to right and left. At one
point there was a thump and a bang which knocked the
vehicle precariously to one side. Heather and Ebbie
screamed, and for a second even Bond thought they would
turn over. He recognised the impact of a heavy calibre bullet,
and knew what it was capable of doing. Miraculously the
BMW righted itself. The castle was to their left now and the
helicopter a long way behind.

Three more shots reached them, one hitting the front
passenger door but causing no damage. The long-range
snipers were almost certainly using night scopes.

'Should we try it on foot?' Bond shouted to Smolin above
the noise.

'On foot they'd get us. There used to be a gap along this
side – overgrown but not properly sealed off.' He sounded
perfectly calm as another shot from somewhere above them
ricocheted past. 'It's our only chance.' He drove without
lights, craning forward to see into the darkness, the engine
whining under stress.

'There!' he called triumphantly. 'Now pray.'

The car slowed as he began to change down, pumping at
the brakes. They were moving right, the wheels protesting
and the back swinging violently.

'Have you ever done any rallying?' Bond called casually to

divert the girls from the alarming experience.

'No!' said Smolin with a laugh. 'But I've done the G.R.U. course — *Scheiss*!' It looked as though they were hurtling towards an impenetrable wall of trees.

'Get down and hang on!' Bond shouted.

There was a violent blow and a grinding noise as the underside of the car pulled across the roots of bushes and undergrowth; then the rustling of branches and foliage parting against the vehicle. While the dense growth had slowed them, the car did not stop. It crunched and bounced, then, as suddenly as they had struck the barrier, they were through and facing a barbed wire fence a good seven feet high.

Smolin changed up, accelerated and rammed the fence head on. This time the impact was more dramatic. Smolin and Heather were thrown against the dashboard and Bond catapulted hard against the back of Smolin's seat. Ebbie came off best, having stayed on the floor. As Bond gave a small cry of pain when his injured arm hit the driving seat she called anxiously,

'James? Are you...Ouch!' as she was rolled back by the jolt.

Half way on to the road ahead, tangled in wire, the car spluttered and stopped. Smolin forced his door open, calling, 'Get out if you can!'

Bond tried the door on his side but it became trapped in the wire so he followed Smolin. Once out, both men scrambled around the car, grappling at the wire with their bare hands. In moments they were cut and bleeding from the barbs, and each cursed in his respective language. Slowly the car was cleared of the tentacles that sprang up as each new strand was loosened.

'Where now?' asked Bond, breathing heavily.

We must dump this car, and get another one,' said Smolin. He ducked to avoid a snake of wire that shot up and missed his face by inches.

'Where?'

'I have a good Rover Vitesse stashed away – that is correct, yes? Stashed?'

'Yes,' said Bond as he tugged the last piece of wire from around the rear bumper. 'You've certainly got this country sewn up, Maxim, with cars stashed away and covert routes in and out.'

They got back into the car. 'Not just me. I'm sure Chernov has more transport near by. We'll be running another gauntlet.'

Smolin twisted the ignition key and the engine coughed and died several times. Eventually it fired. As though nothing had happened, Smolin slammed into gear and, still with no lights, he edged the car on to the road. He turned left towards the Dublin–Wicklow road.

'They'll send the Mercedes after us first, and there will probably be another couple of teams,' said Smolin, 'but our car switch should help. This one I kept up my sleeve. Nobody knows I have it. I did the whole thing alone.'

'Is it far?' Bond asked. He needed to get to a telephone.

'It's fifteen minutes as the crow flies. But have you noticed, the crows don't seem to fly in this country? They litter the roads.'

They were moving swiftly through lanes that appeared to have been constructed from sets of left-over S-bends, overhung by bushes and hedges. Nobody spoke, though Ebbie's hand stole softly into Bond's palm, then was snatched back again as she peered in the half light at the blood flowing from so many cuts and gashes.

Without a word she reached down and lifted her skirt, exposing a generous segment of white thigh. She started to tear at her slip. When she had a sizable piece of light-coloured silk she put it to her mouth, biting to rip it into two pieces, which she then tenderly bound around both of Bond's damaged hands.

'Poor you,' she whispered, 'I'll kiss them better.'

So saying, she bent her head and ran her lips over the exposed part of his fingers. First one hand, then the other, her tongue licking the flesh and her lips closing over the middle finger of one hand.

'I don't think anyone's ever made love to my hands before,' Bond whispered. 'Thank you, Ebbie.'

Breaking the spell, she looked up at him, her eyes wide with innocence. 'I hope your tetanus shots are up to date,' she murmured.

After a couple of miles they turned off abruptly on to a narrow road leading to a large forest. It was completely dark now and the trees were grey against the headlights. Every few hundred yards there were stacks of timber on wooden bunkers. Half a mile farther on they turned on to a track leading directly into the trees. A notice clearly proclaimed: NO MOTOR VEHICLES. PEDESTRIANS ONLY.

'Do you see that, Maxim?' Bond asked.

'We're in Ireland, James. Notices like that don't mean what they say. Anyway, I figured a car-free zone would be the best place to hide a car.'

'Did the G.R.U. teach you that as well?'

'I suppose so. But I'm pretty certain that for all their clever ways Chernov's lads will be looking for this BMW, not for the pretty lady over here.'

He flung the car sideways on, almost grazing the thick trunks of the fir trees before the headlights revealed a mound of branches in the centre of a small clearing.

'Okay, everybody get out. Uncover that car, then use the stuff to hide this one. I have to look to my maps.'

In under ten minutes a dusty, but patently new black Rover Vitesse stood in the clearing, while the pile of branches covered the BMW. Smolin walked a few paces from the nearside front wheel of the Rover, dug into the moss-covered ground and retrieved a small package containing two sets of keys. Bond, standing over him, spoke in a low voice.

'Get the girls into the car, Maxim. We need to talk.'

Smolin nodded. He carefully ushered Heather into the front and Ebbie to the back. Then he walked over to Bond, a short distance from the Rover, where the girls could not hear them.

'First,' said Bond moving very close to him, 'when you were in Berlin, did you have a sidekick called Mischa? Because, if you didn't, Maxim, you should look to your lady.'

Smolin nodded. 'Yes, Mischa was around, but he was a K.G.B. plant. You should know, James, that nothing can ever be straightforward between K.G.B. and G.R.U. We are up to our ears in suspicion concerning one another. You ask about him because he's one of Chernov's killing party. He was in London, wasn't he?'

'That's right. Now, further plans. I just about trust you, Maxim, but I need to know what we're up to. You mentioned throwing them off the scent and getting to west Cork.'

Smolin smiled in the gloom. 'You have special contacts, James. I too. I run two people in Skibbereen. They have a light aircraft. By night we can fly very low. We can escape detection and land, without anyone knowing, in a field in glorious Devon. I have done it several times.'

Bond knew it was feasible. Hadn't Special Branch and 'Five' suspected illegal entry by light aircraft for some years now? No place had ever been pinpointed, yet they knew the lads from the North came in and thought other interlopers did too.

'All right. Chernov wants us, the girls, and presumably Jungle and Dietrich. If we drive to Skibbereen now we won't make it until the very small hours. That'll mean holing up close to our departure point, not the best thing. We all need some rest. There are also things I have to do...the telephones at the castle. You follow?'

Smolin nodded.

'Why don't we drive part of the way tonight?' Bond peered

at his watch. 'It's eight-thirty now. We could be in Kilkenny
by ten o'clock. We could stay there overnight, then continue
the journey late tomorrow afternoon. I presume you can get
hold of your people by telephone. Are they contained?'

'How contained?'

'From K.G.B. doubling.'

'K.G.B. cannot know them. They're mine. This will be the
first time I've taken anyone in with me. Okay?'

'Okay. They won't be looking for a black Rover, but they
will be on the trail of four people. Once we're on the road we
could telephone ahead and book in at two different hotels.
You can drop Ebbie and me off near one and take the car to
yours. We'll have to arrange a meeting for the morning.'

'That seems good. I have two cases in the boot. There's
nothing that will fit you, but it will make the right
impression, yes? The girls can shop in Kilkenny tomorrow,
as long as they're careful. Ebbie has some clothes in that big
shoulder bag, so she may be all right.'

'What kind of papers are you carrying, Maxim?'

'A British passport, international driving licence and
credit cards.'

'Are they good?'

'The best forgeries ever to come out of Knamensky Street.
My name is Palmerston. Henry J. Temple Palmerston. Do
you like it?'

'Oh yes.' Bond's voice heavy with sarcasm. 'You just have
to pray that no Passport Control officer is a student of
nineteenth-century politics.'

'Correct.' You could feel Smolin's broad smile in the
dark. 'They are mainly people whose interests lie elsewhere – aeroplane modelling, railway trains, the novels of
Dick Francis and Wilbur Smith. Very few of them graduate
to Margaret Drabble or Kingsley Amis. We ran a thorough
check through the mail. Simple questions but effective.
Eighty-five per cent filled in our little forms. We said it
was for market research and offered a prize of £5,000

sterling. A man working at Heathrow won the lucky draw, and all the others got small consolation prizes – Walkmans, pens, diaries. You know the kind of thing.'

Bond sighed. At least the Soviets were sometimes thorough. 'Well, Mr Palmerston, don't you think we should get going?'

'If you say so, Mr Boldman.'

They arranged that Smolin and Heather should stay, not in Kilkenny, but at the Clonmel Arms Hotel, thirty minutes' drive away. Bond and Ebbie were booked into the Newpark, near the famous castle, in Kilkenny. In Smolin's opinion it was best that they were completely separated. Surprisingly, they had come across an unvandalised white and green booth marked Telefon only fifteen minutes after leaving the dense wood and had been able to make the reservations from there.

'You can have the bed,' Bond told Ebbie in the back of the car. 'I'll sit up and keep watch.'

'Let's wait and see.' Ebbie's hand slid into his. 'I do know you're a gentleman, James. But perhaps I don't want a gentleman.'

'And I have certain professional duties,' he replied calmly.

Ebbie grinned. 'Duties I might like. I'm sure you do everything in a professional style.'

Smolin and Bond arranged a simple code for telephone contact, and just before ten they arrived in Kilkenny. Smolin passed the Newpark and stopped a hundred yards farther on. He got out, unlocked the boot and hauled out a black travel bag, which he handed to Bond.

'There are a few clothes of mine in there, together with a razor and toothbrush,' he said smiling.

Ebbie had a large shoulder bag which she had taken with her from the Ashford Castle Hotel to what she imagined was to be sanctuary at the castle. As Mr and Mrs Boldman, they were greeted with great friendliness at the hotel. The receptionist told them that the restaurant was closed, but the chef could 'Knock you up anything you might fancy, so.' Bond suddenly realised he was ravenous.

Ebbie began in polite restraint, 'Well, perhaps a light snack. A steak, maybe with potatoes and a green salad; possibly some mousse or profiteroles to follow – oh, and coffee, bread, some wine?'

'Anything at all, madam,' said the receptionist with a smile. 'Anything so long as it's Escalope Holstein, French fries, green salad and fruit salad.'

'That'll do nicely,' Ebbie said quickly. Bond realised she was starving too. He nodded agreement and chose a white Burgundy of dubious vintage and nomenclature. Ebbie asked for some bandages and disinfectant.

'We had a little trouble with the car, and my husband burned his hands.'

All in all, Bond decided, Ms Ebbie Heritage was a treasure. But treasure or not, he could not wait to get at the telephone once they were shown to their room, which was pleasant, if somewhat lacking in originality. That did not surprise him, for the hotel's foyer was decorated in adobe style with a distinct Spanish influence.

'I must do those hands,' Ebbie pleaded, 'and, James, they'll be here with the food any minute.'

Bond gestured to her to keep quiet, reached up to the top button of his Oscar Jacobson jacket and with his thumbnail prised off a strip of grey plastic about an inch long and a quarter of an inch thick. He dialled for an outside line and then the number of Three Sisters Castle, which he had committed to memory. He heard the automatic exchange click through and a second before the ringing tone began he put the piece of plastic on the mouthpiece and pressed hard. For two seconds it emitted a tiny piercing beep not unlike the sound of a muted harmonica. Through the earpiece he heard a small responding beep, meaning that the black grains of plastic wheat he had planted in the castle telephones had reacted to the tone. With the tiny 'harmonica bugs' coming to life he could now listen in not only to telephone conversations but to any sound within thirty feet of each bug. He could have been as far away as Australia or South Africa and have received the same transmission. These tiny, powerful instruments can be activated from thousands of miles away making the telephone a live, ever-ready microphone. At that moment Bond could hear only odd, far away noises, probably from one of the many rooms without a telephone. Softly, he put down the receiver and glanced at his watch. He knew he must continue to activate the bugs until he got a result. Ebbie had been hovering, looking perplexed. She was holding the bandages and disinfectant.

'James, will you let me do your hands? Please.'

Bond nodded, still preoccupied as he debated whether to telephone Smolin. Somebody would certainly be in the castle, if only to tend the injured Ingrid. But the fact that he could pick up nothing meant one thing, that Chernov had every available man, including himself, scouring the countryside for them.

He sighed. 'Yes, okay, Ebbie. Do your worst.'

In fact, she did her best. She was soothing, gentle and very disconcerting. In the middle of her ministrations the food arrived, and they started eating as soon as she had finished.

'I shall bathe after this.' She spoke with her mouth half full. 'I'm sorry I couldn't wait. I was so hungry.'

'That's all right, Ebbie. You've been very kind.'

She looked across the little table that had been brought in for them. Her head was bowed, but she lifted her eyes, half closed, then opened them wide. 'I want to show you every kindness, James. You were wonderful back at that awful castle.'

'I don't need payment, my dear.'

'Oh, but I liked you all those years ago on the submarine. You've bugged the telephones at the castle, yes?'

'You're very astute, Ebbie.'

138   *No Deals, Mr. Bond*

'Astute? What's astute? Is it sexy? I find you very...'

'It means you're very shrewd ... clever at spotting things.'

'But it was obvious, what you were doing just now. We were taught about it when we prepared for Cream Cake – that is such a stupid name. You have listening devices in the castle, yes?'

'Of course I have.'

'Then you're a clever little bugger, James, to be able to listen to things in the castle from this telephone.'

'I think you have the wrong word, Ebbie, but not to worry.' He smiled and her face lit up.

'James, dear man, I hope you don't have to listen to them all night?'

'It depends. At the moment there's nobody there.'

'I hope you don't. Oh, I do hope you don't.'

'We shall see. I must keep trying.'

They finished eating and Ebbie disappeared into the bathroom. Bond wheeled the dining table into the corridor. He was about to dial the castle again when Ebbie came out of the bathroom, dressed only in what she would have called her *Unterkleider*, and very fetching she looked as she grinned unselfconsciously, gathered up her bag and disappeared again.

He tried the castle once more and this time caught a short conversation. A man was talking in Russian to Ingrid, who was obviously very weak. It amounted to nothing and although he waited for fifteen minutes, there was no other sound. He put down the telephone and lay back on the bed feeling tired and now acutely aware of the pain in his arm and hands.

Closing his eyes, he wondered what the next move should be. Like it or not, he would have to reactivate the bugs at regular intervals, and his experience told him that if he heard no more from the castle they should all be on the move within a few hours. If they got back to England in one piece he could take the girls to one of his own safe houses, which he kept well hidden from the Service. He would then report to M with Smolin. At least two-thirds of the mission would have been accomplished. While he was composing his apologia to M, Ebbie returned to the bedroom, her hair glistening and her body only partially covered by an oyster satin négligé.

'The bathroom's free now, James.' She allowed the négligé to slip from her shoulders. 'Unless you have something better to do.'

Bond looked at the young fresh body, which held for him that same urgent attraction of innocence he had felt earlier. Slowly, he moved from the bed and into her arms. Their first kiss seemed to last a lifetime. His hands slid down to the neat silky little buttocks, and he felt his mind shrinking to one great need as Ebbie returned his kiss, her tongue darting and reaching hard into his mouth. He pulled away and looked into the wide open blue eyes.

'With these bandages on, it might be difficult for me to take a bath.' His throat felt dry. 'I wonder if you could…'

'Why don't we have a bath together?'

Ebbie's hand closed around his wrist and she led him unprotesting into the bathroom. She turned on the taps and Bond allowed her to undress him. When he was lying in the warm water she stood over him, naked, to soap his body, her hands and fingers exploring him as she did so. When he was washed clean she stepped into the narrow tub, sliding on to her side and lifting one leg over his so that he took her beneath the warm water.

When it was over, Ebbie dried him with a rough towel, and redressed his hands. This time, he led her back to the bedroom. For all her innocent looks, it was obvious that she was far from inexperienced, for she showed not only great stamina, but also imagination and invention. Through that night they made love to one another three more times, once with a stormy wildness; then with passion — Ebbie above him, reciting a sensuous poem to the rhythm of her own body; and finally with intense tenderness which made Bond think almost sadly of his dead wife, Tracy.

Bond tried the castle several times throughout the night,
still with no result. In the end he gave up and drifted to sleep
with Ebbie twined around him.

He woke with a start, realising that dawn was not far away.
Gently he disentangled himself from Ebbie's smooth body
and looked at his watch. It was five-thirty. Sliding from the
bed, he padded quietly to the bathroom. His hands felt less
sore, though the arm mangled by Fafie still throbbed.
Washing was easier than he expected and by six o'clock,
with dim light starting to show outside, Bond was dressed
and equipped with the ASP, baton and his hidden weapons.

Ebbie still lay in a deep sleep, her fair hair spread across
the pillow, her face tranquil. She would probably need all the
rest she could get that day, so Bond pocketed the room key
and went silently into the corridor. The room service table
had gone, and the whole hotel was wrapped in silence. As he
made his way down to the main lobby, the calm was broken
by occasional sounds of the kitchen staff preparing breakfast
below. Nobody was on duty at the reception desk so he made
his way to the coin-operated telephone, dragging a pile of
Irish change from his pocket.

A decidedly sleepy and disgruntled voice answered from
the Clonmel Arms Hotel, and he had to repeat his request to
be put through to Mr and Mrs Palmerston. There was an
unduly long wait before the operator came back on the line.

'I'm sorry sir, but they've checked out.'

'When?' Alarm bells sounded in his head.

'I've just come on duty myself, sir. But some friends of
theirs arrived unexpectedly, so I'm told. Mr and Mrs
Palmerston left around a half hour ago.'

Bond's nerves shrieked as he thanked the operator and
quickly hung up. What 'friends'? But he already knew the
answer. Blackfriar – General Chernov – had caught up with
Smolin, and it would not be long before he reached Bond and

Ebbie. Whether he had half an hour or ten minutes, it was essential that Bond put himself back in control of the situation. Instantly he dialled a Dublin number. It rang for several minutes before the voice answered sharply.

'Murray.'

'Jacko B. There are problems. I have to make this official.'

'Where are you?' Norman Murray sounded on edge.

'Kilkenny. The Newpark Hotel. I think your friend and mine, Basilisk, has been lifted with the girl you saw at the airport. The rumour about Blackfriar is true. There's a place called Three Sisters Castle...'

'We know all about Three Sisters. We have no jurisdiction. It's Embassy property. Bit of a fracas there, Jacko. Was that you, now?'

'Some of it, but I'm here with the girl from the Ashford Castle Hotel. Got me?'

'Right.'

'We're also due to be lifted. If you can...'

But Murray was way ahead of him. 'I know all about Basilisk, and it's a lash-up. I'll do what I can, Jacko. Watch your back. Official now, you say?'

'Very official and very dangerous.'

'I doubt it, but get out and head for Dublin. We don't have orders to lift you.'

'What do you mean?'

'We were lifting Basilisk and it's gone sour. Now, will you get going?'

'No transport.'

'Well, you'll have to steal something, Jacko. I hear you're good at that kind of thing.' Murray gave a quick laugh and rang off, leaving Bond looking at the dead telephone in his hand.

Ebbie, he thought: I must get her out, even if we have to hide in the hedgerows. As he turned to leave the telephone, another thought struck him. He should try the 'harmonicas' in the castle once more. He dialled the number and pressed the tiny plastic strip on to the earpiece. Suddenly it was filled with a confusion of sounds. Several people were talking in different parts of the castle. What he could hear made him tighten his grip on the telephone.

'They've lost the traitor Smolin and his girl. Shit!' This was in Russian.

There was a sinister laugh, then Ingrid's voice. 'The General's going to be very happy.'

A clearer conversation in German probably came from the Communications Room.

'Yes, message received and understood. Hans,' the voice shouted loudly and an answer came from far away, then closer. 'Hans, the team in Rome have tracked them down at last. Dietrich and the man Belzinger took a flight out last night. Can you get the Chief?'

'He's trying to locate the other pair – radio silence.'

'Break it. Dietrich and Belzinger are headed for Hong Kong.'

'God, I don't believe it.'

'Neither will the General, but get him. Get him quickly.'

Hong Kong, thought Bond. Jungle and Dietrich were really distancing themselves from Europe. The sooner he got Ebbie out the better it would be for all of them. He turned and took the stairs at a run. Reaching their room, he unlocked the door and headed straight for the bed.

'Ebbie! Ebbie, wake up...' His voice trailed off, for the bedclothes were pulled back and Ebbie was gone.

Before he could react to the prickle of danger, a voice whispered close to his ear, 'Don't even think about going for the gun, Mr Bond. You are of little use to me and I'd blow you away, now, in this room, if I had to. Hands on your head and turn around slowly.'

He had heard the voice once before on tape so he knew that as he turned he would be gazing into a face seldom seen in the West – the clean-cut, almost French-looking features of General Konstantin Nikolaevich Chernov, Chief Investi-

gating Officer of Department 8 of Directorate S, K.G.B.
Blackfriar himself.

'A strange meeting, eh, Mr Bond? After following each
other in office paper chases all this time.'

Chernov had a smile on his face and a large automatic
pistol in his hand, while behind him three large men crowded in, like hounds gathered for the kill.

BLACKFRIAR

'WELL.' BOND LOOKED straight into Chernov's green-flecked eyes. 'You're a long way from your usual territory, Comrade General. It must be odd to be away from your comfortable office in the Square, or have they moved Department 8 out to that modern monstrosity off the ring road – the so-called Scientific Research Centre?'

A wisp of a smile appeared on Chernov's lips. Anyone, Bond thought, could have taken him for an influential, wealthy businessman: the slim, powerful body under a beautifully cut grey suit; the tanned, undeniably good-looking features; the personal magnetism of the man, combined with his height – he was well over six feet tall – made him a commanding personality. It was easy to see how this man had become the Chief Investigating Officer of the erstwhile SMERSH.

'You read the right books, Comrade Bond, if I may say so; the right kind of fiction.' He lowered the pistol, a heavy Stetchkin, and turned his head in a slightly diffident manner to give a crisp instruction to one of the men behind him. 'I'm sorry.' He smiled again as though he genuinely liked Bond. 'I'm sorry, but your reputation goes ahead of you. I've asked my people to remove any toys you might be carrying.'

His free hand went up to brush one of the greying, thick wings of hair described so accurately on the file at Headquarters: 'The hair is thick, greying at the temples, unusually long for a member of the Russian Service, but always well-groomed and distinguished by the wings that almost cover his ears. It is swept straight back with no parting.'

Bond knew most of the senior K.G.B. and G.R.U. officers' profiles by heart.

One of Chernov's men, obeying the order, caught hold of Bond's shoulders and turned him around roughly. He ordered him in clumsy English to place his palms on the bedroom wall.

Chernov snapped another command, then said, 'I'm sorry, Mr Bond. He was instructed to handle you more gently.' His accent could easily have been acquired at one of the older British universities, his whole manner being near to deferential. The tone, usually quiet and calm, made him even more sinister.

The man conducting the body search was all too thorough. He quickly found the ASP and the baton; then the disguised weapons: the pen, the wallet and the precious belt which contained so many secrets. He felt the linings of Bond's clothes and removed his shoes and examined them carefully before returning them. In minutes Bond was left only with the tiny 'harmonica' bleeper still attached to the top button of his jacket.

'It's interesting, isn't it?' Chernov said in his near languorous tones, 'Interesting how our masters are always dreaming up new little pieces of technology for us?'

'With respect, you're one of the masters.' Bond willed himself to show the same calmness, for Chernov would be like an animal who could scent fear at fifty paces.

'So I am,' he said with a low-pitched laugh.

'One to be admired, so we are told.'

'Really.' He did not sound flattered.

'Isn't it true that you are practically the only senior officer to survive the 1971 purge, after Lyalin's defection?'

Chernov shrugged. 'Who knows about Lyalin? Some say that was a put up job to get rid of us altogether.'

'But you did survive and helped to build the phoenix out of the ashes of your department. You're to be admired.' This was not mere flattery. Bond knew that a man with Chernov's track record would never fall for such an obvious ploy.

'Thank you, Mr Bond. The feeling is mutual. You too have been resurrected against much criticism, I gather.' He sighed. 'What a difficult thing our job is. You realise what must be done?'

'The price on my head?'

'There's no price – not this time. However, you are on a list. Therefore I would be failing in my duty if I did not achieve your execution; preferably at the Lubyanka after interrogation.' He shrugged again. 'But unfortunately that could prove difficult. To dispose of you will not be a problem, yet my career demands that justice must be seen to be done. Your death has to be public, not in the privacy of the Lubyanka cellars.'

Bond nodded. He knew the longer he kept the man talking there in the hotel, the more chance Murray would have to come to his rescue. Bond had to telephone him. Official or not, Murray would certainly do all that was possible – did he not owe Bond his own life?

'I'm glad you are philosophical about it, Mr Bond. You say you admire me and I would be lacking in honesty if I did not admit to having some respect for your qualities of ingenuity, speed and resourcefulness. You must understand that there will be nothing personal about your death. It's just business.'

'Of course.' Bond hesitated for a moment. 'May I ask what has happened to the lady?'

'Don't worry about the lady.' Chernov smiled, inclining his head to one side in a condescending gesture. 'Eventually she too must pay a penalty, together with the turncoat Smolin and the other traitor in this disgraceful business; Dietrich and her gigolo, Belzinger, or Baisley as he now likes to be called. My duty is to see justice done. You are a most delightful bonus.' He looked around him at his lieutenants. 'We should be on our way. There is much to be done.'

'I'm ready when you are.'

Bond realised that he must have sounded a little too confident, and saw his error in the hint of suspicion that stirred in Kolya Chernov's eyes. For a second the General looked at him, then turned on his heel, flicking his hand in a gesture commanding his men to follow with Bond. They took him along the corridor towards the back of the building and down two flights of emergency stairs.

Behind the hotel stood a large Renault and a sleek black Jaguar with darkened windows. Chernov walked straight towards the Jaguar and Bond was pushed in the same direction. The Renault was obviously either the trail or scout car. Bond was to travel in the comparative luxury of Chernov's Jaguar. A man detached himself from the driving seat and strolled over to open the rear door. He wore a black rollneck and his head was bandaged. Even from a distance, Bond recognised Mischa, the killer who had made the abortive attempt on Heather's life in London. The bandages made him look more piratical than ever, and he stared at Bond with an animated hatred.

General Chernov ducked his head and climbed into the rear of the Jaguar, while the men pushed Bond around to the far side. There was no sign of Ebbie. Another man climbed from the offside door, standing to one side as Bond was bundled in next to Chernov.

Chernov sighed. 'The ride will not be so comfortable. I'm afraid it's rather cramped with three people in the back.'

The guard climbed in after Bond so that he was sandwiched in the middle. Mischa returned to the driving seat, while one of the other men took the front passenger seat. Being a realist, Bond did not need to ponder what might happen if Murray were to miss his cue. Mischa started the engine and the Renault pulled away in front of them. It was to be a forward scout, thought Bond. That was exactly how he would have played it.

It soon became obvious that they were taking the road to Dublin. In a matter of hours they would be back at Three

Sisters Castle. Mischa drove with almost exaggerated care, keeping a steady thirty yards behind the Renault. He did not look back at Bond but his malevolence hung in the air. The man next to Bond kept one arm inside his jacket and occasionally the butt of a pistol showed, grasped firmly in his hand. The General dozed but the man in front remained alert, occasionally turning around or watching Bond in the rear view mirror set in the sun shield.

Time dragged and Bond tired of the monotonous scenery, the views of lush greenery and the untidy towns and villages. Although his mind ranged through every possibility, he knew there was no way he could escape from the car alive. It would be certain death, even on the main roads of the Republic of Ireland. If only Murray would turn up, he kept thinking, there might be a way. For the present he had lost control over the situation.

They covered the miles without incident, finally passing through the narrow streets of Arklow. About three miles beyond, the Renault turned off to the left, up a very narrow road bordered by high trees and hedges and with barely space for two cars to pass comfortably. Clearly this was the road leading to the main castle entrance.

Chernov stretched and woke, telling Mischa he had done well and sharing a joke with him in Russian. Ahead the Renault turned a sharp bend and as they followed Mischa cursed roughly. Around the bend the Renault had been forced to pull up sharply. Two Garda cars were parked across the road and as Mischa applied the brakes Bond glanced behind to see an unmarked saloon covering their rear.

'Stay calm. No weapons!' Chernov ordered, his voice cracking like a whip. 'No shooting, understand?'

Half a dozen uniformed Gardi were surrounding the Renault, and another four now approached the Jaguar. With a slow insolence, Mischa lowered the window and a uniformed officer bent to speak to him.

'Gentlemen, I'm afraid this road is closed to all but the diplomatic traffic. You'll have to get the car turned around.'

'What appears to be the trouble, officer?' Chernov leaned forward and Bond noticed that he and the other man in the rear had positioned themselves in a vain attempt to hide Bond's face.

'It's diplomatic trouble, sir. Nothing serious. There were some complaints last night, so we're having to keep the road shut for a while.'

'What kind of diplomatic trouble? I carry a diplomatic passport, as do my fellow passengers. We're heading for the Russian Embassy property at the castle.'

'Ah, well, that makes a difference, then.'

The man took a step back. Already Bond could see the cars ahead of them had been moved slightly to let the Renault through. He was also aware of men in civilian clothes close to the car. One of them now leaned towards the rear window, which Mischa had been forced to open. Bond did not recognise him, but he had the roving, relaxed eyes of a Special Branch man.

'There were reports of shooting around here last night. You'll understand that people get a bit nervous of that kind of thing. So I'll have to see your credentials, sir, if you'd care to…'

'Certainly.' Chernov fumbled in his coat and pulled out a bundle of documents, including his passport. The Irish S.B. man took them examining the passport carefully.

'Ah!' He looked hard at Chernov. 'We knew you had arrived, Mr Talanov. It's your Foreign Ministry you're from, is it not?'

'I am Inspector of Embassies, yes. I'm here on the usual annual visit.'

'Now, it wasn't you who came last time, was it, Mr Talanov? If I recall correctly it was a short man. Now didn't he have a beard or something? Yes, a beard and glasses. Name of… God love me, I'll forget my own name next, so

I will.'

'Zuyenko,' said Chernov. 'Yuri Fedevich Zuyenko.'

'That's the fella, now. Zuyenko. He's not coming this year then, Mr Talanov?'

'He is not coming anywhere.' Bond detected a slight edge. Chernov, with his experience, would know that the garrulous Special Branch man was playing for time. He was obviously already annoyed. 'Yuri Fedevich died. Suddenly. Last summer.'

'Lord rest his soul poor man. Suddenly, last summer, eh? Did you ever see that filum, sir? It had the lovely Katharine Hepburn in it, and Miss Taylor…you know she has a cottage hereabouts, did you know that?'

'I really think we should be moving, especially if there has been trouble up the road at Three Sisters.'

'Bit of something and nothing I should think, Mr Talanov. But, before you go…'

'Yes?' He sounded stern and his eyes were glittering with more than a hint of anger.

'Well, sir. We do have to check all diplomatic credentials.'

'Nonsense. I vouch for everyone in the car. They are all under my care.'

As Chernov spoke, Bond felt the hard metal of the guard's pistol in his side. He could not risk making a fuss even though he knew Chernov did not want a killing incident on his hands.

Another face replaced the first. 'I'm very sorry, Mr Talanov, as you call yourself, but we'll be taking that gentleman there.' Norman Murray pointed to Bond. 'You're keeping bad company, sir. This man's wanted for questioning, and I think you'll agree he's not a Russian citizen, and certainly no diplomat. Am I right, so?'

'Well…' Chernov started.

'I think you'd better let him come quietly. Out of the car, you.' Murray reached in across the guard and took hold of Bond's jacket. 'You'll come quietly won't you, me boyo?

Then the other gentlemen can get on their way.'

'Quits now, Norman?' Bond did not smile at the Special Branch man. He could see that something had gone seriously wrong. He had seen it as Norman Murray had led the way to his private car and nodded for Bond to get in, leaving the Gardi and S.B. officers to see Chernov's car through to the castle.

'More than quits, Jacko. I'll be for the high jump tomorrow, no doubt about that. There's little I can do for you. I doubt if I could walk the length of my shadow for you and that's a fact. There's some very funny business going on, I'll tell you.'

'What's happened?' Bond knew Murray well enough to see the man was engulfed in a mixture of anger, frustration and concern.

'It's what didn't happen. First, I was wakened before dawn with a message about your man Basilisk. Your friends across the water wanted him pulled in and delivered to them on the quiet, right? Seeing as how we do favours for one another, we sent a couple of cars to the Clonmel Arms where, we were reliably informed, Basilisk was staying with your young woman – the one I met at the airport.'

'You didn't say anything about that when I telephoned you.'

'Because you said they had been lifted. I thought it'd be a nice surprise for you to know we had lifted them.'

'You took the girl as well?'

'We didn't get either of them. They weren't there. I had a call five minutes after you got in touch. The people at the hotel said 'friends' had picked them up. But later they changed their tune. It appears that Basilisk made a lot of telephone calls during the night. Then they came down around three thirty in the morning, paid the bill and left.'

'What about the girl I was with?'

'There's neither hide nor hair of her. There really were

complaints about shooting and explosions at the castle, and one of our people spotted you being brought out of the hotel. But it's a great chance I've been taking meddling with the fella you were with.'

'None of this is good.' Bond felt foolish at his understatement.

Murray laughed. 'You've yet to hear the really bad news, Jacko. Your Service refused to make you official.'

'Damn!'

'You're on leave. There's no sanction for you to be in the Republic, operational. That's what I got. On no account are you to give this officer assistance. On no account, Jacko. That's what they said.'

'In the event of anything going wrong we shall have to deny you, even to our own police forces.' He heard M's voice as they walked through the park. 'Our own police forces' implied everyone else's as well. But why? M had held out on the turning of Basilisk, though that had now to some extent been explained. There had been contact between M and Smolin, probably through Murray, who was the most pliable Irish S.B. man the Service had on tap. Already Bond had run Smolin and two of the girls to earth. Why in heaven's name would the old man go on denying him?

'Norman, you realise who that was in the car?'

'I know exactly who it was, Jacko.'

'Then why didn't you ...'

'Hands off. Those were the instructions from my people, and I gather they are in contact with your own Service. Take in Basilisk and deliver him to us but don't touch Blackfriar. That's what we were asked. Well, Basilisk's disappeared, and ...'

'And the girls as well. The girls were my real responsibility, Norman.'

'I don't want to know.'

'You're not going to know. Except that I have to find those girls, and someone else.'

'Well, you won't be finding them here, not in the Republic. I'm to get you to a secure place we have at the airport and move you on — with a giant boot up the backside.'

'What?'

'You heard, Jacko. We don't want you here. So off you go. Even your Embassy doesn't want you here.'

Bond's mind reeled with questions. 'If we come to a telephone, will you stop for a minute, Norman?'

'Why should I?'

'For old times' sake.'

'We're square.'

'Please.' He spoke gravely. Smolin and Heather had disappeared entirely and Ebbie had vanished in minutes from their room, to be replaced by Chernov. Nasty suspicions were starting to form in his head.

Slowly Murray nodded. A couple of hundred yards along the road they came to a telephone box and he pulled over. 'Quickly as you can, Jacko, and no stupidity. We've enough trouble without you going walkabout.'

Bond had the plastic 'harmonica' bleeper unpeeled from the button before he reached the telephone box. By now Blackfriar would be back in the castle and he reckoned the General would immediately have the telephones checked. Indeed, he was surprised it had not already been done, for Chernov was obviously scrupulously careful. The bugs were nevertheless still in place and he heard the usual mixture of voices. He could make out very little and was about to replace the instrument when he suddenly heard Chernov's voice, very clear. He must be standing right over one of the activated telephones.

'I want every man we have on the streets of Dublin.' His voice was calm and authoritative. 'Bond and Colonel Smolin must be found and soon. I want them both. Understand? They took Bond from under my nose. Then we have the added trouble of those two German women, the damned

Cream Cake business. What have I done to deserve such idiots?'

'Comrade General, you had no option. It just couldn't be helped.' The conversation was in Russian. 'Your orders have been obeyed to the letter. Once we run everyone to earth it will be simple. But the gunfight last night has caused almost a diplomatic incident.'

'Diplomatic rubbish!' shouted Chernov.

Now there was another voice, close to Chernov. 'We've just had a message from Hong Kong, Comrade General.'

'Yes?'

'They've tracked Belzinger and Dietrich. She's opened up the G.R.U. house on Cheung Chau Island.'

'Dietrich's an over-confident bitch. We shall have to move fast. Get a message to Hong Kong. Tell them to watch at a distance. I don't want anyone going in there until I arrive.'

The line began to break up and Bond realised that now, more than ever, it was essential for him to take the initiative. Delving into his pocket he pulled out the few Irish coins that Chernov's man had left him. He put the receiver down, then dialled the castle number again. When it was answered, he spoke quickly in Russian, asking for General Chernov by name.

'This is most urgent! A life and death matter.'

Chernov was on in a few seconds, quietly cursing about secure lines.

'We don't need a secure line, Comrade General,' said Bond in English. 'You recognise the voice?'

There was a short pause. Then, Chernov answered, cold as ice. 'I recognise it.'

'I just wanted to say that I look forward to meeting you again, Blackfriar. Catch me if you can. North, south, west or east.'

He put the accent on east, goading Chernov. Replacing the instrument, he left the box and walked rapidly to the car. Chernov would know Bond was calling his bluff, and that

Bond had a small advantage, with his knowledge of Chernov's likely movements. M would probably have said the telephone call was an insane move, but M was also playing a devious game.

'For a minute there I thought you were playing games with me, Jacko. They've been on to me from Dublin. What country do you want?'

'What d'you mean, what country?'

'You're being deported, Jacko. Your own folk in London have said we can send you to the moon as far as they care. Even your old boss says you've to take the rest of your leave elsewhere.'

'He used those words?'

'Exactly those words. "Tell the renegade to take the rest of his leave elsewhere. Tell him to go missing." That's what the auld divil said. So where's it to be, Jacko? Spain? Portugal? A couple of weeks in the Canary Islands?'

Bond glanced at him, but Murray's face was expression-less, innocent of any knowledge about Jungle's recent visit there.

'Let me think for a minute or two, Norman. Wherever I choose, can you get me out really quietly?'

'As quietly as ghosts. You'll go so silently that not even the Dublin airport controllers will know.'

'Give me a minute then.'

Already he knew exactly where he wanted to go, but first Bond had to think about M's attitude. Controls always worked on the basis of need-to-know, so why had M decided from the outset that Bond should be told he was on his own? And why, when M must know two of the girls had been found and had then disappeared, was he still denying Bond had any rights in the field? Bond was never supposed to meet Smolin, so he did not need to know about him. Was this a case of Bond not needing to know something else?

He tried to reason out the succession of events, using his knowledge of elementary trade and fieldcraft. When would

a control deliberately withhold some piece of vital information from his agent, even when it might put his man at a
grave disadvantage? There was only one set of circumstances that justified this kind of risk, and already there had
been a hint of it in the conversation overheard through the
'harmonicas'. You withhold only one kind of information
– that a trusted agent might be a double. You withhold that
when you do not know who is the guilty person. Bring them
all back, M had told him. All, which meant Ebbie, Heather
or Jungle could be a double. It had to be the answer. One of
the Cream Cake team had been turned and, knowing the
way M's mind worked, Bond had to include Smolin and
Dietrich among the suspects.

They reached the outskirts of Dublin, weaving their way
through the heavy traffic. Why deny him? It was simple. You
deny a field agent when the Foreign Office and the politi-
cians would be seriously embarrassed; or when his targets
know he is getting no assistance. Damn M, Bond thought,
he's playing it very long indeed – long and dangerous. Any
other officer would have called it a day, gone back to London
with his spoils and laid them at M's feet. But not Bond. M
was putting all his money on Bond seeing it through; risking
his man like a gambler, knowing the stakes had risen
dramatically once Blackfriar had shown himself.

'Is there a secure telephone at this place you have at the
airport, Norm?'

'I told you not to be calling me Norm.' Murray sounded
annoyed.

'Well, is there?'

'It's as safe as you can get.' He glanced towards Bond with
a large smile. 'We may even let you use it if you've decided
where you want to go.'

'Can you get me into France, as near Paris as possible?'

Murray laughed loudly. 'You're asking for miracles, so.
You know what the D.S.T. is like. Non bloody co-operative.'

'You live in a country of miracles, Norman. Me, I'd rather

be going back across the water to the good life. You know, the click of willow against a villain's head, the roar of the riot, the scent of new-mown grass snakes.'

'Lord love you, but you're turning poetical, Jacko. Thank heaven the blessed St Patrick rid us of snakes.'

'Did he?' Bond returned the grin, knowing he was about to have all his requests fulfilled.

The secure quarters were inside the airport itself, in a small walled compound, which hid the car and its passengers from any possibility of being watched. Ostensibly, Dublin has one of the most open airports in Europe. In fact, it boasts discreet and powerful security, mostly hidden from public view. When they reached the approach road, Bond realised there were more than the usual number of Garda patrols around.

Inside there was a comfortable waiting room with armchairs and magazines. There were also a couple of plain clothes men who showed some deference to Norman Murray.

'There's a soundproof booth over there with one of the most secure telephones in Ireland,' said Murray, pointing. 'Use it now while I set up your flight.'

'Not until I'm certain you can get me into Paris by tonight,' said Bond coolly.

'It's as good as done, Jacko. You do your telephoning. You'll be on your way with nobody the wiser within the hour.'

Bond nodded. Norman Murray was a very convincing officer.

Inside the booth he dialled a London number. The woman who answered asked straight away if they were scrambled, and he said probably, but that the line was secure in any case. Q'ute had offered help when he last saw her. Bond had known then that it was no idle remark. Just before he left she had said,

'If you need anything from here, just call and I'll bring it to you myself.'

He was calling now, with a long shopping list and an almost impossible delivery time and place but Q'ute took it in her stride.

She merely said, 'It'll be there. Good luck,' and rang off.

Murray was waiting for him, a set of white overalls in his hand. 'Put these on,' he said to Bond, 'and listen carefully.'

As Bond complied, Murray continued, 'The passage through that door leads to the flying club. You're going on a spot of cross-country with an instructor. The flight plan is filed. Permission has been given for you to overfly northern France; they do it all the time from here. This time you'll have a little engine trouble near Rennes, which is your turning point. You won't be able to make an airfield, so your instructor will put out a Mayday and you'll glide into a field: not any old field, but a particular one. There'll be a car and someone to take your place in the aircraft for when the gendarmes and customs arrive. It's got to go like clockwork. Do as you're told and it should be okay. But if you're asked, I had nothing to do with this. You follow?'

Bond nodded. 'Thanks, Norman.'

'The aircraft's directly in front of the building, with the engine running and cleared to taxi. She's a nice little Cessna 182. She would take four at a pinch. Good luck, Jacko.'

Bond shook Murray's hand warmly, knowing that somehow M was still with him, for a reason best known to the old man himself.

The aircraft was drawn up close to the building, and Bond kept his head well down as he walked quickly towards it. He ducked his head under the wing and climbed up beside the instructor, a young, happy-looking Irishman who grinned at him, shouting that it was about time.

He had hardly strapped himself into the pupil's position to the instructor's left before the Cessna was taxiing towards the short runway on the far side of the field. They waited for a few minutes as an Aer Lingus 737 came in from London, then the instructor opened up the engine and the light aeroplane took to the air almost of her own accord. They turned out to sea and began to climb. At two thousand feet the instructor levelled out.

'There we are,' he shouted, 'all set for the fun and games. I'll be turning on course in five minutes.' He moved his head. 'Are you okay back there?'

'Fine,' replied Bond.

He looked around and saw Ebbie's face peering over the back of his seat, where she had been hiding.

'Hallo, James. Are you pleased to see me?'

She planted a kiss on his cheek.

- 14 -
DINNER IN PARIS

EVERY FIELD AGENT worth his salt has his special fall-backs away from home: a bank account in Berlin; a cache of weapons in Rome; passport blanks in a strong box in Madrid. James Bond's was a safe house in Paris; or rather a small apartment owned by good friends who were willing to leave their home at a moment's notice and no questions asked. The apartment was on the fourth floor of one of those buildings off the Boulevard Saint Michel on the Rive Gauche.

They arrived just after six in the evening, following a journey that had gone almost too smoothly for Bond's peace of mind. The instructor had piloted the Cessna all the way and Bond noticed that, once over France, he allowed their altitude to fluctuate to a point where the Paris A.T.C. were constantly calling him up to remind him of his allotted position. The rendezvous itself had been well picked, a lonely spot west of Rennes. They circled above it for fifteen minutes, gradually losing height until the pilot was certain his contact was in place.

He's done this before, Bond thought, wondering when and in what circumstances. Maybe Murray had something on the man — smuggling, or even a tricksy business concerning the lads, as the Provos are always referred to in the Republic. Whatever his previous experience, this went like clockwork. Air Traffic Control called up once more, anxious about the loss of height. The pilot waited for around four minutes as he turned, bleeping his engine and positioning himself for a landing. Then he began his Mayday call, giving a heading and fix that was around ten miles out so that the authorities would take longer to reach them.

'When we're down, you've got about five minutes to get going,' he shouted to Bond. He cut the engine, then gave it another burst: 'A bit of realism for the customers,' he said with a grin.

They drifted over some flat farmland with no sign of life for five or six miles then touched down and taxied towards a clump of trees and a ribbon-straight road lined with poplars. A battered elderly Volkswagen was parked near the trees, almost out of sight from the road. Just as the Cessna's engine stopped, a figure wearing a white overall identical to Bond's broke free from the trees and came towards them.

'Go! God be with you,' said the pilot, already starting to climb out.

Bond helped Ebbie down into the field, stripped off the overall and looked at the man who had joined them. Bond's replacement simply nodded and inclined his head towards the Volkswagen. He handed over the keys and said there were maps in the car. Taking Ebbie by the hand, Bond set off at a trot. The last they saw of the two intrepid flyers was from the car. They had part of the cowling off and were fiddling with the engine. But by this time the Volkswagen was already on the road, heading for Paris. Bond allowed himself time to get used to the car before he spoke.

'Right, young lady. How and why did you turn up again?'

It had been impossible to carry on any detailed conversation on the aircraft, and he was now very suspicious of Ebbie's dramatic reappearance, even if it did have Norman Murray's blessing.

'That nice policeman thought it would be a pleasant surprise for you, James darling.'

'Yes, but what happened to you in Kilkenny?'

'He didn't tell you?'

'Who?'

'The Inspector. Murray.'

'Not a word. What happened?'

'At the hotel?'

'Well, I'm not talking about your daring escape from Germany, Ebbie,' he replied with a certain crustiness.

'I woke up,' she said, as though that explained it all.

'And?'

'It was early, very early, and you weren't there, James.'

'Go on.'

'I was frightened. I got out of bed and went into the passage. There was nobody there so I went along to the stairs. You were using the telephone down in the lobby. I heard your voice, then people started coming in at the other end of the passage. I was very embarrassed.'

'Embarrassed?'

'I only had...only little...' She indicated what she had been wearing. 'And nothing up here at all. So, there was a cupboard – a closet where they keep cleaning things.'

Bond nodded and she continued, 'I hid. It was dark and not nice. But I hid for a long time. I heard other voices and people walking along the passage. When it was silent I came out again. You had disappeared.'

He nodded again. It could just be true, and she was convincing enough.

'I dressed,' she said, giving him a small, uncomfortable look. 'Then the policemen came and I told them. They used the radio in their car and told me there were orders. Then they brought me to the airport. James, I have no clothes, only what I stand up in, and my shoulder bag.'

'Did Inspector Murray tell you what would be happening?'

'It was a risk, he said, for me to remain in Ireland. He said I should go with you, but to give you a surprise. He has a sense of humour. He's a very funny man, the Inspector.'

'Yes, exceptionally droll. Hilarious.'

He still had no way of knowing whether to believe her or not. In the circumstances there was only one course he could take. He must stick with her but keep her in the dark as much as possible, arousing no suspicion in her.

They arrived at his safe apartment, Bond having telephoned ahead from a service area on the A11 Autoroute. There was food in the large refrigerator, two bottles of a good vintage Krug and clean linen on the double bed; no notes or messages. That was always the way. A quick telephone call giving his arrival time and probable duration of stay and his friends would be gone by the time Bond arrived. He did not ask where they went, neither did they question him. The husband was an old Service hand but the trade had never been mentioned by either side. In eight years the routine rarely changed. Everything was invariably ready and this occasion, in spite of the very short notice, was no exception.

'James, what a beautiful little apartment!' Ebbie appeared genuinely enthusiastic. 'Is this all yours?'

'It is when I'm in Paris and when my friend is away.' He went to the desk in the main room, opened the top drawer and removed the false interior. Underneath he always kept a float of around a thousand francs.

'Look, there is steak.' Ebbie was exploring the kitchen. 'Shall I cook us a meal?'

'Later.' Bond looked at the stainless steel Rolex. It would take him the best part of half an hour, given a favourable wind, to get to the rendezvous arranged with Ann Reilly. 'Thank heaven there are shops that stay open late in Paris. Ebbie, I want you to make a list of the essential clothing you need and give me your sizes.'

'We are going shopping?' She gave a little jump, like a small child looking forward to a sudden treat.

'I am going shopping,' he said with great firmness.

'Oh. But, James, there are some things you cannot get. Personal items ...'

'Just make the list, Ebbie. A lady will get the personal things.'

'What lady?' She bridled. Ebbie Heritage was either one

hell of a good actress or a really jealous woman. Bond would have sworn the latter, for her cheeks had gone scarlet and her eyes were brimming.

With a small stamp of her foot she said, 'You are seeing another woman?'

'We haven't known one another for long, Ebbie.'

'That's got nothing to do with it. You have been with me. We are lovers. Yet as soon as we come to France…'

'Hold on. Yes, I am going to see another lady. But I'm seeing her strictly for business reasons.'

'*Ja* – Yes, I know. The funny business reasons.'

'Nothing like that. Now, calm down, Ebbie. I want you to listen to me.' He realised he was talking to her as he would speak to a child. 'This is very important. I must go out. I shall take your list with me. You must on no account answer the door or the telephone. Keep the door locked until I return. I shall give a special knock, like so.' He demonstrated: three quick raps, pause, another three, pause, then two harder raps. 'Got it?'

'Yes.' She was almost sullen.

'Then show me.'

She gave a small shrug and repeated the pattern of knocks.

'Right. Now the telephone. Do not touch it unless it rings three times, goes silent and then starts ringing again.'

The codes were as simple as lovers' signals, but they were equally easy to remember. Bond went through it again, then sat her down at the table with pen and paper while he went round the apartment closing shutters and drawing curtains. By the time he had finished, she held up the completed list.

'How long will you be gone?' she asked in a very small voice.

'With luck, about two hours. Not much longer.'

She pulled herself up very straight. 'Two hours, and I shall smell this other woman's scent on you if you are making love with her. You be on time, James. Dinner will be here, on this table, in two hours exactly. You understand?'

'Yes, ma'am,' he said with a winning smile, 'and don't forget what I told you about the door and the telephone. You understand?'

She lifted her face, hands behind her back, raising herself on tiptoe, and turning her cheek towards him.

'Don't I rate a proper kiss?'

'When you come back in time for dinner we'll see.'

He nodded, kissed her cheek and let himself out, walking down the four flights of stone stairs to street level. He always avoided elevators in Paris. Nine times out of ten in these old apartment blocks the lifts were out of order.

He took a taxi to Les Invalides, then walked back to the Quai D'Orsay, across the Seine and in the direction of the Tuileries gardens. Only when he was certain he had not picked up a tail did Bond flag down another cab, which he ordered back to the Boulevard Saint Michel.

Ann Reilly was sitting in the corner of the small crowded café he had named, only ten minutes' walk from the apartment where Ebbie was cooking dinner. Bond went straight to the bar, ordered a *fine* and crossed to Q'ute's table. It did not look as though they were being watched, but he spoke low.

'Okay?'

'Everything you ordered. In the briefcase. It's just by your right foot and it's safe. Nothing will show on the x-ray machines but I'd unpack and put the whole lot in your suitcase.'

Bond nodded. 'How are things back at the building?'

'Hectic. There's some kind of flap on. M's been closeted in his office for three days now. He's like a general under siege. The grapevine says he's sleeping there and they're taking crates full of microfilm to him. The main computer's been barred to everyone else and the Chief-of-Staff's been with him all the time. Moneypenny hasn't been out either. I think she's lying across his door with a shotgun.'

'That figures,' he muttered. 'Look, love, I've a favour to

ask.' He passed over Ebbie's list. 'There's a supermarket one block down on the corner. Just do your best, eh?'

'I use my own money?'

'Put it on expenses. When I get back I'll square it.'

Q'ute looked at the list and smiled. 'What's her taste in ...' she began.

'Sophisticated,' Bond cut in quickly.

'I'll do my best, being a plain and simple girl myself.'

'That'll be the day. I'll set up a drink for you. Oh, and get a cheap case, will you?'

'Sophisticated and cheap?'

Ann Reilly left the café, her hips swaying almost suggestively. Bond made a mental note to buy her dinner once this was over and he was back in London. In just under half an hour she returned with a flurry.

'I've got a cab waiting outside. I can catch the last Air France flight back to Heathrow if I get a shift on. The case is in the cab. Can I give you a lift?'

Bond was on his feet, following her to the door. He told her to drop him off a couple of blocks away. She kissed him full on the mouth, whispering 'Good luck' as he left with the suitcase and briefcase.

He spent forty minutes back doubling, riding the Metro, walking and using another cab, before he returned to the apartment, within ten minutes of Ebbie's deadline. Ebbie sniffed him suspiciously, but could smell only the brandy and so softened slightly – particularly when he gave her the suitcase and told her to open it. Once more there were gasps of delight as she examined Q'ute's purchases. Bond meanwhile was able to check his own clothes, which were always kept for him in one part of the bedroom wardrobe. There was also a spare case in the flat, so he could pack his clothes and the items from the briefcase later, at leisure.

'The dinner will be ready in five minutes,' Ebbie sang from the kitchen.

'I have to make one telephone call and I'll be with you.'

He used the extension in the bedroom to dial the Cathay Pacific desk at Orly. Yes, they had two first-class seats on their flight to Hong Kong tomorrow. Certainly they would reserve them in the name of Boldman. He quoted his Amex number.

'Thank you, Mr Boldman, that'll be fine. Just pick the tickets up at the desk by ten-fifteen. Have a nice flight.'

He looked inside the briefcase to check that Q'ute had not forgotten the small rubber stamp for doctoring their passports. A sudden horror struck him.

'Ebbie!' he called. 'Ebbie, you have got a passport with you, haven't you?'

'Of course. I never travel without it.'

He went into the living room. The table was set elegantly for a dinner for two.

'You have been a busy girl, Ebbie.'

'Yes. Are we going somewhere?'

'Not until the morning. Tonight it's a romantic dinner in Paris.'

'Good, but in the morning where are we going?'

'Tomorrow,' he said quietly, 'we're off to the mystic East.'

15

THE MYSTIC EAST

The Cathay Pacific 747 Flight CX 290 from Paris made its descent over Lantau Island towards the mainland of the New Territories. There the great jet began its almost one-hundred-degree turn to the final approach, right across Kowloon and down on to Kai Tak, Hong Kong's international airport with its runway thrusting like a finger into the sea.

As the engines whined, giving the machine the last ounce of extra thrust to carry it over the rooftops, James Bond peered out of the window, craning to see the island of Hong Kong below, with the Peak shrouded in cloud.

They would be low over Kowloon Tong now and he thought of its translation, Pool of Nine Dragons, and the story that the late Bruce Lee had consulted a fortune teller before buying an apartment in this exclusive district. The young Kung Fu film star had been told that, should he buy the flat, he would have only bad joss because his name could be translated as little dragon, and nothing good could come of a little dragon going to live in a pool with nine dragons. Nevertheless, Bruce Lee bought the apartment, and within the year he was dead. Bad joss.

The Boeing touched down with the huge roar of the reverse thrust, its flaps fully extended as the speed bled off. It rolled slowly to a halt at the far end of the runway, where the buildings towered to their left. The boat-littered Fragrant Harbour stretched out to the right between the mainland and Hong Kong Island.

Within twenty minutes of landing, Bond was standing

with Ebbie clutching his hand in the garage-like surroundings of Passport Control. Scrupulous, unsmiling Chinese
officials scrutinised their documents. From the moment they
had left the aircraft, he had done his best to spot likely
watchers in the airport buildings; but in the sea of European,
Chinese and Eurasian faces, everybody seemed to be a
potential look-out.

A large Chinese in slacks and white shirt held a board on
which was written MR BOLDMAN. Bond steered Ebbie
forward.

'I'm Mr Boldman.'

'Ah, good. I take you Mandarin Hotel.' The Chinese
grinned widely, showing what appeared to be several sets of
independently working teeth, most of them filled with gold.
'Car here. Inside please, never mind.' The driver ushered
them towards a limousine, opening the door. 'My name is
David,' he said.

'Thank you, David,' said Ebbie prettily, and they climbed
in.

Bond glanced out of the rear window as they moved away
to see if he could spot any car positioning itself behind them.
The search was fruitless, for cars left the arrivals rank all the
time, and most seemed to have just picked up passengers.
What he was looking for was some nondescript vehicle with
two people up front. He caught himself in time – that was
what he would have looked for in Europe. In Asia things
were different. He recalled an old China hand once saying,
'As for watchers, they'll be the people you least expect. East
of Suez they watch in plain sight, and they're a bugger to
spot.'

There were no positive signs as they entered the Cross-
Harbour Tunnel, which they moved through in a slow but
orderly procession of cars, lorries, both ancient and modern,
and those fifteen-hundredweight trucks beloved of the Hong
Kongese, some with tattered awnings flapping and displaying Chinese characters.

Nowadays you have only to return to Hong Kong after an absence of a few weeks to notice changes. It was a couple of years since Bond had been in the Territory and he saw huge differences as they reached Connaught Road. Ahead, to their right, the massive Connaught Centre rose with its hundreds of porthole-like windows, making it look as though it had been designed by an optician; and behind that the almost completed glass triple-towers of Exchange Square. The traffic was still as heavy as the heat outside, while the sidewalks and futuristic linking bridges over the main roads were crammed with scurrying people. On the left he caught sight, through Chater Square, of the huge new Hong Kong and Shanghai Bank Building erected like a large Leggo kit on four great tall cylinders.

Then they were pulling up in front of the main doors of the Mandarin which, next to the high-rise opulence, appeared almost insignificant. The impression vanished when they stepped through the glass doors into the main lobby adorned with crystal chandeliers, Italian marble and onyx, and on one wall detailed gilded wood carvings.

Ebbie's eyes widened. 'This is really fantastic, James,' she began, then took in a sharp breath.

Bond, who had been steering her towards the black-suited Chinese gentlemen at reception, saw her eyes narrow as she peered across the marbled floor at the concierge's desk.

'What is it?' he asked quietly.

'Swift,' she breathed, 'Swift's here. I just saw him.'

'Where?' They had almost reached the main reception desk.

'Over there.' She nodded towards the far end of the lobby. 'He was there. Typical of him. He was always a – how do you say it – will o' the wisp?'

Bond nodded. It was a good name for Swift, he thought, as he began filling in the registration form. Swift had always been a will o' the wisp; a tortured soul trapped between the heaven and hell leading people to destruction. His expertise in handling agents in the field had led many members of enemy intelligence services to their downfall.

Instantly the contradictions and hidden secrets of Cream Cake confronted Bond again. M had asked him to take on a job which, because of its delicacy, could not be an official operation. Yet there were official aspects. Already the conviction that he was involved because someone in Cream Cake had been turned had hardened in his mind. It could be anyone: Heather? The already doubled Maxim Smolin? Jungle Baisley? Susanne Dietrich? Even Ebbie? Damn, he thought, signing the registration card, why had he been foolish enough to allow Ebbie to come with him to Hong Kong? By all the rules she should have been held in safety, yet he, James Bond, had not thought twice about her coming with him. Was it intuition or merely his growing affection for Ebbie? How foolish could a man be when led by his emotions? But then, he had not been led by anything. Ebbie had, in a manner of speaking, been foisted on him. And now there was Swift. Could Swift be the key? Hardly.

'If you will follow me, Mr Boldman, Mrs Boldman.'

Bond realised that the under manager was repeating his courteous words.

'Sorry. Of course.'

He snapped out of the reverie and taking Ebbie's arm, followed the man carrying their papers and room key. They went towards the far end of the lobby past the concierge's desk, turning left to the elevators.

'Tell me if you spot him again,' Bond whispered and Ebbie nodded.

Around them the hotel was functioning with a disciplined ease and efficiency. Gold-jacketed page boys moved swiftly with fixed smiles; one of them wearing a form of skull cap, setting him apart from the rest, marched through the lobby bearing a tinkling bell-hung board displaying the fact that he was looking for a Mrs David Davies. An American couple argued softly near the elevators: 'What ya want, then? We're in a hotel. You want we should move to a different hotel?'

The elevator lifted them imperceptibly to the twenty-first floor, to a light and airy room, with a balcony looking out on the thousand eyes of the Connaught Centre buiding and a large part of the Harbour. Ferries, motorised junks and sampans plied their way fearlessly among the larger craft.

The under manager hovered, making certain the room was to their liking, until the room boy arrived with the luggage and asked if he could unpack for them, an offer they declined.

Once they were alone, standing close to Ebbie, Bond asked, 'You're sure it was Swift?'

'Certain. God, I'm tired. But it was Swift.'

She opened the balcony windows, letting in the sound of Hong Kong's traffic, deafeningly loud, even up on the twenty-first floor. Bond joined her on the balcony, feeling the blast of heat as he passed through the doorway. The air smelled moist, with traces of salt, spices, dust, fish and pork. Below, the traffic streamed unendingly. The water of the harbour twinkled in the morning haze, the white wakes of churning propellers now joined by the long creamy trail of a hydrofoil sweeping west. Three barges, low in the water, weighed down by containers created muddy bow waves as they were towed towards one of the world's largest container ports.

To the left, everything was dominated by the Connaught Centre and the gigantic Exchange Square building. The complex was connected to the Mandarin side of the street by an elegant tubular pedestrian walkway. In the foreground to the right, the world-famous view of Kowloon, Hong Kong – Fragrant Harbour – stretched before them. A pair of helicopters swept down, one hovering while the other landed at Fenwick Pier, below them to the right. The scene of buildings, ships, vehicles and helicopters had a futuristic look about it. Yet as he gazed, Bond suddenly realised that the elusive familiarity he always felt in Hong Kong came from images from the past, from Fritz Lang's film *Metropolis*, that classic made, incredibly, in the 1920s.

'Come on,' he said, touching Ebbie's arm, 'we've got work to do.'

'We have to go out?' She seemed excited at the prospect.

'Just wear something casual.' Bond smiled, but she did not realise that he was joking and rushed to her suitcase. 'Jeans and a T-shirt will be fine,' he added quickly.

He went to the bedside telephone, delving into the memory bank of telephone numbers he carried in his head. Even in Asia he had contacts outside the normal Service channels. He picked up the handset and quickly punched in the numbers. The call was picked up on the fourth ring.

'*Weyyy?*'

'Mr Chang?' he asked.

'Who wants him, *heya?*' The voice was deep, almost gruff.

'An old friend. A friend called Predator.'

'*Ayeeya!* Welcome back, old friend. What can I do for you, *heya?*'

'I wish to see you.'

'Come then. I am in my usual place. You come now, *heya?*'

'Fifteen minutes, never mind.' Bond smiled. 'I shall have very pretty lady with me.'

'So, times never change. My people have saying, "When man visits a friend once with woman, he seldom returns alone."'

'Very profound.' Bond smiled again. 'Is that an old saying?'

'About thirty second. I just make it up. Come quickly, *heya?*'

In another part of the Central District of Hong Kong, Big Thumb Chang put down the telephone and looked up at the man standing beside him.

'He comes now, just as you predict; he also brings a beautiful woman, though if she is European I fail to see how she can be beautiful. You want I should do something special with him?'

'Just do as he asks,' the other said. He had a slow, calculating voice. 'I shall be near. It is essential that I speak with him in private.'

Big Thumb Chang grinned, nodding like a toy with a spring in its neck.

16

SWIFT

BIG THUMB CHANG was so called because of a deformity to his right hand. The thumb was almost as long, and twice as thick, as his index finger. Enemies said it had grown like this from counting the large sums of paper money that came his way from many and varied business deals. He could usually be found — when there was money involved — at a small two-room hovel off one of the precipitously steep streets leading from Queen's Road.

Bond took Ebbie by the scenic route. They went down to the mezzanine floor by elevator and walked through the sumptuous hotel shopping arcade. Over the walkway, from which they viewed the gaudily decorated trams cramming Des Voeux Road, they entered the opulent Prince's Building. Then through another walkway they passed into Gloucester House and the Landmark, one of Central's most splendid shopping malls. Below them, by the big circular fountain, a jazz combo was playing *Do you know what it means to miss New Orleans?* Bond smiled at the sound, which was sweet to his ears. They went down to the ground floor, pausing only for Bond to make a quick purchase — a holdall with a long shoulder strap — before they made their way into Queen's Road by the Pedder Street exit.

It took fifteen minutes to reach Big Thumb Chang's hovel. The door stood open and Chang himself was seated behind a table in the small dark room, which smelled of sweat and stale cooking, mingled with the scent from a few joss sticks burning in front of a small shrine.

'Ah, old friend.' The fat little Chinese grinned, displaying brown teeth. 'Many years since your shadow crossed my miserable door. Please enter my slum of a home.'

Bond saw Ebbie wrinkle her nose.

'You forget, most honourable Chang, that I know your real home is as rich as any emperor's palace.' Bond's eyebrows lifted. 'So it is I who is humbled by coming to your office.'

Chang waved a hand towards two hard and not very clean chairs.

'Welcome, beautiful lady,' he said, smiling at Ebbie. 'Welcome to both of you. Sit. Can I offer you tea?'

'You are most kind. We do not deserve such lordly treatment.'

Chang clapped his hands and a thin young girl in black pyjamas materialised from the street behind them. Chang jabbered instructions to her and she bowed and left.

'My second daughter by third wife,' Chang explained. 'She is a lazy good-for-nothing girl, but out of my duty and good nature I allow her to do small jobs for me. Life is difficult, never mind.'

'We have come to do business,' Bond began.

'Everyone wishes to do business,' said Chang, giving him a weary look. 'But seldom is this profitable with so many to support, and gossiping wives and children always wanting more than I can give.'

Bond looked equally grave. 'It must indeed be hard to live as you do, honourable Chang.'

Big Thumb Chang gave a protracted sigh. The girl reappeared with a tray bearing bowls and a teapot. She placed it in front of Chang and obeyed his directions to pour the tea as though she too were bowed with care and fatigue.

'Your kindness surpasses our miserable needs.' Bond smiled and tapped twice on the table with his fingers to signify thanks to the girl before sipping the bitter tea. He hoped that Ebbie would drink it without any hint of dislike.

'It is good to see you again, Mr Bond. How can I be of

service to you and this wondrous lady?'

Bond was surprised that Chang had come to the point so quickly. It was not unusual to spend an hour or more in pleasantries before getting down to business. The fast response put him on his guard.

'It is probably impossible,' he said slowly, 'But you have done such favours for me in the past.'

'So?'

'I am in need of two revolvers and ammunition.'

'*Ayeea*! You wish to see me imprisoned? Taken away in chains and kept for the bureaucrats of Beijing who will come in 1997 anyway, never mind?'

Already in Hong Kong they were using the Chinese name for Peking – Beijing – as the year approached for power to be ceded back to China. It was ironic that the street hawkers were now selling green caps emblazoned with the red star among their usual tourist junk.

Bond lowered his voice, still playing the game expected of him. 'Respectfully, this has never bothered you in the past. Big Thumb Chang's name is well known in my profession. It is held in great reverence, for it is a password to obtaining certain items forbidden in the Territory.'

'Certainly it is forbidden to import arms, and in recent years the penalties for such things have been great.'

'But you can still put your hands on them?'

'*Ayeea*! With the greatest difficulty. One revolver and a few miserable rounds of ammunition I might be able to find, and that at great cost. But two! Ah, that would be miraculous, and the cost truly exorbitant.'

'Let's pretend you could lay your hands on two good revolvers – say a pair of very old Enfield ·38s – with ammunition, of course…'

'This is impossible.'

'Yes, but if you could get them…' He paused, watching the Chinese shake his head in apparent incredulity at Bond's request. 'If you could get them, how much would they cost?'

'A veritable fortune. An emperor's ransom.'

'How much?' Bond pressed. 'How much in cash?'

'One thousand Hongkong for each weapon, the size not counting. Another two thousand Hongkong for fifty ammunition, making four thousand Hongkong dolla.'

'Two thousand, for the lot,' said Bond, smiling.

'*Ayeea*! You wish my wives and children to go naked in the streets? You wish my rice bowl empty for all time?'

'Two thousand,' Bond repeated. 'Two thousand and the weapons returned to you before I leave, with an extra thousand Hongkong on top.'

'How long you here, never mind?'

'A few days only. Two, three at the most.'

'You will see me beggared. I shall have to send my best daughters on to the streets as common whores.'

'Two of them were already making good money on the streets the last time I was here.'

'Two thousand dolla, with two thousand when guns are returned.'

'Two thousand, and one more on return,' Bond said firmly. There was good reason for his asking for revolvers. He would not trust an automatic pistol begged, borrowed, hired or stolen in Hong Kong. He knew that even Big Thumb Chang could supply only basic weapons.

'Two, with two thousand when you return.'

'Two and one. That's my last and only offer.'

Big Thumb Chang threw up his hands. 'You will see me begging in Wan Chai, like No Nose Wu or Footless Lee.' He paused, eyes pleading for a higher bid. None was forthcoming. 'Two thousand, then. And one when you return the weapons, but you will have to leave five hundred Hongkong as deposit in case you do not come back.'

'I've always come back.'

'There is the first time. Man always comes back until the first time. What else will you steal from me, Mr Bond? You wish to sleep with my most beautiful daughter?'

'Take heed,' said Bond, giving him a withering look. 'I have a lady with me.'

Chang realised that he had gone too far. 'A thousand pardons. When you wish to collect the items?'

'How about now? You used to keep an arsenal under the floor in your back room.'

'And many dolla it cost me to keep away the police.'

'I don't think so, Chang. You forget that I know exactly how you work.'

Big Thumb Chang gave a sigh. 'One moment. Excuse please.' He rose and waddled through the bead curtain that separated the rooms.

Ebbie started to speak, but Bond shook his head, mouthing, 'Later.' Now that anyone from the Cream Cake team was suspect, it was dangerous enough to have her there at all.

They heard Chang rooting about in the adjoining room. Then, quite unexpectedly, the bead curtain parted and instead of Chang a European appeared, dressed in slacks and a white shirt; a tall slim man in his late fifties with iron grey hair and eyes to match. His eyes twinkled brightly as Ebbie breathed,

'Swift!'

'Good day to you both.' He spoke in a flat, unaccented English.

Bond moved quickly, placing himself between Ebbie and the newcomer. Swift held up a forestalling hand.

'Our mutual Chief told me I would probably make contact with you here,' he said softly. 'If that happened, I was to say, "Nine people were killed in Cambridge and an oil fire started at Canvey Island." Does that mean anything to you?' He paused, the grey eyes holding Bond's.

Unless they had M tied up in some safe house and pumped to the eyebrows with sodium pentathol, this was indeed Swift – a noted member of Service – and he had received orders directly from M. Bond always carried in his head an identification code from his Chief, agreed in ultimate security. Anyone repeating it to him must be genuine. The current code, unchanged for six months, had been given to Bond in M's office without a word passing between them.

'Then I am to reply that the sentence comes from Volume VI of Gilbert's excellent biography of Winston Churchill.' Bond held out his hand. 'Page 573. Okay?'

Swift nodded. He had a firm grip. 'We must speak alone.' He clicked his fingers and Chang's second daughter by his third wife appeared behind him.

'Ebbie,' said Bond with a warm smile. 'Ebbie, I wonder if you would go with this girl, just for a few minutes, while we have some man's talk.'

'Why should I?' she asked indignantly.

'Why should you not, Ebbie?' Swift's eyes held a firm command. She resisted for a few seconds and then meekly followed the girl. Swift glanced back through the curtain. 'Good, they have all gone out. We have ten minutes or so. I am here as M's personal messenger boy.'

'Demoted?' Bond asked lightly.

'No, only because I know all the participants. First, M apologises for having put you in such an intolerable position.'

'That's good of him. I am getting a little tired of playing the odd man out. I didn't even know about Smolin.'

'Yes, so he told me. M has asked me to find out how much you do know, and how much you have put together.'

'To begin with, I trust nobody, not even you, Swift. But I'll talk because it's unlikely you could get that code from anyone but M. What I now know, or at least suspect, is that there was something terribly wrong about Cream Cake; so wrong that two agents were murdered and London realised it had to be taken care of. Presumably one or more of the survivors have been turned.'

'Almost correct,' said Swift. 'At least one has always been a double. That became all too apparent after Smolin was left in place; and, yes, we have no idea which one. But there's a good deal more to it than that.'

'Go on.'

'M is being leaned on so heavily that certain people in the Foreign Office are calling for his resignation. A lot of things have gone wrong for him and when the Cream Cake business resurfaced he saw yet another disaster heading his way. He put a plan up to the Foreign Service mandarins and they turned it down flat as too dangerous and non-productive. So he had to go it alone. He chose you because you are his most experienced operator. He underbriefed you, even withheld a large wedge of intelligence from you, because he believed you would eventually put two and two together.'

That sounded like M at bay. No wonder the old boy was so firm about the operation not having his blessing. He remembered Q'ute's description of the situation, in Paris: 'M's been closeted in his office for three days now. He's like a general under siege.'

As though reading his mind, Swift continued, 'M is still under siege. In fact, I'm surprised that he even talked to me. We met under tremendous security precautions. But he won't last if another double is found within his house, or even near to it. You follow?'

'Does, say, Chernov — Blackfriar — know this?'

'Possibly. What you haven't figured out yet I am supposed to tell you. M's pleased with what you've done so far. But now you need to know a couple of facts.' Swift paused, letting the tension build. 'First, the double within Cream Cake has to be eliminated, with no comebacks. Understand?'

Bond nodded. This was not an order M could have given directly. Under the recent Foreign Office ruling, assassination was not permitted. It had been the end of the old Double-O Section, though M maintained that he always thought of Bond as 007. Now he was being told to kill for the Service, and to save M's neck. He felt quite calm about it, for Swift's disclosure had given him a new impetus. M was a shrewd and tough old devil. He was also quite ruthless. His head was on the block and Bond had been chosen to save him. M knew that, of all his people, James Bond would fight shoulder to shoulder with him right up to the end.

'So I've got to finger the double.'

'Right', said Swift with a quick nod, 'and I can't help you there, as I haven't a clue either.'

It could be any of them, or all of them: Smolin, Heather, Ebbie, Baisley or Dietrich. Then another thought struck Bond. 'Good lord!' he said aloud.

'What?' Swift took a step towards him.

'Nothing.' He closed up like a clam, for suddenly he realised there was yet another contestant. He did not even allow himself to think of the ramifications if that were the case.

'Sure it was nothing?' Swift pressed.

'Certain.'

'Good, because there's something else — someone else. To add weight to his position as Head of S.I.S., M requires a coup. The Cream Cake investigation provided the man and the means. He wants Blackfriar, and he wants him alive.'

'We could have taken him in Ireland.'

'And risked one hell of an incident on foreign soil? True, the Irish Special Branch are most co-operative, but I don't think even they would have been that co-operative. No, we have to take him here, on what is still British territory. Here we have rights. That's another reason M sent you into the field, James. As soon as he discovered Blackfriar had been tempted to leave Soviet territory to follow up on Cream Cake, he baited the trap with you.'

'Because I'm on his department's hit list?'

'Exactly.'

That also made sense. M was never squeamish about putting men of Bond's calibre in delicate situations.

'And to help things on their way, I was told to instruct Jungle to head East. Chernov's a determined devil, and he's fallen for it.'

'You mean I fell for it.' Bond looked at him coldly.

'I suppose you did. If you hadn't got out, James, I would probably be dealing with this alone, because Chernov's already here.'

'On Cheung Chau Island?'

Swift gave him a quick, surprised look. 'You're very well informed. I thought that would be my little surprise.'

'When did he get in?'

'Last night. There have been a number of arrivals in the past twenty-four hours. Some came in via China. Altogether, Blackfriar's got quite an army here. He has also taken prisoners. He even brought some – Smolin and Heather. By now I should think he has Jungle and his German girl under lock and key out on the island. It's up to us to sort this out, James. I suggest we meet at around ten-thirty tonight in the lobby of the Mandarin? Okay?'

'If you say so.'

'I'll organise a way to get us out to Cheung Chau. They call it Long Island or Dumb-bell Island here because it's roughly shaped like a dumb-bell. The house is on the eastern side, on a promontory at the northern end of Tung Wan Bay. It's very well situated and custom-built for the G.R.U. Chernov's probably laughing his head off now he's there – at least I presume he's there.'

'Ten-thirty, then,' said Bond, glancing at his watch. 'I have one or two surprises for Blackfriar.'

'You're also willing to give your life for M, aren't you?' Swift was not smiling.

'Yes, damn him, and he knows it.'

'I thought so.' Swift gave a bleak smile, turned his head and called loudly through the bead curtain. At the back of the building, a door opened. Ebbie was the first to return.

'And how's life been treating you, Emilie? I'm sorry, I should say Ebbie.' said Swift.

'As always, dangerously. I feel that the Soviets have a

revenge with me. Is that right, a revenge?'

'A vengeance,' said Bond.

At that moment Big Thumb Chang came back into the room carrying several items wrapped in oilskin, which Bond immediately began to transfer to the holdall.

'You not examine the weapons, never mind?' Chang looked momentarily shocked.

Bond tossed several packets of notes on to the table. Cash had been only a small part of the shopping list he had given Q'ute. He gave the Chinese a twisted, cruel smile.

'Between trusted friends it is not necessary to count the money. Very old Chinese proverb, as you well know, Big Thumb Chang. Now, please leave us in peace.'

The Chinese cackled, scooped up the notes and backed into the inner room.

'When we leave, I suggest you and Ebbie go first.'

Swift's voice had been very soft throughout his conversation with Bond. Now it became almost soporifically calm. It was recognisable from the description on the file, which Bond had studied carefully ('Always calm and usually speaks quietly'). Bond moved to the beaded curtain. He glanced into the inner room to make sure that Chang had retreated through the rear exit, leaving them alone. Satisfied, he spoke rapidly.

'Ten-thirty, then?'

'Count on it.' With an almost imperious nod Swift sent them on their way, back down the steep steps flanked by the stalls of street traders and *dim sum* sellers.

'Swift,' said Ebbie, pronouncing it 'Svift'. She was almost running to keep up with Bond.

'Yes?'

'That is where Heather and I got the idea for using fishes and birds as names.'

'From Swift?' Bond turned his head away from a *dim sum* stall. The food was probably wonderful, but to his sensitive nostrils it smelled pungent.

'*Ja*. Swift is a bird and Heather said we should use code names of animals and birds; in the end, birds and fishes.'

Bond grunted, quickening his pace. Ebbie clung to his arm, struggling to keep up with his long, purposeful strides. They took no detours but went straight back to the Mandarin along Pedder Street, dodging the traffic into Ice House Street. All the time, Bond scanned the crush of Chinese in the streets, feeling a million watchers around them, a thousand imperceptible signals passing between them. Back in the hotel, he went straight to the elevators, almost dragging Ebbie with him.

'Wait by the door,' he told her when they reached their room.

It took less than four minutes for him to transfer the main items provided by Q'ute from his suitcase to the canvas holdall. Then they returned to the hotel foyer. He strode to the main desk, Ebbie in his wake. A pretty Chinese girl no more than fifteen years old, glanced up from a computer keyboard and asked if she could help him.

'I hope so. Is there a ferry to Cheung Chau?' Bond asked.

'Each hour, sir. Yaumati Ferry Company. From Outlying Districts Services Pier.' She gestured in the direction of the pier.

Bond nodded and thanked her. 'We must go now,' he said, turning to Ebbie.

'Why? We are to meet Swift. You arranged ...'

'I'm sorry. Yes I did arrange. But just come now. You should know that I've stopped trusting anybody, Ebbie: even Swift, and even you.'

He became aware of police sirens close by and as they reached the main doors of the hotel, a knot of people was already gathering across the road in the gardens that surrounded the Connaught Centre. Dodging traffic, they dashed towards the crowd just as two police cars and an ambulance drew up.

Bond managed to get sight of the trouble through the

throng. A man lay spreadeagled on his back, blood seeping
on to the paving stones. There was a terrible stillness about
him and the grey eyes looked steady and sightless into the
sky above. The cause of Swift's death was not immediately
apparent, but the killers could not be far away. Backing
away from the crowd, Bond caught Ebbie by the forearm,
and propelled her away to the left, in the direction of the
Outlying Districts Pier.

- 17 -
LETTER FROM THE
DEAD

THE SAMPAN SMELLED strongly of dried fish and human sweat. Lying close together in the bows, looking back towards the toothless old lady who sprawled across the tiller and the twinkling lights of Hong Kong behind her, Bond and Ebbie could feel the fatigue and tension emanating from one another. The afternoon with its sudden changes of moods and events seemed far away, as did the sight of Swift's body in front of the portholed windows of the Connaught Centre building. After the shock of seeing the man lying dead, Bond's thoughts had been unusually imprecise and jumbled. He was certain of only one thing, that unless Chernov had shown monstrous cunning, Swift had been straight. There were moments during the conversation at Big Thumb Chang's when he had doubted that. Now he was on his own and the only chance of fingering the Cream Cake double and getting Chernov alive lay in putting himself on offer, as a living lure.

His first instinct had been to give chase, to head for the island by the quickest possible means. He was in fact half way towards the ferry terminal when he realised that this was just what Chernov might want. He slowed his pace, keeping the holdall close to his left side, and holding Ebbie fast by his right. She had not seen the body and asked continually what was wrong and where were they going. Angrily, Bond dragged her along until the moment when his fragmented thoughts came together and he could think logically again.

'Swift,' he said, surprised at the calmness of his own voice, 'It was Swift. He looked very dead.'

Ebbie gave a little gasp and asked in a small voice if he was sure. He described what he had seen without sparing her. In a way he wanted the picture to be shocking. Her reaction had been unexpectedly restrained. After a lengthy silence, as they almost strolled along the picturesque waterfront, she merely muttered, 'Poor Swift. He was so good to us – all of us.' Then, as though the full implication had struck her, 'And poor James. You needed his help, didn't you?'

'We all needed his help.'

'Will they come for us too?'

'They'll come for me, Ebbie, but I don't know about you. It depends which side you're working for.'

'You know which side I'm on. Were they not trying to kill me at the hotel, the Ashford Castle Hotel, when I was lending my coat and scarf to that poor girl?'

She had a point. Even Chernov would not be so stupid as to kill an innocent bystander in the Irish Republic. Bond had to put trust in at least one other human being. Ebbie was apparently straight and had been from the outset. With some reluctance, he decided he would have to accept her.

'All right. I believe you, Ebbie.' He swallowed, and then went on to give her the briefest details, that Chernov was on the island with his men; that he was holding Heather and Maxim Smolin prisoner, and almost certainly Jungle and Susanne Dietrich as well. 'We're probably under some form of surveillance now. They might even expect us to go charging over to Cheung Chau straight away. I'll say this for the K.G.B., they've become quite classy lately when it comes to psychological pressure. They are putting us under stress at our weakest moment. We're both tired, disoriented, jet-lagged. They'll expect us to make moves automatically. We need time to rest and work out some more effective plan.'

But where should they go? In this place, even though the crowds were constant, you could not hide, for a thousand eyes were watching. He had no safe house at his disposal, only his own experience and the weapons in the holdall, and Ebbie Heritage whose form in the field he did not know. His one chance would be to go through the complex business of throwing a tail — even though he could not spot one. After that, well, it would be a matter of luck; they could try going to another hotel.

Leaning on the wall and looking out over the harbour, he pulled Ebbie closer to him. Three low barges were being towed across the centre of the bay. The usual junks and sampans ploughed and turned. One of the high, double-decked car ferries was nosing out to their left, while two of the Star Ferry boats that ran every ten minutes between Hong Kong and Kowloon hooted as they passed one another in the centre of the harbour. In his mind, Bond went through the various means of running the back doubles in Hong Kong. The Mandarin was out as a resting place, for they were certain to have watchers back there. Kowloonside seemed the best idea.

Very carefully he explained to Ebbie what he must do. Then he went over it a second time. Smiling down at her, he asked if she could go through with it.

She nodded. 'Oh yes, we'll show the devils. I have scores to settle with them, James. At least two — three if you count the poor girl I loaned my scarf and coat to.' She gave a little smile back. 'We will win, won't we?'

'No contest.' He tried to make it sound casual, though he knew that to win here in Asia against the kind of people Kolya Chernov had at his disposal, and with at least one of the Cream Cake team as his ally, it would need very good joss indeed.

They started to walk back along the harbour front, dodging up the open stairs near the Central Post Office to get on to the covered overpass which brought them out on the

Mandarin side of Connaught Road. The offices were closing and the crowds had thickened, yet even among so many people there was a strange orderliness.

'Keep your eyes open. Watch shoes rather than faces', Bond advised her; although as they began to look, he realised how many people wore trainers. A team of watchers would almost certainly be wearing them.

At the hotel they turned right into Ice House Street again. This time they were heading for the red brick ivy-covered entrance to the Mass Transit Railway station, less than a hundred yards behind the hotel. This was the Hong Kong-side, end of the line station known as Central.

The M.T.R. is rightly Hong Kong's pride and joy, the envy of many cities. For efficiency and cleanliness, there are few underground railways in the world that can compare. Certainly Moscow has its huge baroque stations, Paris its fabled Louvre station with *objets d'art* on view; London has its somewhat dingy charm and New York its air of naked danger. But Hong Kong has bright shiny trains, air-conditioned, spotlessly clean platforms and an ordered sense of obedience, evident from the electronic turnstiles to the passengers themselves. They dodged down the steps from the street into the high-ceilinged modern complex. Bond went straight to the booking booth, flashed his Boldman passport and asked for two special tourist tickets, which allowed unlimited travel. He slapped down thirty Hongkong dollars and received two coloured plastic smart cards in return.

All M.T.R. tickets are the size of cards, but the ordinary sort contain electronic strips recognised by the turnstiles. These are swallowed up when each journey has been completed so that they can be reissued, creating a saving of thousands of dollars a year. The tourist tickets, however, each with a printed view of the harbour, allow unlimited travel and so save much time. There are high penalties for damaging the plastic smart cards – as there are for smoking, or bringing food and drink into the hallowed, cool atmosphere of the M.T.R. system. Hence the scrupulous cleanliness.

Still keeping both Ebbie and the holdall close to him, Bond headed down more stairs and on to the platform. A train hissed in, heading for Kowloonside.

They just made it. Settling themselves on the somewhat spartan seats, they studied the simple map that Bond had picked up when buying the tickets. He pointed a finger to the station where they would get out and then began to look around casually. No one seemed to take any notice of them as the train pulled into Admiralty station and then out again to start the crossing under the harbour to Tsim Sha Tsui, a short way up the famous wide Nathan Road. This was where they planned the first jump-off. The trains travelling over to Kowloon followed the same route until Mong Kok or Prince Edward, where the railway branched either to the west bound Tsuen Wan line or the Kwun Tong line, which followed a great curve to the north east. Their train was bound for the latter line, which would take them too far from the centre. Bond reasoned that he should contain the action within a relatively small area for his own ease of movement.

As they alighted, he noticed bunched among the crowd of passengers two well-dressed young Chinese, their eyes carefully averted from Bond and Ebbie. He turned left, as though to make for the exit, noticing the Chinese duo getting closer.

'Get back on again at the last minute,' he whispered as they came abreast of a set of carriage doors. It was an old trick but it could still work. As the doors began to close, he pushed Ebbie in and followed her quickly. To his frustration, he saw the two Chinese do the same thing one carriage down. He told Ebbie to get off at the next station, Jordan, but not until the last moment.

It took but a few moments in the scurrying crowd to realise that the two men were still there keeping pace with them, and too close for comfort. Both wore light grey suits, neat

collars and ties, even in the afternoon heat. They could easily
have been taken for two businessmen returning to their
office. But to Bond's practised eye, they worked with a
polished precision. He had little doubt that another team
was at work, possibly in front of them. They came out of
Jordan station and turned right into the noisy, bustling
Nathan Road, Bond edging Ebbie in the harbour direction.
Smiling, he quietly told her about their being followed.

'Stay casual,' he said. 'Stop and look in the shop windows.
Move slowly. At the bottom of the road we come to the
Peninsula Hotel. We'll try to lose them there.'

The sidewalks were tight with people, more Chinese and
Indians than European. Nathan Road seemed to be a
meeting place of the Eastern cultures. Garish banners overhung the street. At ground level modern shopfronts squeezed
together, yet above them there could still be seen the
ramshackle buildings dating back to the 1920s or 1930s.
Neon and paper signs hung drunkenly at angles, sprouting
to catch the eye, while the omnipresent food produced an
amalgam of smells. There were many camera and elec-
tronics shops, so Bond and Ebbie were able to stop regularly,
as though comparing prices, while they watched for the
watchers.

Bond had mentally christened their tails Ying and Yang,
and they kept pace with a cunning that bespoke thorough
training. Nevertheless, within five minutes, Bond thought he
had latched on to the team in front. A girl and boy, around
eighteen or nineteen, were seemingly engrossed in each
other's company, but they always stopped when Ebbie and
Bond stopped. The boy wore a long, loose shirt outside his
jeans, enough cover for a weapon. Ying and Yang, in their
tailored grey suits had plenty of hiding places for hand guns.
The thought crossed Bond's mind that they could just as well
be an execution squad. Had Swift not already been killed?
No, he reasoned. Chernov would wish to be present at the
end. There should be witnesses from within Moscow Centre.

At last they reached the Peninsula and entered by one of the side doors leading into a bright shopping arcade. Bond remembered someone telling him that this area of the hotel had been the officers' club in the period following the Second World War. He wondered what ghosts of boozy majors haunted the opulent arcades.

As they turned to climb the stairs to the main lobby, Ying and Yang followed them in. Doubtless the younger pair had made for the front of the hotel to complete the box.

'Go ahead,' Bond muttered to Ebbie as he handed her the holdall. 'Take the armoury with you and make for the loo. I'll be in the lobby as soon as I've dealt with this.'

At least this would be a thorough test of Ebbie's loyalty. He nodded to her, smiling and relaxed, as he reached for his cigarettes, placed one between his lips and began to pat his pockets for a lighter. Ying and Yang looked slightly startled as they saw him stop but they could hardly run from their quarry, so they came on, paying no attention until Bond stepped in front of them and asked in English if they had a light.

Close to, they looked like twins with short jet hair, round faces and darting, cruel eyes. For a second they paused and Ying muttered something as his hand went up to reach inside the unbuttoned jacket. When his arm was almost level with his lapel, Bond grabbed his wrist, twisted hard, then pulled down, his right knee coming up with all his strength behind it. He could almost feel the man's pain as the knee smashed into his groin; he certainly heard the gasp of agony. Almost before it came, Bond had spun the man around and jerked him forward towards Yang, propelling him downwards so that the top of his skull caught Yang's face. The blow was head on, for he heard the crunch and felt Ying's body go limp in his grip.

Before anyone appeared from the shops along the arcade, Ying and Yang lay heaped together, only partially conscious. Ying was doubled in pain from groin and head, and

Yang's face looked as though he had met a heavy lump of concrete: there was blood pouring from his broken nose and in all likelihood his cheekbone had been cracked. Loudly Bond called for someone to get the police.

'These men tried to rob me!' he shouted, and there was a jabber of Chinese and English. He bent down and reached inside each man's jacket. Sure enough, they were armed with neat, stubby ·38 revolvers.

'Look!' he said loudly. 'Somebody get security. These men are bandits.'

The outraged noises from the crowd told Bond that they were on his side. He edged back into the growing circle, dropped one of the weapons, slid the other into his belt, where it was concealed under the Oscar Jacobson jacket, and slipped up the stairs.

'Down there,' he said to the two security men who were descending, almost bumping into him. 'A couple of brigands just tried to rob my friend.'

Ebbie waited inside the doors, in a corner of the vast, gilded hotel foyer where waiters scurried around the tables serving late tea, watched over by a silver-haired head waiter. A four-piece orchestra seated high up in a regal box played selections from old and new musicals. Mainly old.

Bond took the holdall, muttering that they should move fast. He headed towards the main doors, his eyes swivelling around to catch the young couple he had fingered as the back-up team. But there was no sign of them either in the lobby or outside in the forecourt. They crossed the road when the heavy traffic allowed and headed towards the harbour front, littered with building sites. Bond's eyes were still moving restlessly to try and spot the other team.

'I think maybe we've thrown them,' he said, squeezing Ebbie's arm. 'Come on, keep going left. The least we can do is treat ourselves to a decent hotel for a few hours. The Regent's just along here. It's a great brick blockhouse of a place, but I'm told it's a strong rival to the Mandarin.'

The view of the Regent was blotted out by vast hoardings enclosing building works, but as they reached the end of these they saw the hotel with its driveway sweeping upwards and the forecourt filled with Rolls-Royces and Cadillacs. It was not the only sight that came into view. As they turned the corner, the young man and his girl friend stepped out directly in front of them.

Bond grasped the revolver butt and was about to draw the weapon when the young man spoke. His hands were clearly empty but the girl was obviously watching his back.

'Mr Bond?' he asked.

'Yes,' said Bond, taking one step back, ready for the next move.

'Do not be alarmed, sir. Mr Swift said that, should any ill befall him, I was to give you this, never mind.' Slowly his hand went to his pocket and he withdrew an envelope. 'You might already know that Mr Swift had serious accident this afternoon. My name is Han. Richard Han. I worked for Mr Swift. All arrangements are made. I presume you dealt with the two no-good coolie hoodlums who were following you. We heard large commotion...'

'Yes,' said Bond, still wary.

'Good. There will be a Walla Walla down by Ocean Terminal at ten forty-five. I will be there to see you both aboard. Ten forty-five, near the Ocean Terminal. Okay, *heya?*'

Bond nodded, and the young couple smiled, linked arms and turned away.

'What's a Walla Walla?' Ebbie asked later as they lay naked in a room high up in the Regent.

It's a motorised sampan,' replied Bond. 'Some people will tell you they're called Walla Wallas because of the noise of the engines. Others say it's because the very first one was owned by a guy from Washington D.C.'

'You are clever.' Ebbie snuggled up to him. 'How do you learn all these things, James?'

'From the official Hong Kong Guide. I read it while you spent all that time in the bathroom.'

They had encountered no difficulty in getting a room at the Regent. Bond had flashed his Platinum Amex card in the name of Boldman and said that price was no object. Nobody even queried the lack of luggage, though Bond supplied a story about it coming on from the airport later. He showed the holdall casually but refused to let anyone carry it for him.

After ordering a simple three-course European dinner for two on room service he had opened the envelope. Inside was a single sheet of paper which contained a short message and a map of Cheung Chau Island.

In case anything happens, I have given this to a young colleague. Richard Han will assist in any way he can. I have arranged transport to Cheung Chau. The woman will drop you at the harbour to the west of the island. You need a white villa which stands almost opposite the Warwick Hotel on the eastern side – ten minutes' walk over the narrow isthmus. Take the lane through the houses just right of the ferry landing stage. The villa is well placed, high up on the northern side of the bay of Tung Wan, looking out across a rather beautiful stretch of sea and sand. Needless to say, the Warwick is on the southern side. To my knowledge there are no warning devices, but the place is always well guarded when anyone's in residence. It has at least one telephone and the local number is 720302. Remember the nine killed in Cambridge and the fires started at Canvey Island. If you get this, I will not be there to wish you luck, but you have it anyway. Swift.

Bond had to accept the note, map and the person of Richard Han as genuine. At least this was a way of getting to Cheung Chau and finding the house. Before the food arrived, he went into the bathroom and checked the weapons and the equip-

ment in the holdall. He decided to arm Ebbie with one of the
·38s. He would keep the similar weapon taken from Ying and
Yang. The rest could be carried in the holdall. Once the villa
was located, he knew what had to be done. You could not
take further chances with a man like Chernov. He went back
to the bedroom, ate a hearty meal, waited for Ebbie to use
the bathroom, then stripped and took a shower. They had no
change of clothes, but at least they were both refreshed and
clean. After towelling himself thoroughly, Bond stretched
out on the bed. In spite of their tiredness, Ebbie displayed an
undeniable inventiveness which Bond found irresistible.
After a short doze, Bond went over the essentials for that
night.

'Do you understand?' he asked at the end of the briefing.
'You will stay where I tell you until I return. After that, we
play it by ear.' He gave her a light kiss on each ear as though
to underline the point.

They dressed and armed themselves, and Bond was
pleased to note that Ebbie handled the revolver and spare
ammunition with obvious experience.

They left the hotel at just after ten o'clock. On the dot of
ten forty-five, Richard Han met them by the large, sprawling
shopping mall known as Ocean Terminal, near the Star
Ferry. He led them away from the main piers, down a path to
the harbour where the toothless old woman in black pyjamas
waited with her sampan.

'She knows where to take us?' Bond asked.

Han nodded. 'And you must give her no money,' he said.
'She has already been paid enough. The trip will take the
best part of three hours. I'm sorry. It's only one hour on the
ferry, but this is the best way.'

In the event, it took nearer four hours, the woman not
speaking a word to them, but leaning back, relaxed at the
tiller.

So it was that around three in the morning Bond and
Ebbie were landed on Cheung Chau Island, seven and a half

miles west of Hong Kong. The sampan had bucked and
rolled at sea but once they neared the harbour the old
woman cut the engine, working an oar to bring them in
noiselessly through a throng of junks and sampans, some
lashed together, others riding at anchor. At last they reached
the harbour wall and the woman whispered something
which must have meant they should disembark. Together,
they scrambled up on to the wide stretch of concrete which
fronted the harbour and Bond lifted an arm in farewell to the
woman.

- 18 -
TUNG WAN BAY

THE ISLAND, AS Bond had already seen from the map, was indeed shaped like a dumb-bell, the south part being much wider than the north, and a short spit of land less than a mile wide running between the two.

Their eyes had adjusted to the dark long before landing, so Bond could make out the buildings ahead. He took Ebbie's hand, made certain that she had her revolver ready and guided her towards the first dark gap leading down a narrow lane. As they drew near he could make out the shape of a clear glass telephone booth, which he decided to use after he had carried out the reconnaissance of the villa.

'You stay here. Don't move, and make sure nobody sees you,' he whispered. 'I'll be back within the hour.'

In the darkness he saw her nod. Ebbie was proving to be less nervous than he had any right to expect. Squeezing her hand, Bond set off up the lane. He felt closed in by the shop buildings which made up the sides of this gulch. After a couple of hundred yards the lane narrowed even further. There was a large tree to the right and he became conscious of someone near by. He stopped, moving only when he realised that it was an old Chinese, flat on his back, snoring under the tree.

After about twelve minutes' walking the buildings gave on to a wide stretch of pale sand with the sea, soft and shimmering, directly in front of him. This was Tung Wan bay. Keeping to the cover of the buildings, Bond edged forward. To his right, a splash of light indicated the Warwick Hotel. He waited, peering around the bay and up to the promon-

tory on his left. High up he could see a grey building with two
lights burning – certainly the villa Swift had marked on the
map. Keeping to the dark cover of the buildings on his left
and praying that nobody was using infra-red night glasses
from the villa, Bond slowly made his way as far as the open
ground. The sand stretched out, white in the blackness,
towards the promontory where the villa stood.

Bond guessed that roughly seventy yards of open sand
separated him from the shadows at the foot of the bluff, fifty
yards of which could be seen from the villa. Taking a deep
breath, he sprinted forward, slowing down to a walk once he
was in dead ground. The sand petered out and the ground
rose steeply, covered with short, spiky grass. Settling the
holdall's strap more comfortably on his shoulder, Bond
began the climb. The grass had no sweet smell to it, and its
roughness scratched at his hands. Occasionally he felt a
softness beneath, as though the whole promontory was
nothing but an overgrown sandbank. It took him ten
minutes of hard work before the steepness levelled off. He
was now on shallow rising ground, still out of sight of the
villa. As soon as the first outlines of the building appeared
against the lighter sky, thirty yards on, Bond dropped on to
his belly, adopting a crawl for about ten yards.

He was now only a few strides from the building. He lay
for five minutes examining the target. It seemed to be a low
white bungalow with a terracotta roof and a series of arches
running along the side, making it look more Spanish than
Chinese. It was set in a circle of garden, surrounded by a
small wall some four or five bricks high. As he looked, it
became apparent that the arches were a kind of cloister
running around all four sides of the villa. The lights he had
seen from below came from a pair of sliding glass doors on
the side overlooking the bay. There was movement behind
the glass, and Bond recognised Chernov himself walking to
and fro, speaking to someone hidden from view.

Bond lay for some time judging distances and impressing

the whole setting on his mind. To the left the ground ran upwards. Recalling the map, he knew that should he choose to go in that direction he would eventually find himself on a path that led back around to the harbour and passed the island's famous temple on the way. He worked out that if he were pursued from the villa, it would take him about fifteen long strides from his present position to the point where he would disappear below the skyline. Then he would have to slow and stop, as a headlong dash would bring him to the steeply angled ground and probably a long, unpleasant fall down the slope to the beach below.

If Bond were to outwit Chernov, he needed to take precautions now. Carefully, he crawled back until he was well hidden from the villa and in the darkness he groped around, seeking soft earth. Eventually the palm of his left hand touched rock. It turned out to be a rough, circular stone about two feet across and a foot high, with an irregular surface. He shifted until he was lying directly behind it. He unslung the holdall and silently opened it, removing a small oilskin package secured with wrap-around tapes – carefully prepared by Q'ute and delivered to him in Paris. Mostly it contained back-up material, duplicating the equipment hidden in the belt around his waist or posing as everyday items spread through his clothing. Dealing with a man like Chernov, Bond did not intend to take chances. Digging into the sandy earth behind the rock, he deposited the oilskin package. He covered this emergency pack with the loose earth and eased himself forward again, taking bearings and hammering them into his head so that, should he have need of it, he could locate the package quickly. Only when he was certain of angles and distances did he retreat again, making the slow descent to the beach.

Some twenty minutes later he was back with Ebbie, who was well hidden in the shadows of the buildings fronting the harbour.

'All set,' he whispered without explanation. The less she

knew the better.

'Are they there?' she asked, her voice just audible.

'Well, Chernov's there, and where he is I suspect we'll find the others.'

He had one of the revolvers in his belt, the barrel slanting to one side. Softly, indicating that Ebbie should stay where she was, he padded over to the harbour wall and dumped the holdall into the sea. They were now both armed, with ammunition to spare.

'We're going to show ourselves,' he told Ebbie. 'We'll just let ourselves be seen but avoid actual contact – Swift's way, like a will o' the wisp. Our job is to draw Chernov out. The house is quite small but difficult to assault. If he's got a few good men there it would be madness for us to attempt any kind of attack. The ground around it is too exposed so it would be suicidal.'

'Should we not send for the police? This is British territory. Couldn't you have that terrible man arrested?'

'Not quite yet.' He did not want her to know that before Chernov was nailed for them someone had to die; that whoever was the traitor within Cream Cake must be disposed of. That had been implicit in Swift's briefing. The double could not be publicly exposed if M was to be brought into safe waters again. What was it Swift had said? 'M is still under siege … he won't last if another double is found in his house, or even near to it.' And now Bond's only way of revealing the Cream Cake traitor's identity was to offer himself and Ebbie on a plate.

'We'll go in a minute,' he said, putting his finger to his lips and heading for the glass telephone booth. He dug in his pocket for small change and then carefully dialled the number quoted in Swift's note – 720302. He heard the ringing tone and then the instrument was picked up. Nobody spoke. He counted six slowly and then asked in Russian for General Chernov. It was Blackfriar himself who answered.

Very softly, Bond hissed into the telephone, 'I'm close.

Catch me if you can,' and immediately cradled the instrument.

He returned to Ebbie and led her back along the lane towards the beach of Tung Wan Bay. This time he did not bother to take any precautions. Instead of keeping well in shadow, he steered Ebbie on to the beach itself. They walked slowly towards the promontory and began the upward climb much farther to the right than before. He wanted to keep Chernov's people well away from the area he had already covered.

Eventually they reached the flatter ground and crawled together towards the house. They stopped only a few yards from the low wall, just hidden from view. All the lights were on now and the sky in the east had already started to lighten. In minutes daylight would make them completely visible. Turning on his side, Bond said he thought they should work their way around to the back.

'We should do this soon, I believe,' said Ebbie, her eyes clouded with concern. 'The ground is very open here. I think they could see us easily from the house if they are looking out.'

A voice came from behind them. 'We seldom sleep for long here on Tung Wan Bay. How nice of you to join us. Now I have the full set.'

Bond rolled, his revolver up and ready to fire.

There were three of them: Mischa and one of the men who had been with Blackfriar when they picked Bond up at the Newpark; the third man, dressed in a well fitting cavalry twill trousers, shirt and a dark jacket, was of course General Kolya Chernov himself, smiling at his triumph and pointing an automatic pistol straight at Bond's head.

'You invited me to catch you, Mr Bond, and I have graciously accepted your invitation.'

- 19 -
MEET THE ROBINSONS

LIKE MANY A safe house in Europe, this villa, set on its promontory with its incomparably beautiful view, was spartan inside. There were the usual signs of soundproofing. Heavy unnatural-looking wallpaper decorated the main living room, which they entered through the large sliding windows. The furniture was functional, the chairs made of bamboo, one table of heavy wood. No pictures adorned the walls; there were no ornaments on the mantelshelf.

Bond had dropped the revolver as soon as he knew the odds and turned to Ebbie, signalling with his eyes that she should keep silent. When he spoke at last, it was to Ebbie.

'Ms Heritage, the gentleman pointing the gun at us has what we call star quality. May I introduce you to General Konstantin Nikolaevich Chernov, Hero of the Soviet Union, Order of Lenin. The list of his decorations is very long, but he is at present Chief Investigating Officer of Department 8, Directorate S of the K.G.B. The Department that was, at one time, known as SMERSH. I suspect the General would prefer it to be still called by that emotive name.'

Chernov gave him a pleasant smile, then, nodding to Ebbie, he instructed the men to take them into the villa. Inside, he spoke to Bond.

'I cannot tell you how glad I am to see you again. I've also been looking forward to meeting your companion. By some stupid oversight we missed you in Ireland, Miss Heritage – or should I more correctly call you Fräulein Nikolas?'

'Heritage,' she answered calmly.

Chernov shrugged. 'As you like. In any case, I am very pleased to see you too. This completes the ludicrous Cream Cake business. All the chickens have come home to roost – and make their final payments, eh?'

Bond had already decided on his strategy. He cleared his throat, coughed and said, 'General, I am empowered to negotiate.'

'Really?' The shrewd eyes met Bond's with an amused glitter. 'You have bargaining powers?'

'Within certain parameters, yes,' he lied. 'Certain exchanges can be offered for those you hold here, for Ms Dare, Ms Heritage, Maxim Smolin, Mr Baisley, and Fräulein Dietrich. I'm sure you would like some of your own people back. We have quite a number in stock.'

Mischa laughed quietly, while Chernov gave a throaty chuckle.

'Everyone connected with Cream Cake, eh? All of those under sentence of death.'

'Yes.'

Mischa laughed again. 'So, what do we do first, Comrade General? Deal with the traitors and spies or put your tame puppets to the test?'

'Well, there's plenty of time, Mischa. Relax. This is a pleasant place. Today will be hot. When the sun goes down we'll put the puppets to work. When that is finished, we can perform the little ritual you seem to long for. With all of them confined here we can take our time. They deserve to go slowly. They wanted us to take Smolin and Dietrich back to Moscow but that could be a little difficult.' He sighed, then looked slyly at Ebbie. 'Now the Nikolas girl here could provide me with a morsel of pleasure before we extract her tongue and dispatch her.' He turned to Bond. 'Don't you agree?'

'I wouldn't know what I'm agreeing to.'

'Really? Let's have some coffee and rolls and I'll explain.

Mischa, has the *amah* arrived with today's provisions?'

'Yes, but I've sent her away again. Today I felt we had no need of outsiders.'

'Quite right, Mischa. Some coffee, then, and rolls with preserves?'

'You should have brought your servant, General.'

'Perhaps. One of these fellows will help you.'

He nodded to the man who stood impassive by the door and at another who had materialised near the window. Both held machine pistols at the ready. Mischa tapped the arm of the one by the door, and spoke to him in Russian. He shouldered his pistol by its strap, and was about to follow Mischa out when Chernov intervened.

'He can help you, but first I think the young lady should be escorted to join her companions. They probably have a lot to talk about. You should make the most of it,' he said, smiling at Ebbie. This time there was an unmistakable chill in his eyes.

Mischa called her over, and the guard prodded her with his pistol. Ebbie nodded and uncurled herself from her chair. She looked first at Bond and then at Chernov. Then she went up close to Chernov and spat full into his face. He reeled back in disgust, but reacted so quickly that even Bond did not see his hand come up to slap Ebbie's left cheek and backhand her right. Ebbie hardly made a sound, taking the blows without even putting her hand to her face Both guards sprang forward, but she merely turned and meekly followed the frowning Mischa from the room. One guard was behind her, the other returned to his place by the window. Chernov was wiping the spittle from his face.

'Foolish girl,' he muttered. 'I could have made the inevitable a little easier for her.'

'For all your veneer of sophistication, you're really a cold-blooded bastard, Chernov, aren't you?'

His dossier at the Regent's Park Headquarters adequately described his devious ruthlessness but could not reflect his

degenerate nature. Chernov could clearly be equated with
the most callous and perverted K.G.B. head of all time, the
infamous Lavrenti Pavlovich Beria.

'Me?' Chernov's eyebrows shot up. 'Me, cold-blooded?
Don't be stupid, Bond. These little girls were used by your
own cold-blooded operations planners. Presumably it was
explained to them what risk they were taking.' He gave a
snort. 'You and I know that Cream Cake was about securing
the defection of the highly trained and experienced officers,
Smolin and Dietrich. To muddy the waters your people
added two extra targets. Well, that worked. But K.G.B. and
G.R.U. could not leave the matter there. Two of the girls
have been disposed of. It would be unfair to let the rest off
with a caution. The intelligence communities of the world
must see that we retaliate to such treatment.' He gave
another shrug. 'In any case, I have orders from my Chairman to carry out summary executions. The bodies are to be
left as a warning, with special marks: a kind of ritual. You
understand?'

Chernov spoke calmly, as though the murders of Heather,
Ebbie, Jungle, Dietrich and Smolin were of as much conse-
quence as the imposition of a speeding fine.

'We cannot negotiate, then?'

'You cannot negotiate with dead people.'

'And what of me, General?'

'Ah!'

He turned, the finger of his right hand pointing at Bond,
but before he spoke there was a tap on the door and the guard
came in carrying a large tray with a coffee pot, cups, a basket
of rolls and jars of preserves. He was followed by Mischa who
held the man's machine pistol. Clearly he would not act as
butler for anybody, not even General Chernov.

Chernov's finger came down. 'Ah!' he repeated.
'Breakfast.'

Mischa left with the other guard. Bond noticed that the
big man at the window eyed the food with some envy.

'You were saying, General?'

'Oh, after we've eaten, my dear Bond. Enjoy my hospitality while you can.'

And with that, he refused to enter into any further conversation. In fact, it was the last he was to say about Bond's future for many hours, for as soon as they had eaten, Chernov issued a series of commands. The other guard came back into the room and with no warning both men took Bond by the arms and hauled him outside and down two flights of stone steps. They opened a stout door and threw him into a small cell, which was completely bare but for a light covered by a metal grille recessed in the ceiling. There were no windows or furniture and only enough space for a man to stand and spread out his arms. Mischa appeared in the doorway.

'Mr Bond,' he said, displaying for the first time an effeminate lisp. He held a bundle of clothes, which he threw on to the cell floor. There were dark blue overalls, nylon socks, underwear and a pair of cheap moccasins. 'They're your size, Mr Bond. We checked with Moscow. The General would like you to strip and put these on.' He gave a toothy smile. 'You have a reputation as a bit of a magician – tricks up your sleeves and so on. The General felt it would be safer this way. Change now, please.'

He had no option. As slowly as possible, Bond discarded his own clothes, together with the precious concealed equipment. He climbed into the overalls, feeling foolish. Mischa took his clothes and slammed the door. Bond heard a heavy deadlock fall into place.

For a while he took stock. There was a tiny hole no larger than a pencil set over the door. He was almost certainly being observed by a monitoring system using minute fibre optic lenses. The cell was obviously located deep in the ground, under the villa. There was no way of escape. His only chance was to get to the back-up equipment hidden in the earth outside the house. Knowing that it might neverthe-

less be of no use to him he crossed his legs and sat impass-
ively, emptying his mind of all thoughts and anxieties,
preparing himself by centring his whole being on a kind of
nothingness.

He did not know how much time passed before the two
guards came again with more food, which he refused. The
men accepted this with ill grace but withdrew.

As time passed Bond controlled both body and mind,
knowing that whatever trial the General had in store for him
he would need all his experience and mental and physical
courage to combat it and even turn it to his advantage,
if he was to save the Cream Cake team and himself from
death.

Instinctively he felt the waning of the day and at last the
door was unlocked and the same men dragged him out and
up the stairs to the main room where he had last sat with
Chernov. This time the place appeared smaller and it was
full of people. He saw outside the long slash of white sand
turning blood red in the sunset.

Looking around him, Bond saw Chernov sitting on a
bamboo chair in the centre of the room. The others were
chained together and he realised there were two new
faces. He recognised the man as Franz 'Wald'
Belzinger — otherwise Jungle Baisley. The face was certainly
the one he had studied on photographs during that first
afternoon, following the lunch with M at Blades. The
surprise came when he saw that Baisley was a huge man. He
must have been well over six feet tall and broad in propor-
tion. He looked even younger than his twenty-seven years,
possibly because of his shock of unruly red hair. He grinned
broadly at Bond, as though welcoming him.

'I think you know everybody except Fräulein Dietrich and
Mr Baisley, as he likes to be called,' said Chernov.

Susanne Dietrich was a slim woman, older than he
expected and with light-coloured, untidy hair. She gave
him a frightened look, as Jungle tried to rise grinning an

American college boy grin.

'Hi, Mr Bond. I have been hearing much about you.'

The voice had German undertones, but more in the syntax than the accent, and he certainly was not going to let anyone know he had an ounce of fear in him.

Bond nodded and smiled, trying to be reassuring. He looked along the line at Maxim Smolin, Heather and Ebbie. Heather smiled back, Smolin winked and Ebbie blew him a kiss. It was good to know they were going to face their fate with dignity. He asked if they were okay. They said nothing but nodded firmly.

'So, I call this meeting to order,' said Chernov, laughing as though he had cracked the joke of the century. 'Or should I call it a court rather than a meeting?' he asked.

No one spoke, so with a wry smile Chernov continued, 'The five prisoners here already know what is to happen to them. They have been informed of their guilt and the reason they are to die. They know too the method of their deaths, which will take place at dawn tomorrow.' He paused, as though savouring the thought. 'As for Commander James Bond, Royal Navy, Secret Intelligence Service – as for him – well, the Department I represent has had an execution order hanging over him for many years now. Are you aware of that, Commander Bond?'

Bond nodded, thinking of the many times he had outwitted and damaged the black heart of the K.G.B., once known as SMERSH.

'Let us not underestimate Commander Bond,' said Chernov, his face becoming serious. 'He has proved himself a valiant enemy: resourceful, highly efficient and brave. It would not be in keeping with my department's practice simply to dispatch him with a bullet, a knife or an injection of racin, the drug our Bulgarian cousins favour. Like the bullfighter, Commander Bond should be given a fighting chance.' He turned with a sinister smile to Bond. 'Commander Bond, do you know what a "puppet" is?

In an operational sense, I mean?'

'One who is easy to control?' asked Bond.

Chernov laughed aloud. 'I am not being fair to you, James Bond. It is the Red Army's Special Forces, the *Spetsnaz*, which we believe to be the equivalent to your S.A.S., who use the word "puppet". "Puppets" are of great assistance during their training. They have been used in the U.S.S.R. for more than fifty years now. Our noble ancestors, the Cheka, called them "gladiators"; then the N.K.V.D. spoke of them as "volunteers", though they are hardly that. SMERSH, under all its different guises, has always called them by an English name, which is strange, eh? We call them "Robinsons", Commander Bond. You may be familiar with them under that appellation. So, I ask you again, do you know what "Robinsons" are?'

'I've heard rumours.' He felt a tightening of his stomach at the word.

'And you believed the rumours?'

'Probably.'

'You would be right to believe them. Let me explain. When someone is sentenced to death in the Soviet Union, it depends upon his place in the community whether he dies quickly or whether his death will be used to serve the state.' Again the grim and chilling smile lit Chernov's eyes like black ice. 'Unlike the decadent British, who are so neatly delivering themselves into our hands by their self-indulgence, their laxity, their failure to see how we will finally take complete control of their politics...' his voice rose to a slightly higher pitch, '...unlike the British who are too squeamish to use the death penalty any more, we use it to advantage. True, old men and women are executed almost immediately. Others go to medical centres; some to assist in the building and running of our nuclear reactors – to do the dangerous jobs. The stronger, fitter and younger men become "puppets" or come to us as "Robinsons". It provides good training for our men. Until a soldier has proved he can kill another human being, one cannot be certain of him.'

'That's what I'd heard.' Bond's face felt paralysed, as though injected by a dentist. 'We are told that they provide living targets on exercises...'

'Not simply targets, Commander Bond. They can fight back, though naturally within limits. They know that should they try and escape or turn their weapons on the wrong people, they will be cut down like wheat. They are, for one exercise, real live opponents. They kill and get killed. If they are really good, they can survive for some time.'

'Three exercises and they are reprieved?'

Chernov smiled. 'An old wives' tale, I am afraid. "Robinsons" never survive in the end. They know they are under sentence so they fight harder if they think a reprieve will come after three ordeals.'

Chernov inspected his fingernails. The room seemed charged with tension. Chernov turned and nodded to the pair of guards, who went out, carefully closing the door behind them.

'When we heard that you, a man on our death list, had been assigned to the clearing up of Cream Cake, I made a request to Moscow Centre. I asked for some "Robinsons", some very good men who had lasted for two exercises and thought they had only one more to win before reprieve. I asked for young men. Mr Bond, you should feel honoured. This is the first time our people have allowed "Robinsons" to operate outside the Soviet Union. Tonight, from midnight until dawn, you will be out on this little island with our four best "Robinsons" intent on killing you. They will be armed and we are allowing you to carry a small weapon as well. But for six hours, in the dark and on ground which you do not know and they do, you will be hunted. James Bond, I would like you to meet your "Robinsons".'

He shouted a command and the door was opened by one of the men outside.

20

ZERO HOUR

AT FIRST SIGHT the four 'Robinsons' looked docile enough. They were free from any form of restraint, watched only by the two guards with their machine pistols.

'Come in,' Chernov said in Russian, beckoning.

If he had expected shuffling, cowed prisoners, Bond would have been disappointed. The quartet marched into the room, their bearing military, eyes fixed ahead. They were dressed in loose black trousers and shirts. They even wore black trainers and Bond reckoned that their faces too would be blackened before the ordeal. There had been no moon last night and there would be none tonight. The 'Robinsons' would become invisible outside in the darkness.

'You see, Commander Bond, they are a good little team. They have worked together before and to good effect – once against a group of six *Spetsnaz*. Five are dead and the sixth will not walk again. Their second mission was against K.G.B. trainees; man to man, four to four.' He gave his habitual shrug. 'K.G.B. are four trainees fewer. Need I say more?'

Bond stared at the men, sizing them up. All were well built, alert and clear-eyed, but one stood out from the rest, mainly because of his height. He was around six-five, towering over the others who were between six and six-one.

'What were their crimes?' he asked, trying to make the question sound casual, as though he were a racehorse dealer checking on pedigree.

Chernov smiled, almost sphinx-like. The enigma in that smile produced a loathing in Bond that he had not before recognised in himself.

'I have to think,' Chernov said, his eyes running along the line of men who stood immobile before them. 'The big fellow, Yakov, was condemned for raping six young women, girls almost. He strangled his victims after using them. Then we have Bogdan, also a killer, though not a rapist. Young men were his speciality. Bogdan broke their necks and tried to dispose of them by cutting up the bodies and spreading the pieces in woodland near his home. He's a peasant, but strong and with no moral sense.'

Bond stopped himself from blurting out the obvious: 'Like you, Kolya. Just like you.'

Chernov continued down the line. 'Pavl and Semen are less complex. Pavl, the one with the bulbous nose, was an army officer who took to converting military funds for his own use. Five of his comrades discovered the truth over a period of two years. Four have never been found. The fifth managed to pass on the information. As for Semen, he is a straightforward murderer, on three counts: his lady friend, her lover and her mother. Very good with a meat cleaver, is Semen.'

'All part of life's rich pattern.' Bond knew the only way to resist Chernov's bullying was to make light of these four monsters who, in a matter of hours, would be out to kill him. 'You say they will be armed?'

'Of course. Two will carry hand guns – Lugers. One will be equipped with a killing knife similar to the Sykes-Fairbairn Commando dagger, which we know is familiar to you. And one will be given a weapon which he likes, a type of short mace similar to the old Chinese fighting irons. It consists of a spiked steel ball hanging from a sharp blade, attached to the end of a two foot handle. It is unpleasant.'

'And what about me?'

'You, my dear Commander Bond? Well, we wish to be fair. You will have a Luger pistol. Parabellum, in good condition, I assure you.'

'I'll have eight rounds,' thought Bond. Eight chances to kill, if he could put himself in the right position.

Chernov was still speaking. 'We have provided you with one magazine half full. So you have four 9 mm bullets, one for each of the "Robinsons", should you be lucky enough to get within range before one of them is upon you. As you will have gathered, this team has been given a walk over the ground. As far as I know, you have not.'

'What if they decide to make a run for it? Grab themselves a sampan and clear off?'

Again Chernov produced his tantalising smile. 'You still do not understand do you, Commander Bond? These men have nothing to lose but their lives — which they keep once you are dead.'

'They think they'll keep their lives.'

'Oh, Commander Bond, don't try to spread dissension. It will not work, my friend. They cannot be turned. They will not run; neither will they believe any stories you may try to tell them — even if they were to give you the time.'

And you know I won't run either, Bond thought. You think you know me inside out, Comrade General. You know I won't run because if I can possibly outwit your deadly foursome, I shall return here and try to save the others. Indeed, Chernov knew him, for that was exactly what he would do. He wondered if Chernov also knew he would try to return in order to unmask the traitor among the other prisoners?

Chernov gave a signal and the 'Robinsons' were marched out, each one meeting Bond's eyes as he turned towards the door. Was it imagination, or did he detect a bleak hatred in those four pairs of eyes?

'You have a couple of hours to rest before your ordeal,' said Chernov as he rose. 'I suggest you make your peace with the world.'

One of the guards came back into the room, ready to lead Bond away, but Chernov took a step forward.

'Let me say something else, just to ensure that you are familiar with the rules. Do not try to be clever. It is possible that you have thought of the obvious scheme, to drop below that little wall which encircles the house and pick off the "Robinsons" as they come out. We know that you are an excellent marksman but please do not even think of trying that. When you are given the order to run, then you run. Any other tricks and my two guards will cut you to ribbons. Should you, by luck or skill, manage to avoid or kill my "Robinsons", I would advise you to keep running, James Bond; to run as far as you can. We shall kill you tonight, I am certain of that, but in the unlikely event that I am wrong, our time will come again and I shall kill you myself. My Department will never rest until you are dead. Do you understand?'

Bond nodded curtly and left with as much dignity as his churning stomach would allow. Back in the cell, he began to consider his chances. For a while, up there with the deadly 'Robinsons', he had almost allowed despair to reach him. Now, alone again, he began to plan. They were giving him a Luger Parabellum with four rounds of ammunition. Well, that was a start. But he would have more if he could reach the hidden back-up package.

The package, worked on by Q'ute and other members of the Service, was for use only in dire necessity in the field. It consisted mainly of lethal weaponry.

Constructed on the principle of the old-fashioned Royal Navy 'Housewife' – always pronounced 'Hussif' – the Covert Operations Accessory Pack, C.O.A.P., was a thick oblong package covered in oilskin, measuring one foot three inches by eight inches, with two long tapes running out from the left-hand side. These held the pack secure with a quick-release knot. Opened out flat, it contained five pockets, each tailored to hold a specific piece of equipment. On the far left were two objects that looked like stubby HP11 batteries. One of these was a powerful flare activated by the button masquerading as the battery's positive nipple. Held at arm's length, it would shoot a pure white-light flare to around twenty feet, illuminating an area of up to a quarter of a mile in radius. Fired at the right trajectory, the flare could also have a blinding effect.

The second battery was operated like the first, though not held, for within seven seconds it exploded with almost twice the power of the old Mills hand grenade. Both batteries contained the untraceable plastique substances that so concerned the anti-terrorist organisations.

The third pocket held a six-inch knife blade fashioned from toughened polycarbon and thus again undetectable by airport security. The blade was protected by a scabbard, which doubled as its handle.

The fourth pocket was almost flat, containing a saw-toothed garrotting wire; while the last held probably the most deadly weapon of all — a pen; but no ordinary pen. Made in Italy, it too had security men worried. With a quick twist, it became a small projectile-firing gun. A jet of compressed air would fire toughened steel needles that could kill if they entered the brain, throat, lung or heart from around ten paces. The pen could be used only three times.

Bond rehearsed in his mind where each of these items could be found in the open C.O.A.P., remembering the many times he had trained in the dark, using all the items by feel alone. He was comforted by the knowledge that he could have everything hidden on his person, or ready to use, within a minute. There was nothing like the threat of death, he thought — as many had done before him — to concentrate the mind.

Having gone through the positions in the C.O.A.P. several times, he could only prepare himself mentally for the test. So he sat as before with his legs crossed and his eyes closed. But this time he went over his recollection of the map Richard Han had passed on from Swift. He knew where the house lay in relation to the rest of the promontory and within the hour knew what he would do. With luck and his expertise combined, he had a chance — though a slim chance — of winning.

They told him that it was eleven-thirty when they came for him. The guards spoke no English, but while one covered him with the machine pistol, the other raised his arm, grinning proudly at his brand new eight-function digital watch.

Chernov waited alone in the main room. The windows had been opened and a few lights twinkled from the cluster of houses around Tung Wan Bay. Across the water on the southern promontory, the Warwick Hotel's lights blazed.

'Come and listen.'

Chernov beckoned him towards the window and together they stepped outside into the warm night air. Bond thought, why not kill now with your bare hands, and be done with it? But that would serve no purpose. He would follow Chernov quickly to the grave, cut down by the man who had stayed in the room behind them.

'Listen,' Chernov repeated. 'Hardly a sound. You realise that around forty thousand people still live on this little island, most of them on the junks and sampans in the harbour, yet after midnight few people stir. There is hardly any night life on Cheung Chau.'

As Chernov spoke, Bond took his bearings, and reciprocal bearings. Directly in front of them the ground sloped shallowly to the place where he had hidden the C.O.A.P. during his first reconnaissance. He could, thank heaven, pinpoint exactly where he must cross the low wall. Below, the beach circled the bay, while to the right the ground sloped sharply upwards. He knew that once over that rise it was only a few hundred yards to a rough road which weaved down towards the central isthmus and the main village. On the way, it swept past the famous Pak Tai Temple, and on to the Praya, or waterfront, with its fish processing factory and hundreds of fishing junks.

Chernov slapped him on the shoulder. 'But we'll give them a little night life, eh, James Bond?' He glanced at his watch. 'It is almost time.' He turned, shepherding Bond inside again.

'Do I get a last request?'

Chernov looked at him, a worm of suspicion in his eyes. 'That depends on what it is.'

'I would like to say goodbye to my friends.'

'I think not. It would be too distressing for them. They are well controlled – particularly the women. I would not like to risk unbalancing that. You realise it is not a pleasant job I have to do in this place tomorrow. It will be best if those under sentence bear the inevitability of death with fortitude. It will make the whole business easier for me. You do understand?'

Yes, thought Bond. The last thing you want is for me to see them now because, like as not, they are one short. The traitor will have been pulled out. Aloud, he said, 'You're a butcher, Chernov. Let's get on with it.'

Chernov nodded, looking solemn. 'You have my word that a full five minutes will pass before the "Robinsons" are unleashed on you. Come, the weapons are here.'

As though by magic the table was now littered with the deadly weapons. There were the three Luger pistols and the long gunmetal dagger – perhaps an inch longer than the old Sykes-Fairbairn commando knife – and the fighting iron. This had a wooden haft some two feet in length with a reinforced hand-grip at one end and a sharp movable steel blade at the other. At the far end from the handle a short length of chain was attached. From this dangled a mace twice the size of a man's fist and covered in sharp spikes. Chernov touched the mace and laughed.

'You know what they used to call these?'

'Morning stars, as I recall.'

'Yes, morning stars, and ...' he chuckled mirthlessly, 'and "holy water sprinklers". I prefer holy water sprinklers.' His hand hovered over the weapons, coming to rest on one of the Lugers. 'This is yours, I believe.' He slipped the magazine out before handing it to Bond. 'Please ensure that it is in working order and that the firing pin has not been removed.'

Bond checked the weapon. It was well oiled and in good condition. Chernov held out the magazine.

'Count the four rounds. I insist on fair play.'

As he followed the instruction Bond was aware that the guard with the machine pistol had stiffened in readiness and that the 'Robinsons' were being brought into the room behind him. He knew that the whole set-up was designed to break his nerve. Chernov was a good stage director and all this drama had point.

'You may load the weapon and put the safety on.'

Bond did so, holding the automatic loosely in his right hand as Chernov continued to speak.

'When we are ready, I shall take you to the window and count down from ten to zero. At zero the lights will be switched off and you will begin your run. Do not forget what I've already told you about tricks, James Bond. They will do you no good. I do promise you, though, on my word as an officer, that the "Robinsons" will not be unleashed for a full five minutes. Make the most of your time. You are ready?'

Bond nodded and to his surprise Chernov held out his hand. Bond just looked at it, then turned to face the window. Chernov paused for a moment, as though hurt by his refusal, before he began to count 'Ten...nine...eight...' until he reached zero.

The lights went out and Bond hurled himself forward into the darkness.

21

EMPEROR OF THE DARK HEAVEN

BOND JUDGED THE leap over the wall perfectly with a combination of skill and luck. Having done his calculations while standing outside with Chernov, he was able to count off the paces as he ran in what he knew to be the right direction. Taking the jump in his stride, he sprinted across the flat scrub until he came to the slope. He went down and rolled so he could not be seen from the house. He was certain he had landed within a few feet of his goal and began to feel the ground around him with the palms of his hands. After a couple of seconds of near panic, his left hand touched the rock. He rolled towards it, scrabbling the earth and dragging out the oilskin package.

On his feet again he turned left, and ran across the slope, aiming to get above and away from the villa as fast as possible. Throughout the run, he counted the seconds. He had given himself two and a half minutes. Wherever he was at that point, he would stop.

He judged that the point he reached in the time was about thirty yards above the villa. There he fell to the ground and placed the pistol where he knew he could grab it. Then he threw the C.O.A.P. on to the ground, slipped the tapes and unrolled the oilskin. By feel alone, in the darkness, he located each item and pulled it from its holder, distributing the weapons around his overall pockets but keeping the flare in his hand.

Breathing heavily, Bond held out his arm, angled the little

battery-like object towards the house and pressed the firing
button. At the same time he reached towards the Luger. He
judged the flare would explode at five minutes twenty
seconds since he had left the house. There was an open
pocket on the right thigh of the overalls, and he jammed the
Luger into it. Then, grabbing the second battery — the small
grenade — he waited.

The flare gave a thumping kick against his hand, then
went up in a dazzling white flash of light. Bond closed his
eyes as the projectile left his hand but opened them immediately the first vivid flash was over. It was as though someone
had bathed the villa and its immediate surrounding area in a
floodlight, just as he had intended. There for anyone to see
were the 'Robinsons', two heading up the rise towards him,
the other two going down in the direction of the beach. One
of the men coming in Bond's direction threw up his arm to
shield his eyes but they both kept going like automatons.
Bond could see clearly that the second pair were not deflec-
ted from their progress towards the beach. He lay still and
silent, clutching the tiny bomb. Already he could hear the
men's heavy breathing as they came on towards him, their
shapes visible in the dying light of the flare.

This had to be judged to the second. If the grenade did not
explode at the right moment, taking out both men, he might
be forced to use the Luger, wasting at least one precious shot.
The panting and heavy footfalls grew nearer, and now he
had only his judgment to go by, for the flare had long gone.
Bond prayed that he had their measure. He pressed on the
nipple and aimed his throw at the path of the oncoming men.

He caught a quick glimpse of the pair — too close
together — as the tiny cylinder packed with plastique
exploded in the air directly in front of them. He ducked his
head, feeling the burn and shock across his own scalp and the
terrible ringing in his ears. Through the explosion he
thought a scream reached him, but he could not be certain.
Stumbling to his feet, he half-walked, half-staggered forward

until his foot hit something. He bent to feel a soft wetness which he knew to be body and blood.

On hands and knees, Bond carefully felt around in the scrubby grass, straining through his buzzing ears for any sound, and trying to marshal that sense of danger so necessary for men in his profession. It was at least two minutes before he found the knife, and another two or three before he located the gun. The charge had, as he hoped, exploded directly between the men, and very close to them. Before his hand closed on the Luger it encountered unpleasant débris from the small bomb. Bond would never get used to the effects of explosions, particularly now that a very small amount of plastique could do so much damage.

His head started to clear, and with the original pistol still tucked into the overall pocket and the other weapon clasped in his right hand, he began to race westwards, heading for the road that would take him down to the Praya.

Chernov had made a point of telling him about the deadly experience of these four men. Now there were only two and it was reasonable to judge that, according to training, they would stick to their route and then probably separate at the village, hoping to catch their prey in the open, or among the buildings running the length of the Praya.

Bond had his own plan of campaign. If he could make the Pak Tai Temple, which was a good vantage point, he would wait there. Let them come to him.

His ears still sang from the explosion and he was aware that his clothes were stained with blood, but he reached the rough road without mishap, moving from the stony surface on to the softer grass at the side. He stopped running now and fast marched, taking great gulps of air in an attempt to regulate his breathing.

After ten minutes he thought he could make out the shapes of buildings ahead. Five minutes later he reached the edge of the village, cutting between dark bushes and feeling gently towards a stone wall he knew must be the temple. Working

his way to the front of the building, Bond reflected on the fact
that at least he had some gods he could pray to now, for Pak
Tai is the Supreme Emperor of the Dark Heaven, and the
temple in his honour also houses his martial gods, Thousand
Mile Eye and Favourable Wind Ear. He could do with the
help of all three tonight to detect the remaining two
'Robinsons'.

The temple faced an open piece of land and for the first
time since the flare and explosion, Bond felt his eyes adjusting to the dark. Within a few minutes he could make out the
flat square and the shape of the temple steps guarded by
traditional dragons. Gently he felt his way towards the top
step. Having reached it, he retreated once more into the
darkness of the temple doorway to his right. There he waited
at a vantage point behind one of the two great stone pillars.
Minutes filtered by, and he knew that the 'Robinsons' must
also be taking their time, moving slowly and silently through
the dark streets.

At least one hour passed. Then the best part of another.
Self-discipline held him from even glancing at the luminous
dial of his watch, as he conducted a careful, regular search
from right to left, then left to right, moving his head and
eyes very slowly, his body becoming cramped through
immobility.

Finally he looked at the Rolex. Ten to five in the morning.
Just over an hour before the game was up and Chernov
would begin his butchery. Bond's stomach turned over at the
thought. As the horrific picture of Chernov at his work slid
through his mind, he caught a movement out of the corner of
his eye. It came from the far right of the square, close to the
house. For a second, a fleeting figure, a shadow appeared
against the lighter band of the sea.

Slowly Bond moved and lifted the Luger, his eyes riveted
to the area where he had seen the shadow. For a moment he
thought that he had imagined it. Then there it was again,
hard against the wall, moving at snail's pace, using the cover

of darkness. He shifted position again, bringing the Luger up as the shadow detached itself from the wall and began to move nearer to the temple steps. It was then that, for all his training and experience, Bond made his first error of the night. Take him out now, said one part of his mind. No, wait, where's the other bastard? That one second of indecision produced the ensuing terrifying minutes.

His training overrode all else: take him out now. He centred the Luger's sights on the advancing shadow. His finger took up the first pressure, then his sixth sense warned of closer danger.

He was standing in the classic side-on position, both arms raised in the two-handed grip and the pain seared through his left arm as though someone had run a burning brand across it. He heard his own scream of pain and felt the gun drop from his right hand as he reached across to his injured arm. And as he swivelled he saw the 'Robinson' with the fighting mace poised for a second blow.

The reaction was automatic, but everything seemed to go into slow motion through the blur of pain spreading from his shattered left arm. He could not recall the man's name, though for some obscure reason his mind wrestled with the problem. He though it was Bogdan, the one who had broken young men's necks and then tried to dispose of them by cutting them up and spreading the pieces around the forest. He could hear Chernov's voice quite distinctly: 'He's a peasant, but strong and with no moral sense.' And all the time Bond was looking into the man's eyes the mace was being lifted very slowly above his head. Then the big steel-spiked ball started to come hard down towards Bond's skull. His right arm seemed to move very slowly, his right leg going back, his hand grabbing the butt of the Luger in the overall pocket. His finger felt for the safety catch. The spikes hissed through the air, coming nearer. The Luger stuck, then came free, Bond's hand twisting, his finger curling. Then two sharp explosions – two shots just as they were all trained — and the scent of cordite. The sharp ting as spent cartridge cases clanged against the steps.

Instantly the slow motion ended and the tempo raced.

The two bullets lifted Bogdan off his feet, popping his arms into the air as though he were some grotesque jack-in-the-box. The fighting iron flew back and Bogdan's body, shedding blood over Bond, fell against the door of the temple.

The pain shrieked back into Bond's left arm and he heard a quick double crack and thump. Stone chipped off the pillar as the other 'Robinson' fired from the square.

Bond doubled up with pain, retching, his vision blurring. He almost keeled over, then saw the shape of the second Luger on the steps. He forced himself to turn, his gun, with two rounds still in the magazine, clutched in his right hand. Turning, he found himself losing his balance, reeling like a drunk with the shock and agony. A voice seemed to whisper near to his ear, 'Get him. Take him out, now.' Automatically, he squeezed the trigger, aware that the weapon was up and his right arm straight. Two shots at a ghost, he thought. Drop the gun and pick up the other one. He went through the routine as in reflex, acting by numbers. Just as he ducked down another bullet whined over his head. His hand caught the butt of the Luger, but he couldn't straighten up.

He dropped on to one knee and raising his head, saw the other man standing over him taking careful aim. He was saying something in Russian and the Luger was huge in Bond's vision.

Then the explosion came and what Bond imagined was his own last cry echoed around the pillared entrance to the Temple of the Supreme Emperor of the Dark Heaven.

22

DEATH OF A
DOUBLE

IF YOU ARE dead, Bond reasoned, you should not feel pain.
His last memory was of the 'Robinson' standing a couple of
feet away from him with the Luger pointing at his head,
ready for the *coup de grâce*, then the dull explosion. I saw, I
heard, I must be dead. But he could sense the waves of
nausea and the stunning pain in his left arm. He knew that
he could move, that his eyelids were moving. He heard a
voice calling to him.

'Mr Bond? Mr Bond? Are you okay, Mr Bond?'

He allowed his eyes to open fully. The sheer blackness was
giving way to the first light of day. He was lying on his side
and into his vision swam the soles of a pair of black trainers
and a grey-black hump behind him, which he knew was a
body. Beside him he saw toes of another pair of trainers. He
turned his head, his eyes travelling upwards from the shoes.

'Are you okay, Mr Bond?'

From this angle he could not see the face properly. The
figure went down on one knee.

'I think we should get out of here pretty damn chop-chop,'
said the dark-haired Chinese boy, smiling. 'You remember
me, Mr Bond? Richard Han. Swift's man. Good thing I
followed you. Mr Swift say that if anything happen, you
might need much help, never mind. He said you would be
here, Cheung Chau Island. Also I should watch your back.'

'You killed the "Robinson"?' Apart from the excruciating
pain in his left arm, Bond felt distinctly better.

'That his name? Robinson? Okay, yes, I kill him. You killed man with fighting iron. I shot this one.' Han held a very large Colt ·45 in his right hand. 'It was correct that I kill him?'

'Too damn right it was correct. Hell!'

Bond squirmed, shifting his head to squint down at his left wrist. The Rolex said five-fifteen. Forty-five minutes, or near enough, before Chernov would begin on the others. Shakily he pulled himself upwards, testing his weight gingerly. All seemed well except for the arm.

'Give me that gun – the one on the ground.'

Han reached out for the Luger.

'There should be another one,' said Bond, peering into the grey light. His opponent's weapon lay to one side of the body. Han picked it up.

'Quickly,' Bond urged him. 'Take out the magazines and put all the cartridges into one. Okay?'

'It's okay. Mr Swift taught me much about guns. Said I was good shot.'

'I agree with him. Look, Han, you know the house to the north of Tung Wan Bay? The house where they kept me?'

'No,' the boy said blankly. 'Swift say you will be here. I watch your back. So, I come here and nobody seen you. I stick around, then late I see these men behaving like they were looking for butterflies in the dark. Very strange. I think, Richard follow these, they are up to no good.'

He would have gone on, but Bond stopped him. 'Listen, Han, there is this house...' He explained exactly where it was. 'Get the police. Tell them it is a security matter...'

'Swift give me a police number Hong Kong. He said it was Special Police.'

'Special Branch?'

'Yes. I am stupid. I think first it is some kind magic root. Then he explain.'

'Okay. You can find a telephone on this island?'

'My father's fourth sister lives here. Has small shop with

telephone. I shall wake her.'

'Ring your number, but tell him to get local police to that house pretty damned fast, chop-chop. Okay?'

'They be there very fast. You going?'

Bond took a deep breath. 'While I've got the strength I'm going, yes. You get police there. Tell them to hold everyone.' Han was already on his way, so Bond had to shout after him, 'Tell them the people at the house are armed. They're very dangerous.'

'Okay. I tell them, *heya*?'

Han turned, one arm raised. Then, in the first light of dawn, the scene turned to one of carnage. There were two heavy thumps and Richard Han's head burst open, spraying a mist of blood high into the air. The body ran three ... four more steps before it hit the ground.

There was the sudden rattle of a machine pistol. Bullets were chipping and smashing into the Temple Wall around Bond. He reacted automatically, governed by his reflexes and training. The muzzle flash had been quite near, to his right. Expecting another burst of fire any second, Bond wheeled, loosing off two rounds in the direction of the flash. There was a hideous scream, followed by the crash of metal on stone and the noise of a body falling.

Bond dropped on to one knee, waiting, silent and still, straining to pick up any other noises, but only the moans continued. Slowly he raised his right hand, conscious again of the acute pain in his other arm. He gritted his teeth, listening. The moaning had stopped, so once more he rose, and took a pace forward. But he was stopped dead in his tracks by the familiar voice.

'Move one more muscle and I'll blow your head off, Bond. Now drop the gun.'

She was very close indeed, to his right.

'I said drop the gun!' The order was sharp, commanding.

Bond opened his fingers and heard the Luger hit the steps just as Heather Dare – or Irma Wagen – stepped from the shadows.

'So?' Bond breathed, feeling the horror of her deception wash over him.

'Yes. So. I'm sorry, James, but you didn't really think the General was going to take any more chances? You did very well. I didn't think you'd be able to get the better of those men. But Chernov was worried. He seemed to sense the possibility.'

'Bully for Kolya Chernov.'

He cursed himself for not having seen through it before. The white raincoat in London – that had worried him at the time, for nobody with even the most elementary training would have worn such a garment on the run. Then there was the offer to share her bed. That too had niggled, particularly when he saw her with Smolin, the two lovebirds.

'No wonder the General was so well advised of our movements,' he said aloud, hoping to bring her closer.

'I led him like a dancer – led you as well, James; just as I managed to hook Smolin into revealing his treachery. We'd better get on with it. My orders are to kill you here, though I thought the precious "Robinsons" would have done the job for me.'

'How long…?' Bond began.

'Have I been K.G.B.? A long time, James. Since my early teens. Cream Cake was blown from the start. When we all had to get out, the orders were to leave Maxim and Dietrich in place. They could have been taken at any point, but Centre thought London might use me once I was in England. They didn't, as you know, so it was decided to deal with all the others. You were a bonus. Chernov came out of safety just for you, James. You find that flattering?'

'Very.'

'On your knees, then. We'll do it the Lubyanka way. A bullet in the back of the head.'

He took a step forward, as though preparing himself. 'And the attempt on your life in London was…?'

'A small charade to help you trust me. Mischa under-estimated you, though. He's been very angry. Now he'll be pleased.'

She took another step closer to him, and Bond shrugged, the pain again angry, tearing at his arm.

'I'll lose my balance if I try to get down. That bastard's smashed my arm badly.'

'Then just turn around, slowly.'

She was calmer than he expected, but she was coming even closer, as though drawn towards his voice. He started to turn, his mind racing with the chances of his being able to take her with only one arm. Then, as she stepped in, her right hand holding the pistol high, he moved.

Turn in. Always turn in towards the body but away from the weapon. It was what the experts taught, and anyone foolish enough to get close with a pistol deserved all she got. Bond wheeled right, knowing the position was good as he turned like a ballroom dancer executing a complicated step. Although his reactions were slightly impaired by the injured arm, he got it right. Heather's gun arm remained rigid for just the necessary length of time. As he came close, her arm and weapon were to the right of his neck. He brought his knee up hard. It was never as effective with a woman, but it still caused a lot of pain. He felt the breath go out of her, and could smell her, feel her body close against his.

As Heather doubled slightly from the impact, Bond's right hand came up to grasp at her wrist. Even with one arm he could execute a lot of force with the downward pull. She gave a little cry when he broke her arm against his knee. The pistol dropped to the ground and bounced away down the steps.

Bond flicked his knee up again. She was off balance and her spine presented an ideal target. His knee caught her in the small of the back so hard that he actually heard the spine go. Then she fell away, her breath coming in little panting jerks. Although she must by now be unconscious, loud whimpering noises came from her throat.

He should have known it was Heather. She had taken the most prized target, Maxim Smolin. He should have seen it from the start. Bond reached out for the Luger. He did not hesitate. One bullet only, straight to the lovely head. He felt no qualms about it. Death was sudden and any nausea came only from the roaring pain in his left arm.

He walked slowly over to the other body. It was one of the two guards. The man was dead, both bullets having caught him in the chest. He had hoped it would be Mischa.

He looked at his watch again and at the fast-lightening sky. Time was really running out now. He would be lucky to make it. Taking another deep breath, Bond clenched his teeth. It was going to be one hell of a run, and lord knew what he could do when he got to the villa. Yet part of the job was done – the traitor had been found and dealt with. The odds on his saving the others were small, but he had to try.

23

CHINESE
TAKEAWAY

HE THOUGHT HIS lungs were going to burst with the effort, for he ran faster than he had since leaving the house with the 'Robinsons' at his heels. The pain in his lungs, combined with the aching of his thighs and legs, helped to take his mind off the agony of his torn and broken arm. Somehow he had managed to take hold of his left hand and secure the arm inside the overall. In his good right hand he held the Luger.

He forced himself on, scuffing the stones and sending up dust from the road that would take him almost as far as the promontory and the villa. He did not even try to calculate how much time had passed, but knew he would be cutting it very fine. Then, after what seemed an eternity, he reached the crest above the villa and sank to his knees, sliding back from the skyline. Using his right shoulder as a prop, he pulled himself up to peer at the building.

Only a few yards below there was a large brown stain, and the remains of bodies strewn as though some wilful child had dismembered a couple of dolls: the two 'Robinsons' he had burned in the night.

Bond caught a movement from the front of the villa. The one guard Heather had left behind, machine pistol at the ready, was crouching near the front wall, watching and alert. Chernov must be edgy, he thought. They would know about the two 'Robinsons' he had taken out close to the villa, and now the other two had not returned. There would be itchy fingers down there, though he suspected Chernov would be watching for Heather's return. The odds had been so heavily stacked against Bond that nobody could have expected him to live.

Chernov would have Mischa inside with him, to help with the ritual killing. It must be very near to the moment of execution now. Slowly and painfully, Bond started to work his way around to the rear of the house, aware of the time bomb ticking away inside the place. He edged downwards and pulled himself to his feet once more. The back of the house was some fifty yards away and he covered the ground quickly, loping somewhat lopsidedly as he had done all the way back from the Pak Tai Temple. Odd, he thought, how your sense of balance went with one arm out of action. He reached the low wall without being spotted and moved silently towards the house.

Suddenly the sound echoed from the other side of the house, the noise he had dreaded from the beginning of his return journey, a terrible piercing scream – female, but like an animal in extreme pain. His mind was lanced by a vivid picture of Ebbie having her mouth forced open, with Chernov wielding a scalpel for the obscene punishment.

At that moment the guard came round the corner of the house to check the rear. The man stopped, his jaw dropping open. The machine pistol came up but before he could fire, Bond's Luger jumped twice and two bullets crashed into the man's chest, knocking him down like a skittle. As Bond stepped forward he thought there was movement to his right, at the edge of his vision, but when he turned, the Luger ready, there was nobody there. A trick of the early morning light.

There was a shout from the front of the garden and the sound of running feet, but before anyone reached the angle of the wall, Bond was on top of the guard. He wrenched at the machine pistol, identifying it almost by feel alone as an Uzi. It was the scaled-down version with the stock folded back; he wondered why the K.G.B. were using Israeli weapons.

Mischa was pounding around the corner as Bond lifted the Uzi, one-handed. He gave Chernov's right-hand man a burst that almost cut him in two. He fired on the run and was at the front of the house almost before he knew it. He yelled at Chernov who stood undecided outside the window unarmed except for a scalpel, his face pale and shocked.

'Drop the cutter and freeze.'

Chernov gave one pitiful shrug, then threw the scalpel into the garden and raised his hands, his shoulders drooping.

Maxim Smolin, Susanne Dietrich and Jungle Baisley were still chained together in the corner, while Ebbie lay strapped to a wide plank set astride three saw horses.

'My God, you really meant it! You bastard, Chernov, you must be crazy.'

Bond's voice had risen to an uncontrolled, murderous yell and Chernov backed away. 'Vengeance is not just the prerogative of the gods,' said Chernov shakily, although his eyes blazed with a mixture of fury and frustration. 'One day, James Bond, one day all the ghosts of the old SMERSH will rise and crush you. That will be vengeance.'

Bond rarely felt the desire to inflict pain but in that moment he saw Chernov being hit by three steel darts from the pen gun: one to each eye and one in the throat. But Chernov had to be taken alive.

'We'll see about vengeance!' He nodded. 'The keys, General. I want those chains undone.'

Chernov hesitated for a second, then his hands moved towards the table and Bond saw the keys lying there.

'Pick them up gently.' Bond was under control now 'Unlock them.'

Again Chernov hesitated, his eyes flickering to a point behind Bond's shoulders. No, he thought, you don't fall for an old trick like that.

'Just do as I say, Kolya...' he began, then the hairs on the nape of his neck prickled and he turned.

'If I were you, Jacko, I'd simply be putting your gun down

on the table very carefully.'

Norman Murray faced him, having come in quietly through the door, his police issue Walther P.P.K. steady in his right hand.

'What…?' began Bond incredulously.

'Kolya,' Murray said calmly, 'I'd leave the keys where they are. Whatever vengeance you're wanting will have to wait, so, because I've a feeling we're going to get some visitors up here soon enough. I'm sorry I'm so late, but it was a bit of a teaser avoiding my own people and the Brits. Not an easy job.'

Chernov made a '*Tchah-ing*' sound.

'Well, when it comes to us getting out safely we'll have to use your man Bond as collateral, will we not?'

Bond backed away. 'Norman? What in God's name…?'

'Ah, Jacko, the evils of this wicked world. You recall that lovely book of Robert Louis Stevenson, *Treasure Island*? Grand book that. You remember the bit where young Jim Hawkins meets the castaway, Ben Gunn was his name? Well, auld Ben Gunn tries to explain to Jim how he got started on his iniquitous life of piracy. He says, "It begun with chuck-farthen on the blessed grave-stones" – playing what we'd be after calling shove-ha'penny on the grave-stones. Well, I suppose it was like that for me. Now will you put that cannon on the table, Jacko Bond.'

Bond turned his back, carefully placing the Luger near the keys.

'Now, hands on your head, Jacko.'

'I've got a broken arm.'

'Well, hand on your head then. You're a pedantic divil, Jacko.'

By the time Bond turned again, slowly raising his right hand, he had slipped the pen from the breast pocket of the overalls, covering it with his right palm. Two traitors, he thought, and the second one an officer of the Republic of Ireland's Special Branch. A man who had a special, secret relationship with the British Service over matters of intelligence, who even co-operated with M himself.

'Good,' Murray continued. 'As I was saying, Jacko, it started by playing shove ha'penny on the grave-stones for me, after a fashion; only my game was the horses. The auld, auld joke – slow horses and fast women. The debts and the lady, one night in Dublin, who had me compromised and trussed neat as a turkey at Christmas. I just want you to know it wasn't a political thing with me, more a matter of money.'

'Money?' The disgust showed in Bond's voice. 'Money? Then why bother to rescue me from Chernov?'

'Now that was a bit of cover. None of us ever thinks we'll blow our cover, do we Jacko? And I was playing it three ways: my own people, you Brits and these fellas. I'm a treble, really, Jacko and I didn't know the cover was blown until I got you to Dublin airport. So that's water under the bridge now.'

'It doesn't matter, Norm. And don't tell me not to call you Norm again, because you're Comrade Norm now.'

'I suppose you're right. I don't know how I'm goin' to like it in yon country. It's goin' to be awful cold there, so it is. But, you see, Jacko, they're most of them on to me now. Your man M's on to me for sure, so I'm getting a lift out with Kolya, here.' He turned towards Chernov. 'And don't you think we should be getting a move on, Kolya? The porpoises must be close behind me now. Treading on my tail, so they were, when I left Dublin.'

Chernov nodded gravely. 'We go as soon as the business is completed.'

During the momentary distraction, Bond was able to twist the two sections of the pen anti-clockwise with the first finger and thumb of his right hand then turn the weapon face forward. His thumb then moved back to the push trigger.

'Norman!' he called, swivelling his body so that he was aligned with Murray's head. He pressed the trigger quickly twice. 'Sorry, Norman,' he said as the two steel darts made tiny red pinpoint holes in the Special Branch man's head, just above the eyes.

'Jacko!' The word came as a reflex, for Murray must have been dead as he spoke, pitching forward, the gun dropping from his hand at the instant Bond reached out and retrieved the Luger from the table.

Now it was done. Those who could have caused scandal were dead. Chernov would be a coup. Only the tidying up and some plausible explanations to the Press were needed.

'Now, Kolya Chernov...' Bond's voice was not as steady as it might have been, for he had liked Murray, '...take the keys and unlock these good people.' He looked at Ebbie. 'When you're free, go to the telephone, darling, and dial the number I give you. It belongs to my own Department's Resident in Hong Kong. You'll have to cover the General while I speak to him. We must go official on this.'

Chernov began to unlock the shackles and Ebbie went to the telephone. The conversation took no more than three mintues. Meanwhile the others were freed. Jungle and Smolin, using their initiative, secured Chernov with the chains. All the fight seemed to have gone out of him now.

Bond put down the telephone, resting his good hand on the table. There was a light touch on his shoulder and a hand slid down to lie on top of his own.

'Thank you,' Ebbie said, her voice breaking. 'James, I have to thank you so much.'

'It was nothing,' he replied.

The pain returned, the dizziness took over, and his legs buckled under him. In a far corner of his mind he welcomed the oblivion.

James Bond came round in a private hospital room. The Service Resident was by his bedside. He was well known to Bond. They had worked together, once in Switzerland and again in Berlin.

It did not take Bond long to realise that his left arm was encased in plaster.

'It's broken in two places and there are some torn muscles.'

'Apart from that,' said Bond, smiling, 'how did you enjoy the play Mrs Lincoln?' It was a very old joke they had shared in the past.

'M sends congratulations, together with some harsh words about your allowing that girl to travel here with you.'

Bond closed his eyes, feeling very tired. 'Girls like Ebbie are not easy to stop. Don't worry, it wasn't my only mistake.'

'He wants you back in London. The doctors say you can leave the hospital tomorrow but you're to stay here for a couple of weeks. Reluctantly our Chief has agreed. The quacks just want to keep an eye on the arm, if you follow me.'

'What about the others?' Bond asked.

'Everything's tidied up. No mess. No questions. Chernov was flown to London this afternoon. You've been out for the best part of a day, incidentally.'

'Open him up.' Bond's mouth turned down, betraying that rare, innate cruel streak.

'We're denying all knowledge at the moment. Our people will put him through the mill before we go public – if we ever do. Ms Dietrich, young Baisley and Maxim have gone as well. Smolin's no use in the field any more, but they'll find plenty for him to do on the Eastern Bloc desk at Head quarters. You just rest now, James. You've wrapped up the last crumbs of Cream Cake and you've no more to worry about.'

'Where's Ebbie?'

'I have a surprise for you.'

The Resident winked and left the room. A minute later Ebbie Heritage came in. She stood looking at him, then approached the bed.

'I put my feet down,' she said, her face breaking into a smile. 'I put my feet down and said I would take care of you.

My surprise was great. They told me yes, okay. We are very grand, James. We even have bodyguards until you're well enough to travel.'

'I guess I might need one.' He smiled and she laid the palm of her hand on his brow.

'That feels very nice,' said Bond. His arm might be damaged, but he knew other parts of his body were in working order. 'Your hand's so cool.'

'There is old Chinese saying,' she said, looking at him sweetly. 'Woman with cool palm has fire under skirt.'

'Never heard that.' Bond's eyes twinkled.

'Really?'

'Never.'

'It's a true saying. I know, because an elderly Japanese gentleman once told me.'

They stayed at the Mandarin, and in spite of the plaster cast enjoyed two very active weeks together.

Eventually they left by Cathay Pacific. As the carpet of lights that was Hong Kong disappeared from sight, the jolly female purser came over to introduce herself.

'Mr Bond? Ms Heritage? Welcome aboard.' She had a broad grin and infectious laugh. 'You had a good time in Hong Kong?'

'Wonderful,' said Ebbie.

'Full of surprises,' Bond added.

'Were you on holiday?' the purser asked.

'A sort of working holiday.'

'So now you return to London.' The purser gave what was almost a guffaw of laughter. 'This route has a special name in Cathay Pacific, you know.'

'Really?' said Ebbie, sipping her champagne.

'Yes. We call this route from Hong Kong, Chinese Take-away, *ha!*'

Ebbie giggled, and Bond gave a wry smile.

'No doubt we'll be back,' he said. 'One day we'll be back.'